His

Brother's

Wife

by

MARY ELLEN BOYD

ACKNOWLEDGMENTS

I would like to give grateful thanks to the following people, who were so
generous in sharing their expertise with me:

The Members of the Minneapolis Writers' Workshop, who taught me more
about writing, plotting, and story development than I can ever express, and
helped hone my skill over the past many years, I owe you all more than I
can say,

Ruthia,
For reading everything I thrust at you,
For what you call "over-analyzing"
(I don't mind, honest!),
And just for being my sister,

And to Yvonne a very special thanks
for our Monday critique sessions.
You helped keep my nose to the grindstone and
gave me the encouragement to keep going.

If there are brothers living at the same time, and one of them dies, leaving no son, the wife of the deceased must not be married to a stranger; her brother-in-law must go to her, and marry her, doing the duty of a brother-in-law to her; and the first son that she bears shall succeed to the name of the deceased brother, so that his name may not be blotted out of Israel.

Deuteronomy 25:5,6

An American Translation

CHAPTER 1

"You shall not covet your neighbor's house. You shall not covet your
neighbor's wife, nor his male servant, nor his female servant, nor his ox,
nor his donkey, nor anything that is your neighbor's.
Exodus 20:17

The land of Gilead, 1157 B.C.

"Levi?" Joshua leaned in the open door of Levi's house, and
looked across the small eating room, the table where a lone plate holding
remnants of the last meal still sat, drying in the summer heat. He called out
his brother's name again. He heard something move inside, beyond the
whitewashed wall holding shelves where more plates and cups and bowls
were stacked neatly, the wall that separated the rest of the house. The sound
had been far too light to belong to Levi. "Hannah?"

"Levi is not here." Hannah's voice, barely audible, came from the other
room, but she did not appear. It was just as well. How could he face his
brother with Hannah's gentle face fresh on his memory, her soft hair the
color of the sand by the river, her eyes the rare green of spring leaves? She

was all softness and delicacy, the top of her head coming no higher than his shoulder –

She was not his wife! An honorable man would not notice such things about a woman not his wife.

Another sound came, a soft squeak in Hannah's voice, a wince put to sound, a wet sniff, followed by – was that a gasp?

"Hannah? Is all well?" He fought down to urge to step inside.

He would be an honorable man. God had given him the strength so far. He would just have to redouble his prayers . . .

"You came quickly." Levi spoke from behind him.

Joshua spun around, hoping his guilt was not visible. A swath of dark hair fell across his eyes, and he pushed it back, a perfect excuse to cover his face for a brief instant. "I heard a sound from Hannah. I thought something might be wrong."

Levi scowled at him. How awful it would be if his brother had seen, and guessed. "She is my responsibility. You need not worry about her."

Despite his efforts, Joshua could not help the glance at the open door. "Did you want to go look in on her? I can wait."

"No." Levi added nothing more, just turned away from the door. His mouth lifted on one corner as he looked at the rope slung over Joshua's shoulder, and the wide leather strap crossing his chest, a brace for the heavy tools hanging down his back, tucked in the broad loops. "You are well equipped."

Joshua shrugged his shoulders and felt the weight of the tools shift. A wooden handle brushed his spine. Levi's request had come at a bad time, to walk all this way and sacrifice a day of his own work, but a debt was a debt. "Your slave said you needed some help. I brought whatever might be useful." His own work would have to be done again from the beginning, for the metal had hardened before it could be properly refined and poured into the mold, but his brother gave him few chances to balance the scales. If Levi were to ask for a month of hard labor, it would not begin to equal repayment.

So he would work today, and he would not complain.

How long would it be before he no longer felt the weight of the gift his brother had given him? Feeling as he did himself about the farm, how the worry pressed in daily, it was hard to understand how his brother could live there and be content.

"Good. I have some tools of my own waiting. Plan to work hard." Levi grasped Joshua's arm in belated welcome, and turned toward the woods, walking off with his large strides.

Joshua watched his brother for a moment as Levi's long steps ate up the ground, and had to brace himself for a day working on the land. How blessed he was at his end, the better end, of their bargain. He had escaped the chains of their land and gone on to another life, where every day brought challenges to his skill. Levi had never complained, and Joshua knew the land was good. He had seen the loads coming in on Levi's donkeys and Levi's wagons, the yield from the barley harvest, the wheat harvest, the olives, the fruits.

But to be tied to the land, a prisoner of the rains, controlled by the seasons and the sun!

Levi broadened the distance between them, not turning around, as if he assumed Joshua would fall into step. Joshua grasped the leather straps. "Huuh!" He barked with the sharp pull as he hoisted the weight more comfortably, and picked up his step toward the stand of trees behind which Levi was disappearing. The hot sun pierced through the fragile layer of leafy shade, dappling both their bodies with moving patches of light and dark.

Levi led the way through the trees into the meadow where they had played as children. This part of his parents' land was held in trust for his own use, or it had been until he turned it all over to Levi. He had forgotten this section.

But then, he had put most of the farm out of his mind the day he walked away to find his own life.

Levi turned around slowly, scanning the grassy field dappled with white limestone. "This is our work for today." He faced Joshua, the sun at his back, its golden rays lightening the pale brown of his hair. "We haul rock."

Joshua scanned the meadow, the limestone tips poking through the ground and dotting the field with white. The grasses had lost most of their green, but the occasional flower still held onto its petals, blue and purple and yellow. But the main color came from the limestone. "Planning on white-washing your house? Or are you patching mortar?"

"Looking to help me with that also, if I am?" Levi's light green-brown eyes crinkled with his smile, but the sparkle of earlier was missing, and he did not answer the question.

Perhaps he had overstepped his bounds, Joshua thought. Really, what Levi did with the house was no longer his concern and a man's house and all that went on inside it was sacred.

As was a man's wife. He stopped to wipe an arm over his forehead, wishing he could remove his sister-in-law from his mind as easily as the sweat wiped from his face. Levi surely knew all that went on with Hannah. If she had truly been hurt enough to gasp, Levi would know and would have gone in to check. And, Joshua scolded himself, he had no place in that house, and she had no place in his mind. He forced his attention back at the rock, a good way to vent his frustration. And heartache.

They collected the loose stones first, hauling the chunks in rope slings to ever-growing mounds around the grassy field for later. Then they turned to the stones that only poked their heads above the dirt. The sun cooked them as they worked. Their spades chopped at the hard summer soil as they found the edges of the rocks. The soft limestone that littered the meadow hugged the ground tightly, and let go only after much struggle. The piles of white rock grew as each newly released one was added. Joshua's shoulders chafed from the rope that scraped his skin through the robe each time he dug his feet in to pull.

"Why did you not do this during the rainy season?" he finally asked as they caught their breath before tackling another limestone chunk. He flopped down to catch his breath against yet another rock that was larger than they expected, the stone scraping the backs of his legs. His robe was filthy. He stood up, his legs protesting, peeled it over his head, and tossed it to one side, then tightened the knot of his loincloth.

"I did not need limestone then," was all Levi said, looking over the white stone's top from his position on the other side. His own robe was stiff with dirt and sweat. He squinted against the sun. "Are you helping, or are you going to beg off like an old man?"

"Who is calling whom an old man?" Joshua bared his teeth at his brother, groaned, and picked up the rope. "I think it will go beneath now." He shoved the end into a small gap at the bottom of the stone. Their fingers tangled as his brother caught the tip of the rope, then Levi pulled it out the other side.

The sun was low when Joshua finally raised a weary hand. "You have enough rock now, Levi, to begin whatever you wish. If I do not stop, I will not make it back home."

Levi nodded, tossed aside the spade he had been using to push dirt back into one of the deep holes they had dug, and flopped on the ground. "I agree."

They lay side by side, as they had done as children, and watched the fragile wisps of clouds drift past. Joshua did not feel like talking. Neither, it seemed, did Levi. Joshua rolled his head to glance at his brother. How different they were, Levi the older, a quieter, more content version of himself, even in coloring. Levi's light brown hair nearly matched Hannah's in fairness by the end of the planting and harvesting seasons after the sun's harshness, while his own features were so much darker, black hair, olive skin and his odd golden eyes, unmuted with the green of his brother's. Levi's hair was straight, while his own dark locks insisted on curling, and falling in his eyes at the most inconvenient times. Levi seemed happy with his roots in the soil, while Joshua had cut his ties to this land years ago. Levi was the sun, while he was the fierce fire of the kiln.

He sat up and looked around the meadow for his tool strap. It was in a jumbled heap of leather and metal a few cubits away. They had made good progress, but so much limestone still peeked out of the hard soil. He walked over and picked the belt up, arranging the straps and sliding the tools in their loops.

"I am going now, Levi. Send for me again if you need me." Levi merely nodded his head, hair rubbing along the dusty ground, and raised one hand in farewell. Joshua started back across the meadow, his legs tired and dragging. He would have to be careful tomorrow. Working around kilns with hot metal was not for the weary.

He stumbled, caught himself against a chunk of limestone almost as high as his chest, and looked down in reflex to see what tripped him. They had looked at the stone and ignored it, Levi ruling it too large to waste their time. Today was for removing the rocks they could, not for digging out stones the ground might not release. Yet the area around his feet was littered with chips of whitish stone. They matched the large rock beside him. He glanced over at his brother, still resting on the ground. Joshua could not tell if Levi's eyes were open, so he did not bother to call. His brother deserved a brief rest, for while Joshua could go back to the village, Levi had more work to do.

It might have been the chips littering the ground that teased his curiosity, kept him there instead of moving on. Joshua bent down to examine the limestone boulder. A hole left its shadow in the shady side of the rock, the small opening nearly hidden by the growth creeping up its sides. He reached inside, but the hole was small. Someone had been working on it, though, it was the only way the ground could be so littered. He supposed it could be a place to keep food cool as the shepherds watched their sheep. Levi had meant this forgotten meadow for a pasture, after all.

Joshua stepped back and measured the rock with his eyes. It was almost big enough for a grave in this land where bodies had to be buried quickly. There was no one dead, no one even ill who might need it soon, and the hole required much work before it could be put to such use. For now, it made a good place for a shepherd to store the day's repast.

Joshua shrugged, anxious to go to his own home, resettled his tools, and walked away.

CHAPTER 2

"You shall make judges and officers in all your gates . . . and they shall judge the people with righteous judgment."
Deuteronomy 16:18

Hannah watched the merchant count the fresh-picked early figs carefully in the basket. Her mouth watered as the sun-warmed scent reached her. She could almost taste them. Just one. . . But, no, she did not dare. Levi might be waiting for her, and he would never allow such a luxury. He would check the coins and ask for prices, and the numbers had to match. If even one fig were missing, he would know.

He always knew. Hannah suspected him of following her, but if he did so, she could never find him, no matter how quickly she turned to check.

"One more," the man muttered, and reached down into the pile. The scale in his hand swayed gently from side to side and found a balance.

The merchant had not met her eyes since the first startled look when she walked up.

Hannah pulled her long sleeve down and tried to hide the ugly wrappings she had managed to fasten around her aching arm. She struggled to ignore the heat as the sun beat down on her over-dressed body. The day was too hot for the robe and wrappings, but what choice did she have?

It had been three days since this last beating. She would not have come today, but her food supplies were low and she could not take the chance Levi would notice how boring his meals had become – and find her.

Maybe she would heal just enough to endure before that happened.

The merchant handed her back her purchase. He still did not meet her eyes. Hannah looked at the basket's handle, and willed her other arm, the one less injured, to move. It had been hard enough to hand the basket over empty. Such a small measure of figs to cause such pain. Her arm, her shoulder, her back, pain streaked like fire as she lifted the basket and its load over the seller's cart.

She had only begun her shopping. Hannah looked down at the basket and its little load of figs, and tried not to think how heavy it would be on the long walk home. She refused to cry. It helped nothing, and when she got back home, how would she explain her tears?

"Fresh lamb's meat," a voice pealed out. "Slaughtered this morning! Fresh!"

Hannah glanced over at the booming voice. A display of copper pans stopped her cold. The face that stared back at her, distorted and orange, had dark shadows around each eye. One was swollen almost shut. A large, ugly splotch puffed out one cheek.

She gasped. No wonder the fig seller had been so uneasy! If only she had known what she looked like before she came! Levi did not permit her to have mirrors in the house. It was hard to get a good look in the wavy image of a hammered copper pot anyway, so she had worked by touch alone, trying to arrange the headdress to cover the worst of the sore spots.

What a poor job she had done.

She lifted her sore arm, unburdened by the basket, awkwardly pulled her headdress further forward to hide her cheek, and glanced around at the crowd. No one was looking her way. A woman in a green robe busily checked the edges of a length of linen. Another counted something in her own basket. Children shrieked in play.

"You had your thumb on that scale!" The sudden shrill complaint, loud and directly at her elbow, startled Hannah into a jerk of surprise. White heat burned down her spine and around her ribs.

"Never! I run an honest business!" The anger coming from the stall made Hannah's wounded muscles tighten.

Hannah left the fruit display, and stepped toward the vegetables. Her legs were stiff, every movement forced and stilted. She had abandoned her bed in the fresh hay in the sheepfold yesterday because the friendly sheep poked their curious noses into bruises and bumped into her, piling new pain on old, nudging her aside as they sought their own comfort, so she had found another last night, under the empty sacks in Levi's own shed. Why he had not looked there yet surprised her, but she was grateful. She would have to find a different place tonight. Three days was a frighteningly long time to go without being caught. She watched for Levi each time she had to venture out to make another meal, peeking out from her hiding place, creeping carefully into the house only when she knew he would be far away.

Why Levi had not come inside the day Joshua had heard her still surprised her, but perhaps it was simply his brother's presence. Joshua had even called her name, and yet Levi had remained outside. He could have strode boldly into that room and pinched and twisted in all the places that would cause pain, all the while crooning the most loving of words for Joshua's listening ears, but he had not. She would not count on such mercy happening again.

Under the spreading awnings that drooped between their support poles at each seller's stall, huge woven baskets sat on wooden tiers, their tempting display sending fragrance into the air. The rich soil of the hills of Gilead produced abundantly: grains, fruits of all kinds, from the common figs, fig-mulberries and olives, to pomegranates, apricots and citron, and vegetables, carrots and beans, onions, peas, leeks and lentils. Her garden produced the common foods, but Levi always found a way to ask for what it did not grow, seeds he would not buy for her – radishes, cucumber, spinach, turnips and eggplant.

So many ways to punish.

Hannah stared at the rich display before her. She had wept and pleaded with God, made endless bargains for the child that would spare her Levi's abuse, but God had not heard her, or if he had, he had not answered, and she had no place else to turn.

She went to set the basket down carefully, trying not to bend. It slipped from her fingers and landed with a soft thump on the ground. She reached across the piles of vegetables for the spinach at the back of the tiers of produce, so far away. The basket at her feet teetered. She leaned down to catch it, too quickly.

"Ooo-oo!" The moan burst out.

No one noticed. Children still played and yelled and ran through the market. Metal clanged from the metalworker's cart. A donkey brayed. Laughter echoed around her. People called back and forth. The woman still complained about the merchant's cheating, attracting a small crowd.

It was a slow process filling the large basket one-handed with things she needed to please her husband. She hesitated over the garlic that scented the air. Should she get some, and add it to her own bowl of stew? Would that keep Levi away from her?

The urge for subtle revenge passed, squashed by the reminder of Levi and the power of his anger. When had she become this cringing creature? How many beatings had it taken?

How much longer could she endure?

Out of the corner of one eye, she saw Joshua, Levi's brother, tall and dark-haired, standing at another stall. She turned her head away quickly, praying he had not seen her. He was tall enough to see over the heads of most of the villagers, he could easily spot her. And if he came over for a friendly greeting and asked about her face, she could hardly tell him the truth, he would never believe it, and she did not feel up to lies. The fig seller had guessed without being told, she was certain of that, but Joshua? Never!

A hand touched her shoulder. Hannah went as still as death, afraid even to breathe.

"Hannah?"

A woman's voice. She took a breath, easing her burning lungs. The buzzing in her ears went quiet.

"Hannah? Is anything wrong?"

She forced a smile and turned. "Hello, Taleh."

Taleh's mouth dropped open in a silent gasp. "Oh, Hannah, this cannot continue." She reached out and touched a spot on Hannah's cheek. Even under her gentle fingers, it set up a throbbing. "Hannah, Javan can help you. He is one of the elders now. He can do something, speak to Levi, whatever will stop this. I thought abuse was not permitted in this land. Why do you say nothing?"

"No!" Hannah heard the fear in her own voice, and fought it back down. "No, please, Taleh, let it go. Please."

"But you should not have to live like this!"

"Has anyone in the market said anything?" Hannah tried to turn her head, but Taleh would not permit it. Her touch on Hannah's cheek was careful, but firm. "I look frightful. I did not realize."

"People *should* know, Hannah. Perhaps that would stop him." Gentle, mild Taleh's voice held a scorn that surprised Hannah. She took Hannah's hands and squeezed carefully, as if she feared the simplest touch would cause more pain. "Please let me say something to Javan. We can fix this, Hannah, we can. Javan can make him stop. Maybe all it will take is the warning that people know."

Misery dragged at Hannah. How could she feel so old, and be only twenty and six? Taleh had ten years more, and seemed younger. Was that what being cherished did, form a shield against time? *What will I look like in ten more years*, she wondered. "Please say nothing, Taleh. Please, for my sake. It will only get worse. Besides, it is my fault. If I could give him a child, all would be well." She tried another smile, but it trembled, so she let it fade.

"Is *that* what this is about?" Taleh's voice was dark with disgust and disbelief. She wiped away a tear Hannah had not even known was there. It left a cool trail. "If you are afraid, come to us. We will give you safe haven. I mean it." Firm words, a promise. "Come to us. We are closest."

Hannah dared not bring another into her own horrors. "No. Your children . . ." she started.

"Javan and I will take care of our children. He was a soldier, you know." Taleh let go of Hannah's hands and started to turn away, then changed her mind and turned back, raising her finger like a scolding mother. "If I see you like this one more time, Hannah, nothing will stop me from interfering. I never thought to see women treated so in this land. I thought I had left all that behind when Javan captured me. I do not intend to let your husband bring such fear into my life again. I will *make* Javan take action, and I will visit you, to keep watch at least, as often as the children will permit me to get away."

Such a tiny woman, so much determination. Hannah knew enough of Taleh's history to know she meant what she said. She had endured life among the depravity and brutality of neighboring Ammon, the death of her own family in war, a trek as prisoner across the desert, the initial distrust of this village, kidnapping – why should Levi frighten her?

A little of the aloneness faded before Taleh's quiet resolve. "Thank you."

Taleh's oldest daughter, a pretty girl of about ten with straight, midnight-black hair, the most recent baby clinging awkwardly around her neck and wailing, pulled at her mother's sleeve. "Mother, please take Saul back. He will not stop crying, and I want to go play with Tamar."

"Thank you, Jochabed. You were a big help." Taleh reached out to caress her daughter's cheek like she had done to Hannah, and plucked her baby away, smothering his sobs against her shoulder and crooning.

Anguish, deep and visceral, squeezed Hannah's heart tight as she watched what she had been denied. She turned away, but Taleh must have seen. She opened one arm and wrapped Hannah in a cautious hug. She said nothing, for what was there to say, but there was compassion in her gaze.

Hannah carried the heavy basket on her good arm away from the busy market, feeling the pain rip through her with every step. It would take longer than ever to make it back home, and the evening meal would be late.

She could not let herself think about it. She clenched her jaw and kept walking.

The edge of the village beckoned, the last of the whitewashed stone houses leaning against the thick rock walls that protected the inhabitants from the dangers outside. Above the walls, Hannah saw the grassy hill give way to the trees that framed the small town. She had almost made it outside.

Just a little farther and she would be safely away from people, away from the threat of being bumped or jostled. Away from the threat that someone else would notice and ask questions, and she would have to come up with a believable lie.

Someone ran past her through the smaller west gate, likely from the lands outside the city, heedless of anything or anyone blocking the way, and shoved her in their frantic haste. Pain screamed through her. Above the agony that clamored within, Hannah noticed voices yelling and the sounds of anxious commotion. She leaned against the rough stone wall of the nearest house, shuddering as she tried to keep well out of the way of the crowd that bore down on the messenger.

The pain eased as she took careful breaths. A strange awareness grew. Fingers pointed at her, heads swiveled to look, and the crowd parted slowly, like the Red Sea in the days of Moses. At its center, she saw the runner, bent over as he gasped rasping breaths. An old man with thinning gray hair, who had clearly come a long way.

Then he straightened, and she looked into familiar faded brown eyes.

Halel, her husband's most trusted slave. Joshua stood by his side, his face a ghastly pallor. He looked in her direction, but Hannah did not think he even saw her.

"What is it?" Her voice scraped like rough gravel.

"Levi . . ." the slave only managed the one word. Hannah waited in numb stillness.

"Levi . . ." he tried again, "is dead."

CHAPTER 3

"He who touches the dead body of any man shall be unclean seven days."
Numbers 19:11

"Put your backs into it, men!"

Joshua pushed a sweaty curl of dark hair out of his eyes, leaned his weight against the big stone, and pushed along with several other men of the village. "Again!" The call came, and Joshua pushed with the others.

The summer heat had dried the grasses into brown stalks. Joshua wished for any green that might have softened the large hill of soft limestone on the far side of the village. If he moved his head the other direction inside the large hollow, he would see the wrapped shapes of the bodies of his parents behind the newly placed body of his brother.

He did not move his head.

Drowned. The word throbbed in his brain. Levi had been wandering drunk and had passed out by the water, so the decision had been from the elders. Levi, drunk? But the wineskin was there on the river's shore, empty, next to an abandoned axe. The limp skin sack still stank of wine.

Oddly, a small boat Joshua did not recognize had been tied to a tree not far away.

"Again! And . . . now!" The man called the cadence, and Joshua bent to the work. The cords of Joshua's neck stood out against the strain as he hurled his grief and rage against the stubborn rock. He sighed against the weight of aloneness in his chest, and gave another shove at the stone in time with the call. The stone slipped forward once, and once more, sliding by tiny bits into place before the hole, covering his family, parents and brother.

On the edge of his vision, he could see the small meadow, the trees that ringed it, their leaves hanging curled and limp in the oppressive heat, as though they, too, mourned with the gathered crowd. Hands covered faces as people rocked back and forth, moaning their grief to the cloudless sky. Heads dusted white with ashes caught the lowering sun. He saw sackcloth, the sign of deep grief.

Amid the din, his sister-in-law stood as though struck deaf, dumb and blind. Wailing from the grievers joined the ache inside him, but Hannah was silent.

The day had begun so simply, just another day. He had left his workshop to purchase a dozen new axe handles to finish newly formed axes, and some silver wire for the other, more profitable part of his business. He had visited with the shopkeeper, and turned to head back to his house and his work when the runner came. Hannah had been in the village, he remembered that, for it took all his effort to pretend she was not there. Despite so many years of practice, it never became easier not to stare at her and wish . . .

After the slave arrived with the shocking, life-altering news, for the first time when around her, he had been blind to her presence.

And now Hannah stood unmoving in the middle of the women, silhouetted against the distant trees, like a graceful statue carved from a solid piece of stone. With effort perfected by years of deliberate avoidance, he turned his attention back to the work.

A final mighty shove, and the rock thumped into place, sealing the hole of the cave. Final. Levi was gone, like their parents a few years before. The group of men stepped back from the grave. His practiced mask carefully in place, Joshua turned to face Hannah.

It was allowed now, finally, *finally*, he could look. He knew what lay ahead.

Did she remember?

Even in the shadows cast from the sun behind her, Joshua could see Hannah's eyes were swollen and dark from weeping, her arms wrapped around her middle as if to hold the pain inside. He knew that feeling, his very body hurt with the loss. He squinted against the glare, grateful that this first look was obscured.

The sun neared the horizon, catching his eye with the last of its rays. He could hardly believe so little time had passed. One day. Less than one day, and his life would never be the same.

Guilt settled more firmly on him. A dream fulfilled, but at what cost? The village elders had said nothing to him yet, but after the week of purification for touching the dead was done, he had no doubt they would find their way to his small house in the village and the workshop he had built behind it.

Barren women were not that uncommon in his land. It was one of the things that had to be endured in life. But an inheritance was now at stake. Levi's land must be protected. His family's name must be ensured and an heir must be raised.

According to the Law, Joshua knew – hoped – the heir was supposed to come from him. He was the closest male relation. After the initial grief had been spent, people would look at him and wonder how he would decide, whether he would accept a barren wife, or suffer disgrace.

There was no choice to make.

The farm was quiet. Hannah stood at the doorway and listened carefully. A sheep whuffled deeply somewhere, and stomped a foot against the hard-packed dirt. The sound carried easily in the cool, quiet night air.

Hannah had to hurry. If anyone found her, some slave who was restless during the night, they might ask questions she did not want to answer. She turned around, grabbed the rough sack she had made from the cloak Levi wore, and pulled.

Pain, her ever-present companion, sent fire through her ribs and down her wounded arm. Hannah froze in place until the heat eased, then pulled again. She bit back a whimper. She could do this, *would* do this.

It took longer than she thought to pull the load across the ground in the dark. If only she dared carry out her plan close by the house, it would save her steps and pain, but that was not possible.

The trees closed around her. It would be foolish to burn the stuff too near the trees, impossible to use the small, inadequate cooking fire outside her door where anyone could see, and she still had to go back for the fire-holder. She had not known the toll this would take on her body, nor realized how much stuff her husband had.

She only knew she would heal faster with these things gone.

At last, she came to an opening. The ground was more dirt than grasses here, little to catch fire. There was no breeze to carry any sparks in this still night when not even clouds moved. Only her, and the creatures of the night.

Hannah dropped the corner of the cloak, knelt, spread the cloak open. Levi's robes lay in a jumbled heap, his belts, his sandals, the loincloths he wore under his robes, the mantles he wrapped across himself on cool days. Most of them were of woven wool. She wondered if it would smell while it burned. A few pieces were of linen, but only a few. There had never been money to spare for buying such a luxury, he had always told her. They had sheep, she could spin and weave.

She hurried back to the house as fast as she could. Wild animals would not worry the pile in such a short time. The smell of man would keep them away until she got back.

No doubt the wild animals had more sense than she ever did.

If she could make the fire hot enough, everything of Levi's would be gone before anyone was awake.

Sweat trickled down the middle of his back from the summer sun's glare as Javan rapped once more on the doorframe. No sound came from inside, despite his call. The planked-wood door stood ajar. He hesitated about stepping inside, despite the welcome the unlatched door implied. *He* might be welcome, his message was an altogether different matter.

He straightened his shoulders and pushed the door wide. Making an effort to brush off the dust from his sandals against the threshold, a habit his wife had struggled hard to teach him so the children would learn from his example and save her work, he entered, leaving the hot sun gladly.

The room slowly took shape as his eyes adjusted to the dimness inside. The lattices had been closed against the day's glare, the thick stone walls muted the heat. He smothered a grin as he looked at the starkness that proclaimed it a man's domain. A bare wooden bench along the wall directly opposite, no back, no arms, just a slatted seat, the first thing a guest would see upon entering. An open door on the same wall led to another room, a stripe of sunlight visible from where he stood. A wooden chair to his left was the sole decoration on that wall, with no pillows on blankets to soften the hard wood frame. It would quickly become uncomfortable, Javan could tell. Against the wall to his right he saw a bed, the blankets jumbled from restless sleep, he assumed, and a small table. An oil lamp, grimy from past fires, hung cold and untended from the ceiling. A spider had made itself a tidy home with the lamp as one corner. Dust liberally coated the entire area, and scraped grittily underfoot.

Yes, Joshua certainly needed a wife. Few men chose to remain alone as long as he had. This might not be so difficult.

Where would Hannah prefer to live for the beginning of her wedded life? Out at the farm, where she had come as a young wife and had left her mark? Or would she enjoy bringing the life only a woman could to this lifeless place until it was time to move to the farm to prepare for the coming year's planting? The slaves could surely handle the fruit harvest and give the new family time to adjust.

Although there were fewer eyes to watch among the slaves than here, where a curious village would gladly enjoy the spectacle and hand out advice, requested or not.

Javan walked toward the open door. He did not know where it led, he had never been inside Joshua's house before, but he knew the kiln was behind the house. Joshua would likely be out there, since the house was so clearly empty.

But it was not as empty as he thought. Javan stopped in the doorway. His quarry sat at a table working quietly, absorbed in his task. Javan said nothing as he watched Joshua turn a tiny round clay mold carefully. The fragile thing seemed too small for his big hands. Joshua was treating the little ball as if it held treasure inside. But then, Joshua did not only make metal axes and hammers and pots. He had another talent. He made gold and silver into things of rare beauty. That small earthen thing might well hold something of great value.

A white cloth lay on the table beneath his careful hands. A hammer, too small for anything but jewelry, sat on the cloth, close at hand. There was plenty of light here, as opposed to the lone other room. The sun had moved during the day, taking the glare toward the front door, where Javan still felt its mark on his toughened skin, but this part of the house had large windows to make the most of the light regardless of where the sun shone when the lattices were opened. It was obvious that, whatever the rest of the house looked like, this room was where he lived.

In a direct line through one opened window, a kiln steamed quietly in the middle of Joshua's property, adding to the warmth of the day. Piles of metals waited next to it, ready to be melted and turned into something new. Even from here Javan could see they had been carefully sorted, copper, iron, bronze.

"Joshua?"

Startled, Joshua's hand closed on the tiny clay bead before he could drop it, and he looked up.

"My apologies." Javan smiled at him. Even though they did not know each other well, he had always liked this young man, not so young now. "I called your name before I entered, but there was no answer. I thought I would find you out at your kiln."

Joshua smiled back. "No, I had some other things to finish. Please, come in." He moved to rise, but Javan waved him back down. Joshua swung a hand to his left, toward the bench at the short end of the table. "Can I offer you something to drink? Wine? Perhaps a bit of bread?"

"Water, if you have it."

Shelves holding plates and bowls, among other eating utensils, sat over the table, within easy reach, and Joshua grabbed a goblet. He looked inside, frowned, and blew a quick breath. Dust puffed out. Javan bit the inside of his cheek to catch the smile. "I must rinse this out first." A red flush crept up Joshua's face. "I was not expecting guests."

"I lived by myself for a time, long ago. You need not explain," Javan said, letting a bit of the smile out. He coughed to cover a laugh as Joshua poured a dash of water in the goblet and swirled it. That first pour went sailing out the window before clear water was set before him. "How have you been? Your grief must be heavy."

Joshua's shoulders slumped as he sat back down. No, not sat, that was too controlled a word to describe what happened, Javan decided. In reality, Joshua's whole body crumpled under the grief and the chair was there to catch him. "It was most unexpected. I keep hoping to see him come striding through the village. I never knew what it meant to be so alone. Parents one expects." His voice cracked at the end.

"I know." Javan was not certain how much this man knew of his own history, the attacks from Ammon that had deprived him of his whole family in a single day. But this was not his grief. Today was about Joshua.

"I am keeping myself busy." Joshua met his gaze steadily despite the red suddenly rimming his eyes and the moisture that left a silver shimmer. "I find it helps. But please, finish your water. You have had a long walk, you must be thirsty."

Javan nodded. "I thank you for your hospitality. It is a warm day." He turned his attention to his goblet, now that the formalities had been observed, however briefly. After a few swallows, he said, "I apologize for interrupting you." He wanted to know more about the man before the rest of the village elders took on the second half of this task. Did any of the others know Joshua better than he did? If the young man refused his obligation, how far would they have to look to find the next repurchaser? "What are you making?"

"A necklace." Joshua gave him a measuring look before he pulled a shallow wooden box near the edge of the table over and ran his finger through a pile of glistening golden beads. "It will be small pomegranates of molded gold strung on a golden wire, with beads of ivory and shells. I hope to get a good price for it." He set the box aside, folded his arms, and fixed a challenging gaze on Javan. One eyebrow lifted.

"I think you will. I might buy it myself for my wife." Javan smiled. "I know what you are thinking. You are right, I did not come here to discuss necklaces."

Joshua sat watchful, that single eyebrow still raised.

"I am here about Hannah."

One small nod.

"You know the law."

Joshua nodded again, that same single bob of the head.

"You must have known we would come." Javan waited again.

Joshua sighed softly, and frowned. "I had expected it, yes."

Javan could not read that sigh. Dread and a refusal? Or resignation and acceptance? "There is an inheritance at stake. Any child of Levi's, if there should be one, would inherit, of course. We must wait to see if she is pregnant. It is possible, although . . ." He shook his head. "After so many years, there is little reason to believe she is with child now."

"Yes."

Javan watched the younger man carefully, but could tell nothing from his face. Joshua had much practice in hiding his thoughts, to do it so well. Perhaps he did not know this man because he did not want to be known. What could he possibly have to hide?

"To refuse means disgrace." Joshua spoke mildly, no expression in either face or voice.

Did he want a way out? He could not force the man to accept. "Yes. Some would understand," Javan said. "You would not be the first to say no."

Joshua gave him a strange, almost reproachful look.

"It has been known," Javan reminded him. "Perhaps not here, not often, but I have heard of brothers who would not." He resisted the temptation to play with the fragile instruments laid out before him. The heavy hammers Joshua used to beat iron and bronze, hanging in a line on the wall from leather straps in their handles, caught his attention. The house might be ignored, but Joshua took care of the tools of his trade.

He gave up trying to read the man. What he did know was good enough, a hard worker, a man whose ability and talent was respected. A quiet man, not known to drink, with no scandal attached to his name. "Your grief is heavy, I know. It has only been a week. We need your answer tomorrow. The period of mourning has been set at one month, and at that time Hannah will have to wed, should she not be with child. The purification week is already gone, but three are left. She will need to be informed, as soon as possible. She, too, has mourning to work through."

Joshua nodded. "Please let me know what time the rest of the elders are planning to convene on the matter. I will be there."

Javan stood. "Yes. I can tell you this much, if you decide to take her, we will all be glad to hear it." He looked down at the handsome man seated before him. Women often stared when he walked past, at the strong-boned face which the neat beard could not hide, at his surprising odd golden hawk's eyes, at his height, his arms corded with muscle, his long-fingered hands. This was a man any woman would be happy to wed. If Joshua agreed, he and Hannah would have beautiful children, should God bless them so. "Perhaps it will not be as difficult as you fear. Widows remarry all the time."

Javan wished he could give a guarantee, promise that all would be well and the marriage be a happy one. He had done a similar thing, taken an unwilling wife during the wars with Jephthah, rescued her from certain slaughter and forced an agreement out of her in exchange, marriage to him or slavery. How well it had worked out. He loved her, more deeply than he had ever expected, and the feeling was returned. His wife. His beloved Taleh. Just thinking about her warmed his heart. Joshua and Hannah had an advantage in that both must have known this was coming. They would have time to adjust, to accept.

But he could give no promise. He could only hope.

.   .   .

Joshua closed the door as Javan's figure disappeared behind the corner of a whitewashed house at the end of the street. Had he given himself away? He thought back over his words. No, surely Javan could not have guessed.

He dared not go back to work on the delicate gold beads. His hands were shaking.

Had Javan noticed? Perhaps they had not been shaking then. Javan had given no sign that Joshua could see, had not stared at Joshua's hands, but he was an elder, used to hiding his thoughts.

During this past week of purification for touching the dead, he had prayed for forgiveness, and wondered why, after committing the sin of coveting his brother's wife, God had seen fit to grant him the object of his every desire.

Perhaps there would be punishment still.

He knew Hannah thought of him as a vague shadow on the edge of her world. From that first shattering day, he had worked hard to see that it stayed that way.

She had come into the village a shy new bride, lovely and sad. Her parents had recently died, the marriage broker brought the information, and her brother needed some easing of the burdens on his shoulders. With the sudden responsibility of his inheritance, his own wife uncertain in her new home, learning to run the family farm alone and needing money to buy slaves to take over work his father would no longer be around to share, he had found a husband for his pretty, and very marketable, sister.

The brother and his wife had been at the wedding, and Joshua noticed immediately that the siblings were so near in age they could almost be twins. But clearly his sister's happiness mattered little. Hannah's brother wore his relief like a bright robe, and the young wife was clearly satisfied.

Joshua remembered standing to one side at the feast, watching his new sister-in-law. He had not loved her then. That came later, near the end of the day.

A bitter love, piercing and heavy with guilt but as unstoppable as the sunrise.

He had seen her set aside her own grief to smile at each new introduction, a smile sweet and filled with hope. Sadness hid in her eyes, slipping out whenever the gaiety around her slowed and each respite let her parents' deaths and her brother's sudden rejection intrude.

He watched her idly at first, watched her struggle to remember names from this unfamiliar place. She laughed at her mistakes easily, her charm reaching out to everyone who paused at the bride-table under the awning in the wide open space before the new house Levi had built to replace the one in which the two of them had been raised, a house that had begun to crumble. The new house was much smaller, but there would be plenty of time and space to build on rooms as children came. They did not know then that there would be no children, nothing had cast a pall on the festivities. Even the sun had joined in the happiness. The day had been warm and bright, the air fresh with spring. A perfect day to feast outside, a perfect day to begin a new life.

Food was spread out on a second long table sharing the shade, further protected by makeshift tents to keep the sun from eating away at the coolness that protected the roasted quails, baskets of warm bread, figs, bowls of nuts and roasted grains, grapes, olives, dates, oranges and early pomegranates, small cakes sweetened with honey and citron, pitchers of water and wine.

Joshua leaned against the closed door and let the memory come back. Finally, after all these years, he could think on that day again. It was all so clear. He could even smell the foods.

Levi had glowed with pride in his choice, his pretty young wife. Joshua knew much about her from Levi's weeks of negotiating and anticipating. He had gone to the end of the line around the bridal table to wait his turn to extend congratulations. He stepped up to the table just as Levi moved away with some of the men.

Hannah had watched him go, this husband she barely knew, her green eyes giving away her vulnerability at being left among strangers. When she turned back, Joshua smiled. "Hello. I wanted to bid you welcome to the family."

Her eyebrows lifted in curiosity.

Had Levi told her nothing about him? "I am your brother-in-law. Jos-"

"Joshua," she interrupted. A bright smile broke over her face, transforming her from pretty to something beyond loveliness. "Of course, I know of you. You are the goldsmith. I was beginning to wonder if you were even here."

He had grinned at her. "I hoped for the line to subside, but it was not going to happen, so I waited my turn."

They both laughed.

"I am relieved I only do this once," she smiled at him. "I would not like the other guests to hear me say this, but I will be glad when it is over." And she blushed, deeply, red rushing up into her cheeks as she realized what awaited her when it was done.

Perhaps it started then.

His next action might have been out of place. He meant it merely as a kindness. But at the joyous pleasure in her face, it became much more.

He brought out a gift, roughly wrapped in fabric. "My brother chose well," he said, and pressed the small gift into her hand.

She carefully untied the simple string holding the fabric tight. A breeze caught the wrapping, blowing it aside, and the gift burst into color in the sun. A brooch of gold, in the shape of a lily, with a yellow stone peeking out of the hammered petals. It had been one of his best pieces, but he only saw her hand, where the golden lily rested as if it belonged there, and her eyes, where the shadows of sadness had finally disappeared.

"Oh, Joshua," she said. "It is beautiful. I have never seen anything so perfect."

And he knew.

He had made excuses, taken his leave with embarrassing haste.

And spent the next six years learning to live with the hole a simple smile left in his heart.

CHAPTER 4

Naomi said to her, "The man is a close relative to us, one of our near kinsmen."
Ruth 2:20

Hannah stood in the doorway of her house and breathed the morning air. *Her* morning air. She ignored the pain in her ribs that stabbed her with every breath and reveled in the scent of freedom, in knowing she could make whatever she wanted for her morning meal, wear whatever she wanted, tell the slaves to do something and know they would listen to her because there was no one to come behind and contradict.

Levi was dead. God had heard her prayers, and if the answer had been dramatic and shocking, she would not be the one to question it. She shoved aside the guilt that nipped at her conscience. She had done nothing to make Levi die.

Unless her barrenness finally drove him to his death.

No! She would not think that way. She could not. She had not given him the wine, she had not pushed him into the river. He had done that on his own. She had survived. It was *her* land now, *her* life. Only her God, and possibly her slaves, knew how dearly she had paid for this.

He had been careless – or foolish. The village knew finally that he had not been perfect. Perhaps they had never thought that of him, no matter how often he told her how respected he was by others. She knew such feelings were beneath her, but she could not suppress the satisfaction of hoping the village wondered what kind of man drank himself too drunk to stand up in a small river after falling in.

And no one had come with an explanation for the small boat.

Hurtful memories hovered around each building, each field, but she hoped time would make them fade and free her from their poison. Levi still lived in her nightmares, but perhaps someday even her sleep would be her own again. It had been only seven days, after all. Not nearly enough time to heal either body or spirit.

She could wait.

She rubbed her sore arm absently, as she had done for the last days every time she thought of her husband.

Through the waving poplar trees that bordered the edge of her land, Hannah saw a bright flash of blue. It bobbed slowly along, moving in her direction. Behind the blue, she saw a yellow patch, and then a multi-colored one. The slow-moving chain of color drew nearer and took form.

Men. Middle-aged, gray-haired and dignified, they came relentlessly on. She looked at the trio, and her heart gave a sinking lurch. Eli, shockingly old to be making such a long walk, nearly an hour on foot, Javan, Taleh's husband and a big man with the first gray marking his dark hair, and Obed, the most recent man to be recognized as one of the village elders.

Oh, God help her! How could she have forgotten? Three men, sent to represent the entire body of the old and wise men of the village. Three men, sent to enforce the Law.

She was so unremarkable – why could they not have forgotten her, left her to the new joys of freedom? Noise built in her head, ringing in her ears, louder and louder as the men walked across the open space and drew up in a line in front of her. Their faces blurred, the forms wavering in tune with the noise in her head, and then all color vanished.

. . .

Hannah heard a sigh. It caught on a little sob, and the sad sound made her open her eyes. A tall shadow shifted, letting a flash of sunlight blind her for an instant before the shadow blocked the glare again.

Memory rushed back. She covered her face with her hands, hiding her embarrassment. Her fingers trembled against her skin, and she hated her fear. They must think her a fool, or the weakest of women, to faint at the sight of visitors.

How could she have forgotten the Law? To think she had believed her life her own! She felt ill, thinking of her blind foolishness, her delirious joy at the wonders of freedom. Hysteria clawed at the back of her throat, hideous laughter that fought for raucous release. Shudders started, odd twitches that toyed with her body as she lay there, unable to find the strength – or courage – to rise.

Someone slid an arm under her shoulders, and lifted her to a sitting position. The feel of a man's touch jolted her the rest of the way to her feet, where she stood, trembling, as she stared into the heart of her nightmares.

"Hannah?' Javan spoke warily. She saw his hand outstretched, as though to guide a wild creature into the snare.

She backed away, coming up sharply against the stone wall of the house. The drooping awning that shielded the door blocked the sun for her. Without the glare, she could see their faces clearly, wide-eyed and uncomfortable. Her stomach turned over, and she swallowed hard.

"Would you like some water?" Javan's hand dropped to his side. "Let me get you some."

That was her responsibility, taking care of her guests, unwelcome as they were. "You must have some also." But she was talking to the air. Javan disappeared into the house in search of the water pail and a cup. She stared behind him at the darkness inside the still-shuttered house, afraid to turn and look at the other men. Foolish to hope they would refresh themselves and leave. But she could not hear their news now. Just a few moments to prepare, a few moments to forget again. "Please sit."

But there was no place to sit except the dirt, unless someone dragged out the bench from the table. There was, however, the small three-legged stool leaning against the side of the house, the stool she perched upon while cooking. It was hardly sufficient for Eli. She motioned to it anyway, hospitality forcing her courtesy. "I have only this?"

He smiled, his wrinkled face crinkling. "I have used less. I appreciate your kindness." Obed helped him down onto the stool, and the old man leaned against the house with a sigh.

Just then Javan came out, carrying the pail in one hand, four cups cradled easily in his other. He took over the duties of host, and Hannah let him. Her hands were shaking, and she did not want them to see.

Let them forget, she prayed. *Let them refresh themselves and go.* The prayer grew in desperation as the water level in the cups lowered, the bottoms raising higher in the air with each swallow.

She should offer another drink, give them dried fruit or bread. She could not. She did not want them here, and her prayer built. *Make them go, make them leave.*

But the prayer was not answered. After draining the cup, Eli set it on the ground and rose slowly to his feet, with some help from Obed. He turned to her, and Hannah felt her heart clench. He spoke first, by virtue of his age. "You and your husband had no children. Please forgive us our boldness, but are you with child now?

She dared not lie, tempting though it was. God had ways of making sure liars were found out. "No." She tried not to blush, but her cheeks heated. Men knew these things about women. They were all married, they knew about a woman's cycles, but how could they know what a shameful thing Levi had made her own monthly times, the beatings she endured each time she proved herself barren? The mockings at her missing womanliness, the blame for wasting his precious seed?

She could not bear their delay. Best to know and get it over with. "How does Joshua feel about this?"

In his raspy, old-man voice, Eli said, "It is good that you know why we are here."

Good? Hannah let his comment pass. She turned to Javan. Taleh knew about Levi. Taleh also loved – and trusted – her husband. He was big, and dark-haired and brown eyed, but that meant nothing about the man. Outward appearance meant nothing. Levi had been sunshine packaged as man, light-complexioned, hair almost her own color, and green-eyed, but nothing about the inner Levi was bright, evil in a misleading package. If Levi had been all soft colors and evil, did that mean dark hair was the sign of good?

Javan wore yellow, and Hannah thought she saw something of Taleh in the color. Taleh trusted her husband, and he cared enough for his wife that he would wear a yellow robe, but Hannah did not know if Taleh had followed through with her threat to tell Javan what she knew and saw. He might be standing there in ignorance.

Although, whether he knew or was in ignorance, he would still have to do this. Would he not?

Eli, the oldest, what hair he had left the white of frost, wore the blue robe that had first caught her attention, a dignified color for a dignified man. His scalp was dotted with brown spots, she knew because she could see the top of it. Age had bent and shrunk him until he could hardly seem a threat, but she could not convince herself to trust him. His eyes were too shrewd, or perhaps just because they were faded into near colorlessness, they seemed to see right through her.

Of all of them, the third man standing there, tall and regal in his Joseph's coat, Obed worried her the most. His light brown hair was brightened to Levi's color by the morning sun, but his eyes scared her, odd and gold and piercing. He was new to the village elders, which meant he had not yet been on many decisions. She knew of his history, his Ammonite wife who had caused him such grief. The woman had tried to flee back to her own country to sacrifice the child she carried. Obed had caught her before she crossed the border, then married someone else to raise the baby once he sent her away. Hannah knew only that his second wife was the village midwife, and that the child nearly sacrificed was now a sweet-faced, brown-haired, green-eyed girl of fifteen.

No, Obed would not be quick to trust a woman's word.

She turned to Javan, with his playful yellow robe. Did she tell him everything? "Tell me, please, how does Joshua feel? Should he not be with you?

Has he refused? Who will take his place?" Her heart beat with dread, pounding bitterness through her body. The nightmare was already here. Joshua had given her a gift once. One gift. One gift meant nothing. After he owned her, if he agreed, would he be as bad as his brother? No other woman in the village had accepted him. That alone terrified her. She would have to do what no other woman was willing to.

Perhaps he had not asked one yet. In a nation that valued marriage as much as Israel did, a single man was great cause for concern.

If not Joshua, who else was in the family to whom she could be tossed like helpless prey? She knew nothing about the family. Levi had not seen fit to share his relatives with her. This wonderful gift of her freedom – had God truly set her free from Levi only to bind her to another?

If only there was a way out, an escape!

"He has not refused," Javan said. He sounded pleased.

Of course, she thought bitterly. If Joshua refused, no doubt the elders would have to go to much effort to find another kinsman to replace him. This way was so much easier and more convenient for everyone.

Except her.

She looked at the three waiting men, while her mind struggled for some delay, some excuse, like a rabbit in a snare, tugging against the restraints. But the trap held firm. There was no way out. Too many years of living according to Law, of obedience and belief, crowded in on her.

She opened her mouth to plead for mercy, but the men were so satisfied, so pleased. They had a Law to follow, too. She had been stupid all those horrid years, keeping her secret. Or was it Levi's secret? If she told now, who would believe?

Taleh. But Taleh could not help her now, could not stop the Law.

If only she had conceived! If only that last time, weeks ago, had borne fruit! But it had not, and he had kept her from his bed, only finding her to hurl accusations about her uselessness and beat her. The one respite, banishment from his bed, would not have lasted much longer, he would have used her again, if not for conception, at least for relief of his needs. The other, well, for the other, there had never been a respite. She sometimes wondered if he took pleasure in using his fists.

And it would all happen again, before she had a chance to heal. She did not know what she had done to make her God so angry with her.

The men waited patiently.

Her spirit broke. She could feel it, the last remnants of hope and happiness dissolving with inexpressible pain. She bowed her head. "When?"

"The end of the month. Three weeks away. He has agreed to give you this time. It is good of him. Once it is over, he will come for you." Eli's intake of breath sounded loud in the quiet morning air.

Hysterical laughter bubbled up. Hannah could not catch it this time. It burst out, the sound wild in the still meadow. Three more weeks. He would give her three more weeks!

"Hannah!" Javan's voice snapped against her, angry and harsh.

The laughter died.

How could she have lost control like that? Hannah felt the bile rise and hoped they would leave before she disgraced herself.

Javan smiled at her, but it looked uneasy. "Do not worry about the land. Joshua may once have decided to turn his own parcel over to Levi, but he remembers enough to direct the men. The land will not suffer. The child he will try to give you will find his hereditary possession well cared-for."

She had the wild urge to slap his face. More than just him, all three of them. They were condemning her to horrors beyond what they could possibly know, and they dared *smile*?

"What time?" She was surprised she could speak around the nausea.

"At sunrise on the thirtieth day, Joshua has told us." Obed spoke for the first time.

She felt hollow inside, drained. "I will be ready," she said, and heard the emptiness in her voice. She looked down at her bare feet, peeking out beneath her robe. "I must put on my sandals. I apologize for greeting you in such disrepair."

Javan looked at her, a strange expression on his face. "There is no need. Our task is done. We just came to bring you Joshua's acceptance of his responsibility. We will not intrude on you further."

He frowned, and Hannah felt the old fear creep along her spine.

The men made their farewells and left, walking slowly back down the gently sloping path that led through the thin woods to the village.

She ran on shaky legs to the corner of the house, braced herself with one hand against the rough stone, still cool in the weak morning sun, and vomited.

CHAPTER 5

God said to Abraham, "Don't let it be grievous in your sight . . . In all
that Sarah says to you, listen to her voice."
Genesis 21:12

Javan watched his wife pull the small, well-worn hand loom into place on
the floor. This was the time of day he liked best, when all six of their children were in bed and it was just the two of them again. He had added onto
the back of the house as the children began to arrive, but this part was much as it
had been when he first brought her here. The cedar table for eating but with
more benches now, and oak shelves that held their pottery, plates and cups and
bowls, filled half of the large room. This half of the room was for sitting and talking. During the day the floor was covered with goat's hair or feather pillows for
the children to loll about on between their chores. The lone bench they had at the
beginning of their marriage was still there, softened with blankets. The wood
had been well used. He ran his fingers over the smooth edge and remembered
Taleh lying on it when her first pregnancy was discovered and she felt so ill.

The windows had been shuttered for the evening. The house was still warm, he could have opened the windows for air, but it would get cool soon enough and he wanted to keep the moths away from the burning oil lamps, some hanging from the beams overhead, some on tall iron stands.

Those stands were Joshua's work. And that brought him back to the subject he wanted to talk to his wife about.

Taleh slid down with the grace that he still loved to watch, and seated herself next to the loom. It clicked, slowly at first, then picked up speed, rhythmically counting the rows as she worked on another robe, picking up where she had left off the night before. He wondered idly which of their children had outgrown their clothes this time, then leaned back against the wall behind him. Taleh's black hair shimmered in the lamplight. He loved to watch her, even after all these years, loved to watch her work, loved the vitality that came from her every move, loved the soft humming she did unknowing when she was happy.

What a treasure he had plucked from the Ammonite war.

He needed her perception now. She had endured much before he captured her, and often could see things he could not. "Wife?"

He waited until she carefully set down the smooth wooden shuttles on the warp threads that stretched along the loom. She fixed her dark gaze on him. "Yes?"

"Today, Eli and Obed and I went to see Hannah, to tell her that Joshua had agreed to perform brother-in-law marriage."

She turned abruptly back to her weaving. Her hands were trembling. The wooden sheds that only a moment before had lifted smoothly to make room for the shuttles jerked now. The rhythm was lost, and the uneven vibrations danced along the warp.

She never turned away from him unless she was very angry. What had he said?

He held his tongue when the shuttle caught on a thread and she muttered in frustration as she tried to untangle it. The batten stick slid off her lap and rattled on the stone floor.

Javan fought the urge to get down and help her, but he frowned in sympathy as she struggled to untangle things. The shuttles slid through again, the sheds rose in order again, but the smoothness had not returned.

This marriage of Joshua and Hannah seemed to upset everyone: Joshua and his closed face, Hannah and her panic, Taleh and her anger. What did everyone know that he did not?

"I am worried for her, and I do not know why. You know her, perhaps you can help me understand."

"What did she do?" Taleh's voice was as stressed as her weaving.

"She fainted first, then later she laughed like one gone crazy. I would swear she had forgotten all about this law before we arrived. Her spirit seemed broken, as if this news was the worst possible she could hear. I felt as if I should apologize for providing her with a new protector."

"Oh." Taleh gave up on the loom. The jerky noise stopped, and the wooden frame gave a final shudder.

Javan did not think his wife was surprised at Hannah's oddities. Had Taleh been there with them at Hannah's door, he suspected she might have been ready for such a reaction. He waited for her to say more. Instead, she picked lightly at the newly woven threads as though removing lint. This was not like his wife. She had not even looked at him since his announcement.

If she would not speak, he would. "She needs a child."

Taleh's head jerked back up, and her midnight eyes met his in alarm. "She is barren."

"I know that." He bit back his irritation. "Perhaps she will be successful with Joshua. It does happen that way."

"Perhaps."

Javan scowled at his wife. "Taleh, I know you have something to tell me, something you are hiding. It might help me understand. Out with it. Speak to me."

She rubbed her forehead, and took a deep breath. "What can it hurt now?" she said softly. She was not speaking to him.

"Hurt what?"

Taleh looked at him with sad eyes. "Levi beat Hannah horribly."

He inhaled sharply, an ugly sickness sliding into his stomach. What he had assumed was from weeping – how could he have been so blind? He closed his eyes and slid down to slump on the wide bench, splaying his legs for balance. He opened his eyes again. "I saw nothing before, and I have known the man for years. Are you sure it was from him? A farm can be a dangerous place. How do you know?"

"She was very skilled at hiding her bruises. If you men had taken the time to look at her arms at the funeral, you would have seen they were badly bruised. One was even bound – poorly, as if she had done it herself, with no one to help. I fear it might have been broken. And more than her arm. Every breath pained her."

Javan looked down at his precious wife, and rage boiled. How could a man do such a thing? And to Hannah, so slender, like his own woman. Taleh had been stolen away once by a man who cared nothing for her. Javan had got her back safely, before she could be harmed. And had seen that the man died for it.

Taleh was still talking, cleansing herself of the secret she had kept. "Her face was bruised, up near the hairline so she could cover it with her headdress. There was a big bruise on her cheek, as well. You men must have thought her swollen eyes were from weeping. I know that is not the case. I saw her at the marketplace before ever the news came. I do not believe she shed one single tear. Ask around the market. See if some still remember what she looked like that day. It was not that long ago."

Taleh was on her knees now, as if pleading. "The bruises were getting old. She must have waited before coming to the village. And it was not the first time. It happened many, many times, each one worse than the last. She would not permit me to tell. I am surprised Levi did not succeed in killing her."

She rose to her feet, and crossed the room to kneel again at his side. "Husband, is there no way to stop this marriage? Hannah does not deserve any more misery. She finally has her freedom. I actually saw her smile yesterday. She does not know I was watching. I have been walking over to her house, just to make sure she is surviving."

Taleh cupped her hands around Javan's face. "Javan, Hannah is only now able to use that arm. If he had found her instead of drinking that day –"

Taleh's voice trailed away. Her dark eyes held him as surely as her hands, gentle imprisonment. "Javan – stop this marriage. Please?"

Javan caught her hands and kissed them as he pulled them away. He wrapped his arms around her and held her close, needing to be gentle, to wipe out the vision of violence. Still, he had to ask, "How can you be sure it was Levi? A farm is a dangerous place."

"I am positive. There is no doubt." Taleh pulled back slightly, and braced her hands on Javan's strong chest. "Have you ever seen a more defeated woman? More subdued, more withdrawn? Levi has been torturing his wife, and none of the people in the village ever saw until this last time, or ever dared speak if they did. I am ashamed how long I waited to tell her I even knew. The day Levi's body was found, I told her I would tell you, and you would stop him."

Javan hid his smile of pride. How simple she made it sound, that she would tell him, and he would fix everything. He kissed her forehead, and let her continue.

"She was terrified, and begged me to say nothing. She feared he would attack her again. It was her fault, she said, since she had not given him a child."

"He beat her because she was barren?" Prickles of disgust filled his mouth, like a dish of spoiled meat.

"Yes." Taleh grasped his arms, and tugged, as if to shake him into submission. "Please, stop this marriage?"

Javan rested his forehead against hers. "No, wife, I cannot. It is the Law." He leaned back with a heavy sigh. "It all makes sense now. I do not know why I did not see it before."

"She was too clever at hiding his abuses." Taleh let go of his arms, and leaned back on her heels.

"He was too clever at hiding his nature," Javan corrected. How obvious it all was. Now that he had all the missing pieces, so many things made sense, the separateness Levi clung to, holding everyone away, no visiting with others, no reciprocal invitations to his house, the silence of their slaves, how Levi even had kept Javan, his closest neighbor, away so subtly. He was always busy, with no time for a casual conversation.

And Javan had been so busy himself, with his family, his own farm, his responsibilities, that he had accepted the excuses and lived as a virtual stranger to Levi and his wife.

It made him ill to think what blindness he had shown, not just he but all the older men of the village. There had been a monster in their midst and they had all been happy to ignore him.

What a pity Levi was beyond their reach.

How well did he know the brother? He would watch this time.

Where was the money? The sun splashed through the opened windows onto the gray stone floor, giving much needed light. Leaving the lattices open was a risk, the slaves might see, but she could not afford to miss a single possible hiding place by saving her examination for the privacy of night. Hannah sat back on her heels in the eating room and shoved her dusty fingers through her hair. A pale swath abruptly fell back across her eyes. She pushed it aside in a flash of furious frustration.

There was no place left to look in the house. She had just finished searching the shelves in the eating room, had emptied the other set of shelves, the large shelves that held the blankets and pillows in the room where they sat at day's end, or rather, where Levi had sat in pompous majesty on his carved wood chair and she had shivered with fear in her smaller chair nearby. She was never allowed to sit in the bench against the opposite wall. It was too far away. No one had ever sat on that bench, but she had checked it anyway to see if anything was loose that would hide a bag of gold, perhaps a hidden layer of wood under the shiny top. But no, there was not a place under any board to hide anything.

She had even pushed the heavy mattress off the bed in their sleep room with her legs to see if anything rattled inside, but it was only straw and tree needles. And now she had to figure out how to get it back on.

Where had Levi hid their – his – coins? She knew he had sold seeds, the monies she had used to purchase that last basket of food for him had come from that supply, knew she had not purchased anywhere near enough to have spent it all. She could not get away without Levi's coins. The days were slipping by, she had no way of stopping time, she had given her word to the elders, she had said she would go through with this marriage, but she could not! How hypocritical of her to have agreed at all. She should have thrown herself on their mercies and begged for release.

She could not marry Joshua. She could not marry again, not ever. Not even for a child, not even for Levi's inheritance. Let the birds and beasts have it!

She glanced heavenward, almost expecting divine retribution to strike her. "I am sorry," she called out, hoping Heaven would hear and forgive. "Please help me!"

There was no retribution, no thunder from heaven. Did God understand? If He did, why was there no way out?

She had never heard of a woman refusing this kind of marriage. Never. She would be the first. But she did not have the courage to stand up to the elders, the village, or Joshua, not before, and not now. Finding Levi's coins was the only way, if there were enough to pay for her flight.

Joshua had done well for himself, she knew. His business thrived with all the work the villagers gave him, all the pots to make, and swords and spades and axes.

And brooches. He had given her a brooch.

If only she could use Joshua's money to flee. He certainly must have enough.

Panic tightened her chest again, as it had last night and yesterday morning and every time she thought about what lay ahead. God had set her free once, how could He let this happen?

Where would she go? She had asked herself that same question for days, and never found an answer. Her brother would not welcome her. His wife in particular, if things had not changed, certainly would not. Hannah could not think of any reason her sister-in-law would have changed her opinion. She did not know to this day what she had done to so annoy her brother's wife, and make her demand Hannah leave. No, there would be no help from that quarter. She would have to find another place to run. She had skills to support herself, and she could glean on the edges of the fields for her food, always left untouched for those like her, not just field corners, but fallen sheaves and fallen fruit, food for those desperate and determined enough to harvest for themselves.

She was certainly both.

She would think of that later. First she must find the funds to get her away. She would decide how far to go based on how many coins she found. If there were enough at all . . .

Where were they?

Panic came again, fiercer, faster, stronger.

No money, no coins. No escape.

What was she going to do? Hannah dropped her head in her hands and sobbed, the tears trickling through her fingers like winter rain.

CHAPTER 6

"When a man takes a new wife, he shall not go out in the army, neither shall he be assigned any business. He shall be free at home one year, and shall cheer his wife whom he has taken."
Deuteronomy 24:5

Joshua wiped the top of the smooth wooden table again, and stepped back to see if he had missed any corners. The faint morning light was kind to his efforts. Hannah would be here soon, and see it in the bold light of full day. His house must meet with her approval.

He looked around the room. His tools were still on the shelves he had built for them, the hammers hanging on the wall. Would she mind that he had usurped so much of their eating room for his work?

He wanted her to approve. He wanted everything to be perfect for her. Joshua bent over and took a closer look at the small bowl of the flowers he had smuggled from the field into his house last night. Their petals had begun to curl. He stuck a finger in the bowl. It had dried over night. He reached for the pitcher that always sat by the table, and poured a little water in the bottom, and hoped it was enough.

Today was the day. The waiting was over. The month was passed.

He had not talked to her yet. He had kept himself distant for so long. From that devastating day of Levi's wedding, Joshua had been very cautious, intent that no one ever guess. They had conversed so easily on her wedding day – her *first* wedding day. Now he feared his tongue would cleave to the roof of his mouth, and he would stand there, as speechless as the most callow youth.

In all the six years of his brother's marriage, he had exchanged barely a hundred words with Hannah. Perhaps that number was even too large. But he had watched her, Oh! how he had watched. Carefully, so carefully. He had stored up memories, holding them close during long nights when loneliness threatened to smother him.

Hannah was his now. Every time he thought of it, discomfort and wonder and fear roiled in him.

Six years of torment and pain were almost ended. How strange, how very strange life was. Somehow he had imagined God must be angry with him for the feelings he had not quite been able to control. Yet He still granted Joshua this dream.

Hannah, of the quiet and soft-spoken manner, the gentle green eyes in a face of delicate beauty, the cloud of light brown hair that she kept so carefully hidden beneath her headdresses, and that too-slender body.

He would have to get her to eat more, and add some flesh to her bones. Everyone knew that a woman needed to be more rounded to carry a child safely. Perhaps her very thinness had kept her barren all those years.

Some of the villagers, his friends who knew nothing of his feelings, congratulated him on his obedience to the Law. They thought him reluctant to wed her. How surprised they would be! From comments made when he was not supposed to be able to hear, he knew most of the village worried about him ever having a child from barren Hannah. Perhaps, like Javan, they looked for him to take another wife just in case no heir came. How surprised they would be if they knew he would take her – and gladly – even if word came from Heaven that they would never have a child!

If no child came, he intended to have his brother's oldest slave be his heir. Abraham had planned to do that, and if Abraham could, he could see no reason why he could not. Joshua would remove the land from their lives rather than have it hang over her head as a shameful thing, a constant reminder of her barrenness. He would share her sorrow, just as his brother must have, for Levi had never taken another wife, either.

He would – somehow – convince her that he loved her as much as Levi had.

He washed the stone floor quickly, then took the clay bowl with the dingy water from his final cleaning and stepped to the door. The dirty water arched in a brown-tinged rainbow before it splashed onto the thirsty ground. He shook the last few drops off the bowl, brought it back and set it on the table. He dropped the ragged swatch of linen he had used to clean his house into it.

Time must be going past. He had been up so early, he no longer knew where the sun was in the sky. Had he forgotten anything? His floor was clean, the table was clean, even his bed was covered in clean new linen, a gift from the women in the village who always enjoyed a wedding. He had washed the front part of the house just the past night.

The sun peeked through the window.

Hannah was waiting for him to arrive.

His new undyed linen robe lay on the new sheet on the bed, the bed that took up one corner of his simple house. The bed on which he would finally make Hannah his wife. Every time he thought it, his heart gave a leap.

Only one thing tainted his expectation.

He would have to be better than his brother. He wanted to be loved more than she loved Levi. And he hated the competition, but was as power-less to feel it as he was to stop the sun from setting.

A water jar and soap waited on the small table. Each moment brought the time closer when she would be expecting him to arrive.

Joshua washed himself, taking special care on his armpits so no smell would offend. The fresh robe, almost white, befitting the day, slid stiffly down his body. It had been a long time since he had a new one. Clothes were not something he needed concern himself with. Questions chased each other around his mind. How would she receive him? Was she surprised he had accepted his duty? Pleased? Disappointed? Relieved at the chance to try for a child?

If there were others who had gone through this situation in Israel, he did not know them.

He stepped outside. Javan was leaning against the frame of his door with the air of a man losing patience. He moved politely out of the way as Joshua pulled it shut. "Joshua."

"Javan. Did you come to make sure I would follow through?"

"No." Then one side of Javan's mouth lifted in a faint smile. "Well, yes, perhaps, but that is not my only reason to be here."

Joshua's eyebrow lifted.

"It is customary for the bridegroom's friends to escort him, just as it is customary for the bride's friends to prepare her. My wife is at Hannah's even now. Did you think you had no friends to accompany you on this happy day?" Javan's eyes were watchful, measuring.

If he was expecting Joshua to be reluctant, he would be disappointed.

Or perhaps not.

Joshua smiled unevenly. "No. I knew full well there would be many who wanted to join me, but this is not the usual wedding and I did not know what was appropriate, so I turned all the offers down." He did not want to admit how grateful he was to see Javan there. This was not the way he ever imagined getting his first wife and Hannah – well, Hannah had not spoken to him in person, and only now did he know for a certainty that she would be ready for him when he arrived.

He thanked God for the kindness of Javan. The walk would be easier with him along.

Javan motioned toward the street, and returned his smile, only stronger, and with encouragement. "Shall we be off?"

Joshua's knees suddenly felt weak, but he made himself start walking.

Ragged donkeys carrying packs of woven baskets bulging with wares, clopped past, leaving their musky scent behind. People walked along the dusty street, going about their business in the early coolness. They stopped to wave and call greetings as Joshua and Javan passed.

"You will have a beautiful bride!" "May you both be blessed with many sons!" "God's blessing upon you this day!"

He felt them watching even after he was past. How many would be waiting, watching him return to his home later with his bride? It felt as if the whole village was on the street as he passed, people finding an excuse to be outside so early in the day. He turned to Javan with a wry grin. "I did not expect this to be such an event. I had been asked if I wanted company, but I did not know what Hannah preferred, and the circumstances are –"

Javan cut him off. "A wedding is a wedding, and after the sadness of Levi, people need a reason to rejoice. Had you wished, you would have had a grand procession to accompany you to Hannah's house. I would have given you any advice you needed." He heaved a deep breath, as if readying himself to begin dispensing his knowledge regardless.

Joshua hoped, no, prayed, that Javan would not ask why he had not gone to anyone for company. The risk of letting slip his hidden love and despair had been too great, and even now the secret must be kept. "I had to do this on my own," was all he would let himself say.

In silence they passed through the huge gate set wide in the city's protective wall. Women, so many women coming back from the well with their water jars dripping, smiled, although some were clearly wistful. Joshua felt his cheeks warm.

At one time the water source lay within the city's walls, but after the war with Ammon so many years ago, the villagers had drawn into themselves, pulling what was left of their city behind the walls that still stood. There had not been enough stones left to enclose the well within the walls. It lay close, and Ammon had been defeated, so no one troubled that the women had to go outside the gate to draw water.

"We should expand the walls," Javan muttered.

Joshua grinned at the reminder of Javan's years as a soldier, and the slight tension between them eased.

Javan looked over at the younger man, walking with apparent calm at his side. What kind of man lay beneath that mild exterior? Were he and his fellow elders condemning Hannah to more misery? He had been fooled by Levi. Was Joshua different from his brother?

The Law was the Law and must be obeyed, but he would be more at ease if he could see what lay ahead, and if it was only good.

They walked up the sloping hillside that ringed the village, toward the forest at the top. Sheep grazed on the grass, gray-white bumps against the green rapidly wilting in the summer heat. Little boys watched over their fathers' flocks and played together with sticks and rocks, just as Javan and his long-dead brother had done, as his sons now did.

Small bushes decorated the hilltop with low-hugging emerald. Poplars waved above, forerunners of the deeper woods that closed around them as they reached the small plateau. Wild olives grew short and gnarled in dark green clumps. The tall, drying grass brushed against their legs in stiff brown stalks as they walked abreast on the narrow path. Javan had walked this same path sixteen years ago, his virgin bride nervous and afraid at his side. Funny how the memory came unbidden, prompted by circumstances. He smiled suddenly, biting back the urge to laugh. He doubted Joshua would appreciate it.

He remembered Taleh's worried eyes as recent as this morning's waking, and sobered.

"How do you feel?" he asked suddenly, to break the silence.

Joshua gave him an odd glance. "Unsure. Worried. How did you think I would feel?"

"Unsure. Worried." Javan kept his concerns inside.

"I know you better than this, Javan." Joshua turned his attention back to the path. "You wait for me outside my door, and walk me to Hannah's house. You did not go to this trouble for the pleasure of a walk you make several times each week. You are filled with advice and suggestions and I am at your mercy. If you have something you need to say, say it."

He would assuage his wife's worries, and his. "You will be patient with Hannah?"

"I may have been alone for years, but I am not without perception when it comes to women. I hope she will . . . adjust, but do I expect it soon? No." He frowned. "I feel as though I have stepped into a contest. 'Levi could not give her children, can Joshua do better?' I am sure the village women will be counting months." He sighed, and gave Javan a piercing look. "The men, as well."

Javan nodded. "No doubt. Does that bother you?"

"I can hardly do worse than Levi, can I?"

Worse. A strange choice of a word. Did Joshua know what had passed between Hannah and his brother? He had not thought so, could not countenance such a lack. It was bad enough the whole village missed it, but to turn Hannah over to a man who could know and ignore, it would be a crime against Hannah and their God. Taleh had been convinced no one knew the full horror. The market sellers had seen the bruises, they could not have been missed, his wife said, but the rest . . .

Javan could warn, he could begin protecting Hannah. He clapped a hand on Joshua's shoulder, and stopped him. "Joshua, do not expect much from her. I will not tell you how to handle your marriage. You know as well as I that these situations are always . . . complex. Hannah is a woman and women are more fragile. We are to give them care, they are our responsibility. I would give my life for my Taleh. I am not embarrassed to admit it. Abraham loved his wife, as did Isaac and Jacob love theirs. To love a woman does not weaken a man. Let no one tell you otherwise."

He took a breath to calm himself. He needed this man to consider him a friend, because he would stay near and watch. "I wish happiness for you and your wife. My farm is as close as any others. Whatever help I can give you, never be afraid to come to me and ask. Will you do that?"

Joshua gave the hand resting on his shoulder a gentle squeeze. "I will need a friend, I think. And I will need and welcome your advice."

Javan nodded in relief. It was one step, a small one, but it would do.

CHAPTER 7

Isaac brought her into his mother Sarah's tent, and took Rebekah, and she became his wife. He loved her. So Isaac was comforted after his mother's death.

Genesis 24:67

Hannah watched, sick with nerves, as her new husband came along the path. His robe was crisp, clearly new, the soft bleached-bone color of fresh linen. He had purchased a new robe for the occasion, but she did not delude herself that it was to honor her. More likely because it was expected. She could not fault him. Was not she, herself, here because it was expected?

Javan came, too. She blushed, hot color rushing up her face, remembering her odd behavior when he came to bring her news of this marriage. She had not seen him since. She did not want to see him now.

Why had he come, this village elder? To ensure she would be here, waiting? That was hardly necessary. Taleh was here, after all, standing behind her, tightlipped and unnaturally subdued.

Hannah looked down at her white robe, and held the trailing ends of the headdress that served as her wedding veil out of the way. It was better than watching the two men come. The veil sat like a weight on her head, this symbol of submission. She had used a bolt of fine cloth Taleh had brought over early on in the waiting, too sheer for a robe. She had never found a headdress heavy before.

Here she stood, like a willing participant, covered in all the signs of compliance. She could not condemn Joshua for his new robe and his hypocrisy when she had done the same thing.

She was not going to look up, but she did, and was instantly sorry, for the men were closer, past the stand of trees. It was all happening too fast, her last moments of freedom slipping away with his every step. Once upon a time, she might have enjoyed Joshua's appearance, his handsome face, his height, his strength. Of all the unwed men in the village, he commanded the most attention, that height, his broad shoulders, the thick dark hair that stuck to him in tight curls when he was sweaty with work, his strong-boned face, his quiet demeanor. Young girls tittered when Joshua passed, staring after him with eager eyes. Silly children. Once she might have been one of them, but no longer. The giddy young woman who had welcomed her status as wife had died a long time ago.

A man's strong arms were a threat, she had learned from painful experience, and Joshua's over-large size terrified her. How easily he could tower above her and thunder commands down on her head. His face spoke of unyielding character, while she had lost her own over the years, beaten from her, smashed down with fists and words and unending cruelty.

If only she could have stopped this! What a millstone this farm was! Levi had hated it, and its very existence was now trapping her.

The men kept coming, across the span of drying grass that stretched from the woods to the door where she stood. Only Taleh's presence kept her in place.

Joshua had waited long to marry, even though it was rumored that his gold creations fetched a good price. He had much work in addition to the jewelry he had given her long ago, copper pots and mirrors, bronze basins and pans, metal locks with matching keys for doors, knives and other weapons so useful against the wild beasts that roamed the nearby woods.

She hoped his work would keep him very busy.

That was yet another thing to worry her. He could afford several wives, yet he had not taken even one. Perhaps his expectations were so high no woman could meet them. How could she ever measure up, she who had never measured up before?

And now his choices were taken from him. Was there another young woman he would have preferred? She did not know if having another woman in the house, having him divide his attention between them, was better or worse. She could hardly be the favored wife, but neither did she want to be the hated one like Leah.

She took a moment for a desperate prayer. God, please let him not take his frustrations out on me.

Such a brief time of freedom. One month, thirty days, to relish, to live on in the years ahead. She had barely tasted the euphoria of having her life be her own.

Joshua walked with a firm stride. If he had regrets, they did not show. Her heart pounded like the hoofbeats of startled horses, louder with each step he took. He was close enough now that she could see his face. It told her nothing. He neither smiled nor frowned.

She could look no longer. Let him think she suffered from modesty, rather than terror. If she did not look, she might not vomit with her churning fear. Taleh had urged her to eat, but she could not swallow. She should have tried harder. If her stomach was not so empty, it might not feel so sick.

A hand touched her and she jerked away before she realized it was Taleh. "Hannah? Your husband is here."

Husband. She had just thought that word herself mere moments ago, but now it was real. The formal walking to his house, the witnesses Javan and Taleh, the leaving behind of one life for another.

Husband.

Sandals, on large feet, stopped directly in range of her down-cast eyes.

"Hannah?" A man's voice, soft, even, she thought, warm.

She gathered her tattered courage, and let her gaze slide up, over the dust on his ankles, over the hem of his new robe with the blue thread, the matching blue sash that wrapped his waist, the broad chest that stretched the linen into flatness and hid wrinkles, the neatly trimmed dark beard that framed his lips, forming again to say her name.

"Hannah? Are you ready to leave?"

Her eyes closed the final tiny gap to meet his, that startling golden so different from Levi's green-brown mixture.

A small bit of the panic that had smothered her for the endless day just past released its grip. For the first time, she realized how terrified she had been of looking into Joshua's face and seeing Levi's eyes.

But the eyes that looked back at hers were nothing like Levi's cold ones.

He smiled, and his eyes smiled, too.

Her eyes skittered away, and the maidenly shyness became real. Her stomach settled, much to her surprise. He was not Levi. Only time would tell if that was better, or worse.

A hand lifted into her vision, a long-fingered hand with calluses on the broad palm. For perhaps the first time ever, she could not remember, her brother-in-law reached out and ever so gently took her hand.

Something strange trickled down her spine.

"You must have clothes you wish to bring. If you will show me where they are, I will carry them for you. Will you invite me in?"

He asked her permission? "Oh, of course." What a fool she was, to stand there when there was work to do! She had even seen the dust on his sandals. Had Levi not trained her better than this, that she had not even offered to wash his feet? "I am so sorry. I can fill a bowl with water in a moment for your feet. Please excuse me."

The panic was there, old fears and remembered beatings, endless years of disappointing Levi and equal numbers of years of punishments for forgetfulness and mistakes. She moved to step away, but he did not release her hand and she was brought up short.

"There is no need for that. My feet will only get dirty again on the way back to the village. If you could just get the things you want to bring today, I will carry them."

For a fleeting moment as she turned, her gaze met Taleh's.

Taleh smiled, and touched her arm. "Go in," she whispered, and leaned forward to brush a kiss on Hannah's cheek.

Hannah stepped toward the door, and this time, Joshua moved with her, her hand in his strong grip. The door had been pulled shut, she remembered doing that, thinking he would drag her off without delay.

She eased the door open with her free hand, waiting for him to step inside first, as befitted his stature as the man, but he waved her ahead. "This is your house. You go first."

It had never been her house, not really. Joshua said nothing, just waited. One eyebrow went up over his hawk eyes. Hannah stepped through the doorway, and felt those eyes boring into her back.

He was close behind her as she entered the dim house. This was so unlike her first wedding, when everyone had come here to watch her be fed and welcomed as Levi's bride. There were no crowds today – but there was Javan, a respected village elder, and Taleh.

She stood still as her eyes adjusted to the dimness inside. Joshua looked around. His face gave nothing away, no approval of her skills in the house, but no disapproval either.

Hannah looked at the room she knew so well, trying to see it through his eyes. The stone floor had been swept and scrubbed, no dust collected in the corners of either floor or walls. The two wooden chairs, one slightly smaller than the other, had soft cushions of goat's hair she had labored long on, weaving the blue-striped coverings tightly so they would last. The small table where she put Levi's cups sat close to the larger chair, within easy reach. Too easy reach, remembering the times he had grabbed her hair, slapped her, taken advantage of her having to come near to minister to his needs. She would not miss that chair.

A long bench sat against another whitewashed wall, a place for the visitors who had never been invited. The table in the other room, unseen from where they stood, was clean, for no one had thrown food at her for a month, and the benches were neatly lined up where no one would catch a foot on their protruding wooden legs.

Surely there was nothing for him to find fault with. The unlit lamps were even clean, using busywork this past month to chase away the night-mares when they came.

Through the second doorway was the bedroom where they had slept, cut off from the rest of the house by a curtain of plain linen. She did not want him to step inside that room.

Joshua let go of her hand finally.

"Please . . . sit down. I will . . . go get my things." The room felt small, with him so close. Her voice was suddenly breathless.

He looked oddly uncomfortable. "I can stand."

She knew what that meant. It meant, *I am in a hurry, and you are causing me further delay*. A warning. Levi had been very good at those hidden warnings. She had learned them all.

"Yes. Well, if I may have just one moment . . . " Her voice trailed off, and she fluttered a hand toward the curtain. "I will be quick."

He nodded, and rubbed the back of his neck. "Yes."

She darted behind the curtain.

Joshua turned his back on the curtain to look at the pristine cleanness of Hannah's house. His own suffered by the comparison. He should have hired one of the village women to clean.

His mind turned to Hannah, as always, but without the guilt of before. Joshua and Hannah, now. Never again would Levi's name be joined with hers.

She had acted afraid when he arrived. He supposed that was only natural. He looked down at the hand that had held hers. He could feel her soft fingers still. When he reached for her hand, the gesture had been so . . . natural. Necessary.

He would have to take care with her. Javan had been right. Women were to be protected. Hannah would need even more protection, she was so frag-ile, her bones so small.

She was as lovely as his memories had colored her. Years of hopeless longing had added nothing. He should have removed her veil and looked at her hair, but that might have been too great a liberty to take so soon.

He paced the room, avoiding the chairs, uneasy with so much perfection. No doubt his own house would soon resemble this one, everything carefully in its place.

It would take some getting used to.

What was causing this delay?

Hannah looked at the bedroom one last time. The pegs on the wall were empty. Levi's clothes were long gone. That early morning fire had done its work well. Probably the slaves could have used his robes, but she could not endure seeing them.

The small box where she kept the few jewels Levi had given her early in their marriage perched on the little table. It held nothing she cared to bring with. Hannah looked down at the brooch, Joshua's gift from that other wedding day, held tightly in her hand. This one thing she would keep. He had smiled at her, and said, "My brother chose well." She remembered the touch of the fabric covering as he pressed it into her hand, remembered feeling the hardness of the gift inside, remembered her curiosity, and the wonder when she first saw it with the sun shining through the gem and giving it life.

The golden lily still looked new. It should, Hannah thought with sudden bitterness. As time went on and no pregnancy came, as Levi's cruelty grew from the initial sharp words that began their life together into fists, it had disappeared one day, and she had grieved for it. If she had not been searching the house for money these past weeks, she would never have known what became of it.

Why had Levi not destroyed it? The only answer Hannah could find was that it reminded her husband of his brother, and not of her. Had it reminded Levi of her, had she ever had a chance to wear it, he would have smashed it to bits, she was certain.

No doubt Joshua would expect to see it.

Hannah slipped the lily into a headdress that served as a sack.

Life had to be safer in the village where people could hear, it simply had to be.

He could not run the farm from the village. What would she do when Joshua decided to move here?

Soft shuffling noises in the silent house caught his attention. The curtain rustled aside, and she stood in the doorway, a large parcel held in either hand. Her chin was lifted bravely, but when she looked at him, her eyes caught him. Frightened eyes.

Hannah was truly afraid.

He wished he knew if that was normal. Marriage was such a permanent thing. He pretended a certainty he did not feel, and gestured toward one of the parcels. "Can I carry something for you? It is a long walk."

"If you wish." Hannah held out her arm, with one bulging sack clutched so tightly her knuckles were white.

He eased the sack from her grip, and turned toward the door. He was nearly there before he realized she was not following him. He looked back. She had not moved.

This was clearly not a woman who wanted to marry again. Levi was gone. It was time to face the living, not hide with the dead. "We must talk about this. Come." He held out his unencumbered hand. "Sit with me." Hannah stiffened as he eased her toward Levi's chair.

As he tried to push her closer, she went rigid, and arched away, planting her feet on the floor in defiance. "No! Please! You sit there." Her voice was surprisingly loud.

Joshua looked down at the chair. He let go of her hand, and just stared at it.

She could not stop her reaction. He must know it was Levi's chair, it was so clearly built for him, large and male, solid arms and thick legs, and higher back. No doubt he was imagining six years of happy scenes, herself and Levi as a comfortable, married couple sitting here in peace. It was only right, she supposed, that someone somewhere mourn him, since she certainly would not.

He sat down in it. Hannah moved quickly to her own, smaller chair before he could change his mind, slipped into it, and waited.

Joshua slid his hands over the worn wood arms. His mind seemed far away. He abruptly gave a sharp sigh and faced her. "Hannah, I know this is difficult for you. I want you to know that I do not expect you to forget Levi. I will not forget him ever, and he was only my brother. He was your *husband*. I will not hold it against you if you need to grieve for him a while. I will do whatever I can to make this adjustment easier for you. I believe I can make you happy." His eyes seemed to plead with her.

For what? Agreement? To be unmarried again would make her happy. To be off the farm would make her happy. She was getting one of the two, and she would have to make the best of it.

The thought was enough to make her weep, but she controlled her despair.

Joshua scrubbed his hands down his face abruptly, and released a sharp sigh. "Come, we must be going back to the village. Javan and Taleh have waited long enough." He scooped up both bundles, and stalked to the door, leaving Hannah to follow alone.

CHAPTER 8

*All the people who were in the gate, and the elders, said, "We are
witnesses. May Yahweh make the woman who has come into your house
like Rachel and like Leah, which both built the house of Israel."*
Ruth 4:11

It was a long walk back to the village through the forest, with the birds
calling and small creatures scuffling in the brush. Joshua was glad. He
did not know what to think of his wife. Every time he moved close to her, so
many reasons to do so on the path, she pulled away. He did not expect her to
throw herself into his arms, but he had wanted some acceptance. It would
make this night easier, taking his brother's woman.

He needed to talk to Javan. The women separated them, making questions – and answers – impossible.

Taleh tried for bright conversation. Hannah's lovely robe, the veil, the
sunshine, the perfect day. Hannah responded in single words. Or one word,
"yes." Yes, it was a lovely robe, a lovely veil, yes, there was sunshine, yes, it
was a perfect day.

At last they passed the final hill. The village lay beneath them, the flat wooden roofs barely showing behind the protective stone wall.

And all the villagers were gathered outside the gate, waving palm branches and cheering. Someone jangled a tambourine, someone else blew a horn. Flowers littered their path. Everyone wore the finest robes in bright colors, a bouquet to match the petals on the ground.

Hannah stopped and stared. Joshua thought he saw panic on her face.

And then she smiled. Strained, tense, if one looked closely, but then, he did not like being the center of so much attention either. If he had it to do his way, they would walk quietly through the village and slip into his house.

That was not the way it was done. A marriage had to be witnessed.

This one certainly would be. And if so many witnesses was what it took to let him see her smile for the first time today, the first time he had been able to see it in six, nearly seven, years, then he would welcome every villager. His throat closed tight, his eyes burned. His heart swelled to fill his chest, and pushed at his ribs.

Hannah had smiled on their wedding day.

They walked down the path, crushing the flowers underneath and releasing their fragrance. The scent became oppressive, but Joshua would not complain. He had not expected so much.

Javan touched his arm. "I thought you both deserved a celebration. The village needs it as much as you. It is time to put mourning behind us all."

Joshua looked over, grateful for the distraction. "Thank you."

Hannah forced herself to keep walking toward the smiling faces that waited for them to approach. There were no bruises to hide, no injuries to protect. It was safe to be seen.

And it was easier to smile than she anticipated. She would be living here, and people would be nearby. If she screamed, someone would hear. What could be hidden in the country would be out in the open among so many people.

The celebration was clearly as much of a surprise to Joshua as to herself. It should hurt that he had not planned to celebrate their wedding. It did not.

He had not gone into this marriage of his own will. Neither had she. It was better there were no pretenses of happiness between them. But they would accept the villagers' gift with courtesy. It was a good way to start.

People closed around them as they passed through the gates. There was much slapping of backs among the men, hugs from women who had been mere faces in the marketplace for Hannah.

A small child, a little girl with dark, curly hair, clung to her mother's leg as Hannah drew near. The mother leaned close to her daughter. The bustle of the crowd forced her to speak loud enough for Hannah to hear. "Someday that will be you, and you will be just as happy."

The little girl smiled shyly at Hannah before hiding her face again in her mother's skirts. A little girl. Hannah could not tear her gaze away.

Another chance for a child. That was what this was all about. A child. Hannah tried not to look at Joshua, but she could see him in her mind, his golden eyes, his dark hair. If there was a child, it would be a beautiful one.

She could not let her hopes get too high. The fall would crush her.

"Javan says it is a time to set aside grief." Taleh spoke directly into her ear. "If you ever need help, come to us." From behind Taleh, a fat, gray-haired woman was closing in. "For Joshua's sake as well as your own, keep smiling!"

It was good advice, and just in time. The fat woman greeted her as though she was a long-lost friend. "Hannah! Hannah!" She wrapped Hannah in a giant hug that nearly lifted her off the ground. "We rejoice with you! A second chance! And Joshua! Now, there is a man to get the job done!"

Her words rang out even above the crowd. Hannah blushed painfully as raucous laughter broke out. Gaiety surrounded her. Noise, loud voices, laughter, and the smell of food cooking, goat meat, beef, leeks, onions, lentils, beans, cumin, dill and mustard, fig cakes, dates and bread, cheese and wine.

It suddenly felt like a wedding. The tambourine reappeared, and the jingle of its bells rang sweetly on the air. A lyre caught the tune, and a line formed. Women took their places, stomping their feet in rhythm, clapping their hands above their heads. The men formed opposite them, swaying with their women.

Hannah knew the steps. They came back to her from some forgotten place in her mind. Joshua took his own place across from her. Forward, and back, the bells chiming up and down the line, the lyre singing in the air, they moved in the dance.

Hannah watched him in his place across from her own swaying body, this new husband of hers. He was smiling all the way to his eyes that held hers. Her veil swirled with the movements of her hands. Hannah only saw it in the edges of her sight, for her gaze could not leave his.

The dance came to a crescendo, every dancer dewed with perspiration in the last few thundering steps.

She was laughing with the rest.

Taleh was back. She caught Hannah's hand, and pulled her away, then looked around to ensure no one was close enough to overhear. "It will be all right, I am certain. Joshua is nothing like his brother. I have been watching him, and how he looks at you. He looks away every time you turn to him, but he is a happy man today. It will not be the same as before, I am certain."

Her words sucked the laughter away. Taleh, Hannah thought to herself, was not going to be alone in the house with Joshua this night.

The sun was setting. Joshua appeared suddenly at her side, her parcels that they had left under a table somewhere early in the day slung over one shoulder. Dishes smeared with food, streaks of lentils and bits of broken bread and fig cakes and leftover bones sat about on other tables carried out for the celebration. Scents lingered on the air, meat, bread, onions, and perfume. Women collected the crockery slowly, tossing the bones for the dogs to drag away and worry.

Hannah was tired. She had managed to laugh, as Taleh had ordered, but the crowds were leaving and Joshua would be taking her home. She could not hold her smile any longer. Her last moments of freedom were gone.

Taleh was here, again. She had stayed nearby all day, and Hannah was grateful for her presence. It would show Joshua she was not totally without protectors, even if they did live outside the village walls.

"Come, wife," Joshua said, and held out his hand to her.

She had to look at Taleh. Her friend was frowning fiercely at Joshua. Hannah fought the hysterical urge to laugh at her friend's protectiveness, standing up to the giant in front of them. Taleh did not even reach to Joshua's armpits, and yet she dared to try to intimidate him.

And Joshua merely frowned back, an exaggerated frown. Did his eyes twinkle? "Hannah," he said again, only this time he took her hand and held tight. One corner of his mouth twitched. "Thank you, Taleh, and your husband, so much for this day. Dances and musicians and a feast, everything a wedding should be. I know this was all your planning. It was a good gift, and we are grateful."

And then, before Hannah could say anything, before she could even marvel that Joshua was amused at Taleh's unspoken threats, he tugged her away.

Hannah stayed quiet as they walked through the bustling streets, past the scattered groups unwilling to let the festivities end. Houses lined this part of the village, some small and squat with the roof parapet easily seen, others taller, more than one story, taking up long stretches of the street. Olive trees peeked around from behind every house, the ubiquitous fruit growing as easily here in the village as out in the country. Some houses set a little away from the street had the vital trees in the front, the branches drooping over their heads.

Limestone was everywhere, walls of houses and fences and whitewash on brick, and the setting sun reflected golden off its light surface. How bright it must be in midday! Most of the lattices were opened now, to let the evening coolness in. Hannah could see oil lamps flicker to life in some of the windows as they passed.

People nearby.

She did not walk this alone, though she might as well have for all the attention the man at her side paid to her. She could not figure Joshua out. He responded to the greetings and calls shouted at them with simple nods. His jaw beneath the neat beard was set. She would have thought him unhappy, but he never once let go of her hand.

They stopped in front of a door. Joshua pushed it open.

His house. They were here. Hannah hung back, her feet feeling stuck to the rocky street. He gave a slight tug on her hand. Hannah forced her legs to move, stepping carefully over the threshold. The house was dark, as dark as the future she dreaded.

Joshua pushed the door shut, and it slid on its pivots, thunking against the frame, cutting off the light from outside. He let go of Hannah's hand and pushed the bolt home.

"Come, follow me." He turned and walked through the dark room toward the opening for his workshop, making his way easily through the familiar house. He listened to the sounds behind him. A delay, and soft footsteps, womanly footsteps, light on the stone floor.

He had longed for that sound for six years. The hairs stood up on his arms in delight. Hannah's soft breathing whispered in the stillness.

She was here. Hannah was finally here.

He moved through the doorway into the brighter room beyond with all its windows. The lattices were closed to keep the house cool, but it was still lighter than the other room had been. His workshop was clean, as he had worked so hard to make it, but what would Hannah think?

"My house is small," he said, "but it will be enough for a while. You must tell me what changes you wish to make. This has been my workroom, but I also have my meals here. If you need to use the shelves for something else, you must tell me." He waved a hand vaguely around the room, not wanting to actually point out its many deficiencies.

Hannah looked up at him, her eyes startled. He met her gaze fully. "I will see how it works first," she said.

She was clearly not a talker. "You must tell me what to change."

"Yes," she said.

This was not going at all like he wanted. If only she would respond easily to him! "Sit, please." He waved toward the table and slipped Hannah's parcels off his shoulder and onto the floor. "We need to become better acquainted. You are as much a stranger to me as I am to you." Joshua added the smile that served him well with women.

Hannah sat. She toyed with the bottom edge of her veil.

He leaned against the wall, doing his best to seem relaxed. "This –
between us – this marriage – is as strange to me as it must feel to you. You
have been married before, I have not, so it is harder on me. I have been alone
a long time, I will need your help adjusting. You must remind me when I
forget that I am not living alone. We must be honest and tell each other what
we think. Even if you do not believe it to be what I want to hear, I need to
know what is on your mind. We cannot have a marriage without that."

Very pretty words. If she were young, she might be convinced. She hardened
the yearning, broken part of her heart, and abruptly looked away, for fear he
see her doubts. This room was unlike the barren room she had first entered
with so little furniture it was clearly just for sleeping. This room was where
he lived. Tools on the wall, small shelves with little boxes for something, no
doubt his work, a few sparse dishes and cups on more shelves, and cooking
pots clearly an afterthought in this, so much his place. A bowl of wild
flowers sat in odd contrast on the table.

"Would you like to go outside? My kiln is there, if you want to see where
I spend much of my time." He stepped away from the wall.

She had been staring at the lattices, but she could feel his gaze on her. He
was watching her, and closely. A chill crept across her skin. She would have
to be very careful with this man. "If you wish," she said.

"It is not what *I* wish, Hannah." His voice was firm. "I know this house.
But all of this is strange and new to you. I want you to become familiar with
it. This is, after all, your new home."

So many pretty words. "Yes."

Joshua looked at his new wife, diligently avoiding looking at him, finding
endless fascination in closed lattices, and could not guess what she was thinking. He took a chance. Her head drooped, he could see her weariness in the
shadows under her soft green eyes. Her skin still glowed from the dancing,
and he forced his hands to stay at his sides to keep from reaching out to
stroke the rose-petal smoothness of her face. A curl of wheat-gold hair slid

from under the veil. "Hannah, you are not betraying Levi, no more than I am. This is the Law. The crime would be if we were to refuse to obey. We must try for a son. What was not possible with Levi might be possible with me." He moved closer to her.

Hannah flinched. He knew she tried to hide it, but she was not quick enough, and he was watching her very carefully. A child might not be possible, he had faced that and accepted it. She would never hear words of reproach from him, no matter how many years passed without children. "Come outside. Let me show you what I do." He pulled her to her feet and leaned down to see her face. "I can make whatever you wish. Set me a task, make a challenge, and it will be my pleasure to form it for you. Gold, silver, copper, iron – pick whatever you wish." He led her through the door. The smoke from the kiln was faint on the air. The excitement he felt whenever he began to create with his metals and his hammer lifted within him.

Near the kiln, close enough but not too close, he drew her to a stop. "Did Levi tell you I hated farming, and wanted only to work with metal?"

"Yes, he said that much," she answered. "He told me once that you had a gift."

Rich pleasure filled Joshua. Levi said he had a gift. "This is my kiln," Joshua said, looking down at it to hide his pride. He would have to impress her, make something new for her with all the skill at his command. "Let me show you how it works." He bent down, grabbed a stick that sat propped against the kiln wall, and held it out to her.

Not a simple stick, Hannah saw as she tried to lift it and it did not move. It was tied tightly to a large leather bag fastened to the kiln.

"My bellows," he explained. "It fans the fire, and keeps it hot enough to melt my metals. When the metal turns red, it is ready to be molded or hammered, or poured. It takes a long time to read each metal. They are all different, each with its own strengths and weaknesses."

His hand closed over hers, and for one heartbeat simply held it. His thumb slid over her skin in one faint caress. Hannah went perfectly still, refusing to let herself jerk away in reaction. Without warning, he pumped her hand – and the stick it held – up and down.

"See?" He let go and reached an open palm toward the kiln as though feeling the air. "The fire is already heating. Now, you do it."

She lifted the stick – and the bellows – in time with his smiling count, and pushed it back down. The fire did not change – no, it did! A little more yellow in the heart of it, and a puff of heat. She felt an unfamiliar thrill of accomplishment.

A big hand stroked her shoulder, making her jump. She thought she heard a sigh, but Joshua's voice was calm and even. "Very good. A little more practice and you might become an apprentice."

She turned to him in surprise. "Me?"

"Only if you are very careful. I will not put you at risk, but if you wish to come and watch, and help when I can be here to keep you safe, I would be glad to have you." He patted her shoulder, and then his hand dropped. It clenched at his side, one tight grip, and then it was loose and free again. It was a big hand, and it made a big fist.

She tried not to look at that hand. She did not know what she had done. But then, she never did, never had.

"Enough of this." Joshua took the stick out of her hand and leaned it back in its place. "We cannot stand by the kiln now, it will be too hot." He moved her a few cubits away, in the direction of the house. "So, now that you know a little of what I do, what can you tell me about yourself?"

Hannah's mind was suddenly empty. "What do you want to know?"

"Everything."

Telling him everything about herself would take too much time, or no time at all. He put a large finger under her chin, his touch warm and startling, and lifted her face until she was staring into his golden eyes. A frown puckered his forehead.

Something in those eyes slipped past her control, a yearning that tugged at the same desire in her. Hannah blurted, "I had a garden."

"A garden?" The frown was still there, as if this was the last thing he expected to hear.

"I grew vegetables. Levi –" She caught her breath, as if something had almost slipped out. "I always wanted flowers, but – " There was no good way to finish the sentence. "We can always eat vegetables."

"There are always plenty of vegetables in the market. I know little about flowers, but I will have to find some for your garden." He removed his finger from beneath her chin.

Hannah felt a smile start. He was only trying to placate his new wife and she was gullible to even believe the words, but if he meant it, and she thought maybe he did, what was a small thing to him – well, he could hardly know what that would mean to her. "Thank you," she said. "I would like that very much." Time would show whether she was a fool to trust in him this little bit.

Joshua shrugged her thanks away. "I want you to be happy here. If you know the kinds of flowers you want, I will see if someone has them to sell." He reached for her hand. "Let us go back inside."

People would hear if she screamed. Hannah consoled herself with that and with one bracing breath, stepped back across the threshold.

CHAPTER 9

"Better is a dinner of herbs, where love is,
than a fattened calf with hatred."
Proverbs 15:17

Joshua aimed all his frustration at the cold rough edge of the iron axe head. The iron hammer whistled through the air with the force of his blow. A small portion of the thick edge flattened to knife sharpness as though made of papyrus rather than metal. He measured his swing and aimed again, hoping this time would release some of the torment inside.

He had no patience for the fine detail work he normally loved, no patience even to lay out the larger molds to fill with liquid iron for nails, latches and keys. No, he needed to raise a sweat, to punish himself for whatever he had done wrong the past night.

He had thought to serve himself, find release from years of longing, knowing the reckoning would come later.

Come it had.

He winced at the memory.

Despite the hot sun, despite his exertions, he felt cold prickling along his spine again. He swung the hammer once more, and another section of the axe blade flattened with a single blow.

Everyone knew that, in a marriage, the two came together not knowing what to expect. And Hannah had been married before. She was the one with the most experience, six years in his brother's bed.

He had been careful, he was certain he had. She had been afraid. Down to the bone afraid, and what should have been a pleasure for both of them had been completed but only just, and every touch and every movement felt like a mistake. Should he have waited? No, that was a foolish thought, and he had already waited so long he could not have given her a single day. What is more, he felt then and felt still to have waited would only have fed her fear.

Of him.

What had he done to make her so afraid?

He swung again, even more fiercely. The sound of metal on metal rang in his ears, the noise bouncing off the wall of his house, coming back to him in an echo. BR-R-R-AAANNNG!

The vibrations raced up his arm. He saw with strange detachment how the skin trembled like a pond when a rock has been tossed into it. The echo faded, leaving behind quiet until the village sounds drifted in, audible now with the clanging gone, a donkey complaining in grating tones, children calling with happy voices, the muted rumble of bargaining, arguments and laughter from the marketplace.

He bent over, letting the iron hammer fall to the ground with a thunk. His lungs heaved for air. His breath sounded like the bellows he used to heat the furnace, whistling with effort.

Joshua picked up the hammer again, and turned back to the iron axe head. He had drained off the worst of his frustration. He could work calmly now, and think. The hammer came down, smoothing another section. The heat pushed at him, stifling and sweltering. He swiped at his brow with an equally sweaty forearm. The hammer slipped from his wet fingers in his distraction.

Joshua jumped, but not quite in time. The hammer thudded on his toes.

"Yaah!" He bit back stronger words, and shook his foot to make the throbbing pain ease.

Someone tittered behind him, feminine giggles smothered behind hands. He turned eagerly, despite the heat in his face.

But it was not Hannah smiling at him, eyes dancing with amusement. Instead, Miriam, the bane of his existence. Shallow, self-centered, and absolutely determined to have him for her husband. How many times had *she* asked *him* for marriage? Exactly that many times he had threatened to tell her father of her flirtatious ways. He might as well have been talking to a tree.

And here she was again, the very day after his wedding, dressed in her finest linen, boldly standing where his new wife would certainly see her if she chanced to look out. He knew her better than to think she cared about any talk she might cause. Sweat trickled down his face. He did another swipe with his forearm and cursed the men in his land who chose more than one wife. They only gave ideas to women who thought they would be happy to share.

"Are you not even going to greet me? I should like to meet your wife. I have not had the pleasure." Her voice was high-pitched and childlike. She thought it appealing. He did not.

"My wife is resting," he said tersely and untruthfully. He expected to see hurt in her eyes. His marriage must have come as a blow to her pride, even though he had never given her any indication that he would ever consider her for a wife. Miriam was hard to discourage. He did not remember seeing her at the festivities, but then, he had not been looking.

Miriam tilted her head, and her warm brown hair slid over her shoulder. His gaze followed the curls before he realized it. He snapped his attention back to her face.

She was smiling smugly. "You never even talked to me yesterday."

So she had been there.

Miriam pressed her hands to her heart. "You have no idea how difficult it was for me to smile," she went on. "But I did. Even though it should have been you and me."

Remonstrations were useless with Miriam. "There were many people there. I am certain there are others I missed greeting as well."

"But I know," Miriam continued, as if he had not spoken, "I *know* that you only married her because you had to. And I am willing to wait until you can choose another without exciting comment from the village."

It was too much. Hannah did not have to listen to this. And neither did he. "Miriam, listen to me and listen well. I did not marry Hannah because I *had* to. I did not marry her because it was expected. I *wanted* to marry her. Very much. I have no interest in finding another. I did not marry you when I was free. And I will not marry you now. I do not know how much more plainly I can say it."

She stared at him, shocked, for only a moment before recovering. Her eyes narrowed in speculation. "You cannot have wanted to marry her. She was not a virgin. You only say that because you would have been reproached if you said no."

Joshua stepped back. Miriam followed him.

He hoped, without much faith, that Hannah was not watching.

"You cannot fool me." Miriam whispered the words, showing some discretion at last. "But you are brave to accept your fate so cheerfully. That is why I love you so." She gave his tunic a light, possessive pat before finally stepping away. "I will not give up hope." With that ominous statement, she walked away.

Joshua took deep breaths, and forced himself back to a semblance of calm. The window still stood open, the lattices pushed wide. There was no movement inside, but Hannah was there somewhere.

How much had she heard?

The wall was rough against Hannah's arm. She felt foolish, hiding out of sight, able to see but not be seen. Perhaps she should go out there and tell Joshua he did not have to worry. He could take another wife, she had decided, she would not complain.

She had often wondered why Levi had not done that very thing. Another wife might have given him children. After all those years, she decided Levi enjoyed hurting her, liked the excuse her barrenness gave him.

It was probably not the true reason, but she could never find another.

She had been watching Joshua pound on his metals while she chopped vegetables, the two of them with their similar tools but with such different manners, hers controlled, his violent and troubled. She had wounded him somehow.

The meal sat on the table, half-prepared, next to that odd bowl of flowers. She did not know what she felt as she watched him with the young woman who had walked so boldly up to her husband, whose name she caught in one sharply spoken sentence. Miriam. And Joshua clearly shared a history with her.

The conversation fluctuated between indistinct and understandable, Joshua's deeper voice and Miriam's high tones. As the young woman stepped closer, Joshua backed away, the gesture so unnecessary. Hannah shook her head as she watched. He did not need to put on a show for a wife he was forced to marry. Granted, Levi had also, but only at their wedding.

A happy day with a bitter ending. Last night had been such a different start. Joshua's hands had been only gentle, his touch soft, even his lips tender, but that would change. The only question was, how long did she have to wait?

Joshua's voice rose, and his words came, clear and harsh. "I did not marry Hannah because I *had* to. I did not marry her because it was expected. I *wanted* to marry her. Very much. I have no interest in finding another. I did not marry you when I was free. And I will not marry you now. I do not know how much more plainly I can say it."

Hannah froze in place, and listened in numb surprise. Joshua *wanted* to marry her?

No, that was too much to be believed. She was barren and no man in Israel wanted such for a wife.

But it was a kind thing to say, and she was grateful for his tact.

. . .

Joshua slipped into the workroom, closing the bottom half of the door quietly behind him. Hannah sat at the table, her back to him, wielding a knife on something. Her blue robe made a bright splash of color in the functional room. He noticed her position with a grimace, back to the window, spine stiff.

Whether or not she had heard anything, she certainly had seen.

A platter of meat left over from the feast sat in the middle of the table. The pieces had been cut into easy portions. Cloves of garlic sat among leafy greens. The flowers he had picked for her were even there. Round, thin loaves of bread, more leavings of their wedding celebration, had been piled atop each other on a shelf. Somehow she had managed to find space for everything without moving a single one of his tools.

She had only to ask and he would have cleared room. He had offered.

Hannah shoved a pile of peeled turnips to one side. She did not turn, but reached for another root from the pile beside her. She seemed absorbed in her work, but Joshua was not convinced.

He deliberately scraped his sandal against the stone floor. She turned around on the bench, then rose quickly to her feet in the manner of a slave, in respect, as if it were required. The bench scraped backward against the floor in protest. She looked down at her hand holding the knife, and did a strange thing. She tossed it aside as if she had done something wrong, not looking to see where it fell. The little knife fell to the table, doing a strange flip before coming to rest against a fat turnip. The root rolled in a small circle, its purple cone revolving like a child's wooden top before it settled to rest.

He looked up from the vegetable to see her eyes on him, wary and distant. Her thick, sand-colored hair settled slowly about her shoulders. She had not covered it this day, and something inside him rejoiced. It glowed, shimmered, as it moved about her shoulders, a beautiful covering.

He wanted to stop and enjoy the sight, but those eyes held him at bay.

"That was Miriam," he said awkwardly, wondering even as he spoke if he would do better to ignore the situation entirely.

Hannah nodded.

"I am sorry you had to see that. She means nothing to me."

Hannah nodded again.

No questions, not even a raised eyebrow. Just simple acceptance. He took heart. "She is a spoiled child who thinks she can get whatever she wants just because she wants it. And for a long time, she has wanted me."

This time the nod was a bit more noticeable. Yes, anyone, even one who did not want to notice, could tell that.

He rubbed a hand over his beard. The sound scraped in the quiet room. Something about Hannah, some uneasy stillness and waiting, prompted him to ask, "How much did you hear?"

She looked away, out the window.

A frantic pounding from the front of the house startled both of them. In the single breath as they whirled toward the noise, he saw relief clear on her face.

"Master Joshua! Hannah! Are you there?"

They moved as one through the doorway to the main room. Joshua got there first, running across the open space as the pounding went on.

He jerked the outside door open.

Halel stood there, his hand raised for another blow. Disheveled, out of breath, his face red and wet from effort, his eyes big with fear, "Forgive me," he gasped. "It is bad – bad news."

Hannah stood behind Joshua, struck by the similarity to another day, another report of ill brought by the same man.

"Tell it!" Joshua snapped.

"One of the slaves is ill and I fear he will die. His wife is ill, also. There was a child in the house with them."

Hannah stepped from behind her husband, surprised by her own boldness. "What is this illness?"

Joshua turned slightly, and set a big hand on her shoulder.

Halel hesitated for an instant. "It is strange to me, a bad, bad fever. They were not well yesterday, but I did not expect – "

"Illness comes this way sometimes," Joshua said.

Hannah looked at him in surprise. Levi would have screamed in anger, and hurled abuse at whoever was unhappy enough to bring the news.

Perhaps Joshua was saving his anger. Perhaps the ears of the villagers stopped him.

Joshua gently moved her out of his way. He strode to the bed, pulling his sweat-stained robe off, leaving only his loincloth, and paid no attention to either her or Halel, still standing in the door. He tipped the last bit of water from the pitcher onto a rag, and swiped his face and armpits. His muscles rippled as he reached for another robe from the peg in the wall. She felt herself blush.

He was moving back across the room before he tied the wide linen belt across his waist. "Well, man, let us be going."

Hannah stood where she was as he passed, waiting for him to remember her. She had done nursing before. Levi had expected it of her, and she knew she had skill. She had promised herself, as the time of her marriage had drawn near, that she would be strong in this marriage, but it was easier to promise than to do.

He reached the door. "Joshua?" She blurted the words before her fragile courage failed.

Joshua turned, and raised an eyebrow in question.

"I know healing." Her heart was pounding and her lungs were tight. Being brave was a terrifying thing.

He stared at her face for what seemed a long time. "Come, then. I know little of tending illness. I have never been sick enough to have to learn. You can be of help."

"Thank you." A little glow started deep inside. *You can be of help.* She would show that she had some worth. He might find value in her.

Before she could move, Joshua caught her with a hand on her arm. He nodded at Halel. "Carry on. We will catch up." He turned back to her, and small frown lines pleated his forehead. Her skin was warm where he touched. He did not pinch or squeeze or do any of the other tricks Levi had been so good at.

"I do not care for Miriam." His gold eyes willed her to believe. "If she tells you anything, even the day of the week, do not believe her. If she does anything to torment you, you must tell me."

"Yes. I will."

His lips curved into a sad smile. "I wish you meant that. Well, there is time." He took a deep breath. "One more thing. Hannah, there is no need to rise when I enter the room. I do not care for the gesture. Do not do it again." He caught the back of her head in one large hand and before she had time to think, or react, or panic, brought his mouth down on hers, his lips warm and gentle, his beard soft.

Then he ushered her out of the house, down the hard-packed dirt street.

CHAPTER 10

*"What will you give me, since I go childless, and he who will inherit my
estate is Eliezer of Damascus?"*
Genesis 15:2

T he waving leaves of the thin forest showed quick glimpses of the
house she and Levi had shared, and a wave of dread washed over
Hannah. Halel's hand closed gently on her elbow, as if to give her comfort.
Or did he merely mean to help her over the rough ground?

"Halel?" Joshua's voice caught her by surprise. After the first flurry of
questions he had asked of Halel, questions that sounded like he might actually have a care for the slaves who were total strangers to him, he had been
silent on the trip. No one seemed to feel like speaking, and they had been in
a hurry. "Where are they?"

Halel led them around the large house, the one that had been Levi's so
recently. Behind it, across a broad gap of grass and sand, the slave sheds
stretched out in a neat row toward the left, but the row was the only thing
straight and tidy about them. The wooden structures were hardly more than

a flat roof drooping on four tottering walls, each structure barely big enough for two people much less entire families. The row framed one edge of the empty field behind, harvested during the spring months and now laying fallow. Dried stubs of grain stalks still poked from the baked ground. Did Joshua remember enough from his days on this farm to recognize what the stalks had been?

Several of the sheds had single windows cut into one wall, lattices closed tight against the growing heat of the summer day. Or as protection from a terrible sickness, Hannah thought.

Between the shorn fields and the decrepit hovels, the farm looked utterly unloved. No one would live here who had another choice.

If anyone knew that, she did.

A small group of brown-haired children played in the scant shade left by the midday sun. They looked up as the group drew near, watching with wary eyes.

How much longer before the seven years allotted for slavery were over and they would have to be freed, Hannah did not know. One of so many things about the running of this farm she did not know, and should have. She had not even thought to find out during her precious month of freedom, but they were here already when she wed his brother, which made it six years, at least.

Joshua stopped by the children and looked down at them. She could tell nothing from his face. He looked for another moment, and the children suddenly and silently ran away, scattering like bees from a disturbed hive. Joshua watched them go just as expressionlessly as he had first taken notice of them, then turned and walked toward the small huts. "Which one holds the sick slaves?"

"This one," Halel replied, and waved a hand toward the shuttered house near the end in front of which he already stood.

It was time to see how much of her healing skills still remained.

As Halel turned, the sun caught the side of his face. The hole in his ear lobe showed dark against his skin, the sign of voluntary servitude for life.

At least, Joshua thought, he would have one slave that had to stay.

He needed to check the countries from which his slaves came. Those from other lands could be kept indefinitely, but any Hebrews would have to be released at their time. Seven years was the limit, and Levi and Hannah had been wed for six. When had Levi purchased them?

Think of something else besides those two together! He looked at the children, fixing his attention on them so intensely the children shivered visibly and went still, their eyes going wider, if that was possible. They finally broke out of their terror lock, and without a single scream, not even a whimper, they whirled and tore away silently, as if afraid to make any noise.

Joshua watched them disappear over the sagging poles of the wooden fence surrounding the orchard beyond, puzzled at so extreme a reaction. The children had all looked Hebrew, from his own nation. Hebrew children, sold into slavery with their parents to pay off debts from hard times. What must it be like to feel outcast in their own land?

He looked away from the little figures. Halel was already stopped before one of the small ragged buildings near the end. He waited in strained silence until Joshua joined him. The old slave shoved the door open, and the smell of sickness came out, a heavy wave of unwashed bodies, stale, acrid sweat and rancid vomit mingling on the smothering, hot air.

Joshua gagged.

To his surprise, Hannah eased around him, fearlessly pushing the door wider. He moved to grab her, but she was already inside. He followed her. Something had given her the courage to go first. He wanted more of that from her.

Just not here.

He stepped inside and gaped. If there had at one time been any kind of floor, it was long gone. He was standing on hard-packed dirt. Low shelves, little more than ragged discarded wooden boxes on the floor, lined one wall, holding a few cracked clay plates that actually looked clean, some small sagging woven baskets made out of the rushes he recognized from the river that ran through his land, worn, rusted iron pots, and clay cups. A handmade table with one lone bench at its side held dirty plates, the remnants of food so dry and hard on them. Joshua wondered how many days passed since they had been taken ill. He imagined them struggling to the bed in the first attack of sickness, too sick to clear things away.

Wooden pegs poked from the cracks of one wall. Joshua stepped closer. They looked handcarved, done by someone who could not afford – or for some reason had not requested – bronze or iron nails. He would have gladly made them himself if they had asked. He counted the scanty number of garments hanging there. Four. Two robes, both so faded the original color had long been lost, and two cloaks, equally worn and frayed. How anyone kept warm in the winter's icy rains in those he could not imagine.

These people had *nothing*. It was no wonder they were sick. The only wonder was that it had not yet spread to the rest of the slaves, if their lives were all like this.

Hannah stood silently a couple steps further in, a strange expression on her face. It was hard to read her with his body blocking most of the light, but if he had to put a name to that, it would be guilt.

He followed her sad gaze to one side of the hut. The place was so small it could hardly be divided into purposes, but a narrow pallet sat in one corner on a wooden bed frame, the ropes holding the four sides together dark with age and rotting. A man and a woman, husband and wife, lay on the thin pallet, barely breathing. Both faces were flushed with a dry heat that chapped their lips and deepened the lines in their faces. Illness had burned away the fullness of features, leaving the skin sagging on the bones, and wrinkled.

Hannah walked over to the bed, and leaned down, trying not to get too close until she could determine what this was. The Law had isolation requirements for certain sicknesses, but this did not look like one of those. Seen up close, death was not far away from either of the people on the makeshift bed. It was no wonder, in the sad house with the few possessions and the pitiful food. The pallet was tattered, the straw poking out of the thin fabric that should have protected them from its sharp stalks. Levi must not have permitted them to replace it, either the rushes or the covering. She saw no loom to weave anything, clothing or bedding. And when would the wife have had the time to weave, anyway?

The woman looked vaguely familiar, but it was hard to be sure. Her sunken eyes fluttered, and her lips moved. No sound came out, but Hannah knew what she asked.

My baby.

Halel had mentioned moving a child. Did it lie sickening in another hut? Had it carried whatever sickness was in this house with it?

A twinge of dread at being so close to such desperate sickness tripped her heartbeat, but Hannah's mother had known healing and had taught her daughter. It had been many years, but Hannah believed the knowledge would come back.

It had to.

Joshua looked as appalled as she felt, Hannah noticed when she turned around. He did not seem to notice her gaze. Beneath his tan, his skin had gone pale. Green tinged his mouth, and for that moment, Hannah thought he might vomit.

Someone should check the other dwellings. Hannah looked from one man to the other, waiting for either of them to suggest it.

Neither did.

"Have any of the others – " she began.

Halel answered before she finished. "There was one with a mild fever two weeks ago, but no one else has been ill since."

"Until these." Joshua said her very thought.

She walked back to the table. It wobbled when she put a hand down. The plates rattled quietly, settling back when she lifted her hand. The crockery would have to be smashed and burned. There was too much sickness to take the chance, and the Law suggested such an act for leprosy. This was not leprosy, but no one could be sure of ever getting them clean. She was not going to try.

The pallet would have to be burned as well. To leave them on such a thing would be a waste of her efforts, and she dared not fail.

And the table! It was hardly worth the effort of cleaning, as well. Surely Joshua would agree to get them a new one, with all four legs even. Perhaps a second bench.

What had her mother used to fight sickness in the house? She remembered the onions and garlic, hung from the rafters and left to dry, spreading their healing powers on the air.

She turned to Halel and put her thoughts into words. "Are there onions in the fields still? Or garlic?"

"I believe there are some of each in one of the sheds, hanging to dry."

"Already tied and strung?" He nodded. It would save much time if they did not have to dig and wash them. And time was precious now. "Bring several bunches of both. We must hang them in here. They will clean the air. I need fresh water, as much as you can bring, and cloths. They must drink."

Joshua shifted his weight, and Hannah turned to him, old fear whispering at her. She should have talked to him first, she should have asked, instead of giving such a command. But her husband nodded to Halel, seconding her command. "Find a woman to help."

"Yes," Halel said. "If you can wait for me, my lord, I will show you the sheds."

"Please be quick," Hannah said, and did not even look at Joshua after she spoke.

"I will go get them, if you can show me which shed." Joshua turned toward the door, his movements slow and aching, like walking through deep water. He felt as though someone had slapped him very hard. He had to get out of this house, had to get away, had to *do* something. He could not understand what his eyes were showing him. How could they *live* like this? Levi, the brother he knew, would never have left his slaves in such conditions!

The woman was Hebrew, one of their own people! The whole country knew better than to live in filth. Cleanliness was part of the Law. And to allow it on his own land – how, *why* would Levi permit this?

At least Hannah, his lovely new wife, could still think. He certainly could not.

Halel followed him out the door, much to Joshua's relief. He walked away from the house before he turned to the slave, his fear turning into anger that poured out of his mouth. "This is shameful! Did you see the mean pallet, and the straw sticking out? Why do they have such a filthy bed?

When was it last changed? Where are the rest of their clothes? I could not even see a place for a child in there! Where could they fit one? No wonder they are sick! There is no food on the shelves, no ends of bread even to go dry. Nothing could come to such a state in a few days!"

Halel said nothing. He merely looked at Joshua as if he were disappointed.

The words almost stuck in Joshua's throat. "What are the other slave houses like?"

"They are all much the same." There was no anger in either his voice, the words, or his eyes. Halel's voice was mild, almost pitying. The slave moved past, and started across the dusty ground toward the rest of the sheds.

Joshua could not follow him at once. It was impossible, simply impossible, that none of his brother's slaves had enough. Unless there had been troubles, not enough money perhaps to purchase new beds and new cloth. That hardly made sense. The weather had been good. The rains had come on time, the sun had shone strong and warm. The farmers had brought in good harvests. *Levi* had brought in good harvests. Joshua had seen the overflowing sacks on the burdened donkeys with his own eyes.

"What happened here, Halel? Why do they have nothing?"

Halel did not answer, just hurried toward another separate row of buildings. Despite the old man's age, or perhaps because his own mind was still stunned by the barren shed with death hovering inside, Joshua had to hasten to keep up.

At a shed at the far end of the row, Halel pulled a key from under his sash, and put the key in the lock. It was slow to turn, and complained.

This shed had been built by his father before he and Levi had even been born, Joshua remembered. He watched the slave struggle with the lock almost as if this was the first time he had used the key. There had never been a lock on this shed. Locks were to keep out thieves. This was a fertile area, with food aplenty and field edges open to free gleaning for all those willing to work. No one was hungry enough to need to steal food here.

Except Levi's slaves. And Hannah. Hannah was so thin she worried him.

Levi had looked well-fed the last time he had seen him.

What had gone on here?

Halel tugged on the knob, sliding it along the opening cut into the wood of the door. The heavy door swung open slowly, releasing the faintest whiffs of grain, drying fruit, and spices, faraway whispers of onion, oregano, mint and dill.

Joshua's eyes adjusted to the dimness, and he took a cautious step past Halel inside onto the stone floor that kept out the rains and the pests. The old slave waited outside as if needing an invitation to enter.

The shed, longer than it was wide, was nearly empty. He could only stare in dismay. Strings of something round dangled above his head, nearly indistinguishable in the darkness, and he brushed them away. Two limp bags, not even half-filled with grain slouched against one wall. No baskets, no sacks, no clay jars sealed against time and predators. Six months had passed since the vegetable harvest, four since the grain harvest, but should there not still be some left? A good farmer planned ahead, at least for seed for the next year. This would only make a few loaves of bread!

"What has happen to this place?" He turned to Halel, shadowed against the bright light from outside. "This is impossible! Where are the supplies to feed the slaves? To plant for next year? The trees are heavy with fruit, I can see the olive harvest will be just as rich. I know the fields produce just as much and abundantly as the trees and vines out there. So tell me, Halel, *where are the seeds for this coming year's planting?*"

Halel said nothing, but Joshua could see the man was nearly as surprised as himself. Over the surprise, Joshua sensed a growing anger, the first such reaction from the mild man.

Stepping further into the stifling darkness, Joshua scanned the shed. No matter how hard he looked, or wished, the shadows held nothing. "There must be another shed. Where did Levi store the rest of the supplies? There is not enough."

Still no reply.

He turned back again and faced Halel. "Was Levi in danger of losing the farm?"

Halel's face was in darkness, the sun was at his back, coming in through the door in a single narrow beam, hiding any expression there. "That is information your brother never shared with me, my lord. Levi held his own counsel. I am but a slave." Anger edged Halel's voice.

What had his brother intended to do with the slaves over the winter? The only thing that would have kept them alive is if he turned them over to someone else. Without slaves – or children – Levi could not manage the farm alone. If he went by the testimony of his eyes, Joshua would think Levi had no plans for his land. But whatever Levi had intended, he had kept it hidden from everyone.

Who was the man in his brother's body?

"The onions?" Halel reminded him. Joshua started, pulled back into the present. "And garlic? Do you see them?" The old man stepped into the shed, away from the blinding sun, but his face was expressionless.

Yes, Joshua thought, think of something else. But dying slaves and cures in onion and garlic hardly dispelled the ominous thoughts that crept into his mind. He reached up and caught a loosely woven sack that swayed just over-head and brushed his hair. His fingers followed the string netting into the dimness to where it was looped over a nail. The sack slipped free easily and tumbled down into his hands.

A muffled scent tickled his nose. Garlic.

Across the shed, he saw Halel catch another sack that had slipped free. "I have onions here." Halel sounded triumphant, moved a step away, and reached up for another shape hanging over his head.

"I have garlic," Joshua said.

"Good." Halel sounded like the one in charge, his voice strong, a man used to giving orders. "We should take these to Hannah quickly." He seemed to remember who and what he was, for he added in a totally different voice, "My lord."

Joshua looked up from the netted bag into Halel's brown eyes. "What were you before you were sold as a slave, Halel?"

Halel's eyes became mild again, the same calm Joshua was becoming used to seeing. For the first time, Joshua realized that mildness hid secrets. "The onions and garlic?" Halel reminded him, ignoring the question.

He would not press. "Let us see if Hannah can begin with what we have. We can come back and look for more." Joshua motioned the slave out the

door, and pulled it shut behind themselves. Halel did not bother to lock it
with the key he wore, what was the point? They carried their small, precious
bundles to the hut in silence.

It already smelled better. The door stood open, and the hot, dry air
moved around them as they stepped inside, onto the hard-packed dirt floor.
The lattices had been opened slightly, giving subdued light to the shadows
inside. Hannah sat on the bed with the sick couple, washing the woman's
legs with smooth, gentle strokes. The woman had been stripped of the
smelly garment she had been wearing, and lay unconscious on the bed, a thin
covering over her from shoulders to knees, oblivious of Hannah's tender
care.

Someone must indeed have brought Hannah water, for a clean, large
bowl filled to the top sat on the dirt floor near her feet. Joshua recognized
the cloth she was using from the color, the blue of her gown. She had torn a
piece off the bottom of her own robe. The white inner garment showed
beneath the jagged bottom edge.

"What are you doing? She should be kept warm!" Joshua's hand clenched
around the neck of the sack he held.

"She is already too warm. This is what my mother taught me."

Hannah sounded like she knew what she was doing, which was more
than he could say for himself. She had obviously worked hard with whoever
had come to help during the short time they had been gone. Patches of sweat
darkened the back of her robe, and left wet rings under her arms. Brown dirt
streaked the robe. She had pulled her hair back from her damp face and tied
it with a blue string she found somewhere, probably from the ragged bottom
of her gown – again. She would have no gown left at this rate. Her sleeves
were rolled above her elbows. Her arms were so slender for the work she
had done.

Another bowl of well-used water, dingy and covered with an evil-
looking coat of slime, sat on the table.

She must have sent the helpers away. No doubt she feared for their
welfare. Joshua wanted to grab Hannah and whisk her away as well from this
place of awful sickness. If he knew of another with the skill to take her place,
he would. He had not endured the past six years to lose her now.

"We found onions and garlic," he said, keeping his voice quiet to hide the roiling fear inside.

"Thank you," Hannah's soft voice was even softer, not to disturb the man and woman on the bed.

He had to force himself not to grab her and run out of the house. "What shall I do with these?" He raised the sack of onions he held, and stepped closer, as if his very presence could protect her from whatever illness lived in this house.

He would burn this place as soon as he could.

"Can you find some place to hang them?" Hannah went back to her slow strokes. "Nearest the bed, if possible. They must be old and dry by now, and we need as much of their aroma as we can manage."

He would work by her side during this crisis, and perhaps that would be a start in breaking down the wall between them. Joshua looked up at the low ceiling. Splinters poked out from the rough wood. Any one of them would do nicely.

"My mother washed away sickness with herbs." Hannah's voice came again. "Rosemary and oregano will clean the table and shelves. I will need a lot of each."

"Of course."

"I will cover the floor with it, and I have to burn rosemary for the air as well." She paused to think. "I remember juniper berries. And dill, and mint, and parsley. I am quite certain I have some in the house. Dried sage, as well. I will need that." She sounded more confident, still a mere shadow of the laughing Hannah he remembered, but this was not a place for smiles.

He would dig up whatever remained in Levi's fields, and anyone else's, if it would get them enough. He grimaced at the list, hoping to remember it all. "Is there anything more?"

"Hot water, as much as you can carry."

She had wanted to run from him yesterday. He knew that without doubt. They had to be near each other now, she could not run away. But for Javan and Taleh's presence, Hannah would not have been waiting for him when he came. It was a painful thought, and Joshua had to turn away. He reached up again for the splinters in the ceiling, and hooked one bag. It held, barely, but it would do until he could retrieve more nails.

He felt Hannah's eyes on him. Turning his head slightly, he stole a look.

Her gaze was fixed on his chest. Her breath came quickly, and her hand stilled, the feverish woman forgotten. Afraid to let her know he saw, Joshua wondered if his robe had a tear.

Or was she seeing something she liked?

For the first time since his wedding, Joshua felt a flicker of hope.

CHAPTER 11

*In those days Hezekiah was sick and dying.. . . Isaiah said, "Take a cake
of figs."*
They took and laid it on the boil, and he recovered.
2 Kings 20:1, 7

J oshua muttered frequently about burning the hut, but Halel pointed
out that there was no place yet to move them, and they would only
bring the sickness. Hannah, Joshua and Halel washed everything that
could be washed, but Joshua insisted on burning the plates, and anything else
in the boxes. Hannah agreed with him. She brought the blankets out to the
fire herself. There were enough at the house to spare.

"Straw?" she reminded the men, and slaves were sent out to collect what
could be collected. Several women began weaving a new cover, but it was a
long process.

"I will do my best," she answered when Joshua asked what to do until
then.

They scrubbed oregano into the table, and washed it off with hot water.

Joshua had found the herbs, from where she did not ask. More oregano littered the floor, crushed underfoot with every step, adding its rich scent to the air already thick with spices. Hannah tried to remember her mother's cures. Small clay bowls sat around every flat surface, holding smoldering mixtures of dried rosemary needles and juniper berries.

She had crushed several onions, using the mash as a poultice on both the man and his wife. Hints of the mint tea she had tried to make them drink lingered in the air. Happily, most of it had stayed down. The air was thick with scents, soothing, biting, burning, so thick it could almost be eaten.

Despite her husband's urging, and with a stubbornness she had not known she still had, a stubbornness she would not have been able to tap without the fear that this small family would die, one small thing she could do to atone for Levi's neglect, she refused to move from the hut. She hardly dared step away from the low three-legged stool Halel had placed next to the bed, except brief moments to breathe air unscented with herbs. Their lives were in her hands, and she would not let herself fail in this.

Joshua and Halel kept the other slaves away from the tiny house. Hannah suspected it had taken little to convince them not to come. She asked about the baby, and so far the news had been good. Another woman had been found with enough milk to feed it, and Joshua had seen the infant and brought the report to Hannah himself.

At last the new pallet was done. Joshua eased the man off the old pallet, while Halel lifted the woman. Hannah fought the old, smelly straw mattress off the rough bed and tugged and pulled the new one into place.

Still, the fever raged in the two on the bed unimpeded.

She had done everything she could remember. What had she forgotten? The sick pair thrashed about with heat during the stifling days, and shivered with the cold at night.

The rag in her hands was warm from their feverish bodies.

"Hannah?"

She dropped the rag into the bowl in startled surprise, and turned slowly, her back stiff from too many hours leaning over the low bed.

Her husband stood with his hands braced on his hips, a frown tugging his brows over his hawk eyes. "Come to the house. You cannot stay here day and night. You are already overtired. If you continue like this, you will be no good for yourself, or for them."

His words hurt. "I have done my best. I do not know why they will not get well, but I have not been neglecting them."

"I did not say that. It was not criticism." Joshua came over to her, and knelt at her side. "You are so tired that you look as sick as they do. Perhaps if you get a good night's sleep, you will remember another remedy that might be the one they need." He reached up a hand to smooth her tumbled hair away from her face.

Hannah tried to stay still when he reached out to touch her, but she was so tired. At her flinch, she saw his lips tighten. She could hardly bring herself to care. She was so tired, and the slaves would not get well.

"Come to the house with me." His voice was soft, coaxing.

She reached down for the wet rag, one last wash to cool the fevered flesh, but his hand caught hers. "No. I told you to go and sleep. Leave it."

The constant worry about the slaves held her back for one moment. "They need watching at night. They try to throw off their coverings and then they get chilled. They are so fevered they do not even know they do it."

"I can do that as well as you. I have helped you for days. I trust I will not make too many mistakes alone." He held her face in his big, calloused hands, and his touch was surprisingly gentle. "Hannah, you must sleep. As your husband, I order you to go to the house. I will stay here and watch."

His beard was unkempt, the first time she had seen it so. She looked into his golden eyes, so close to her, glowing in the lamplight. Worry set heavily on his face.

Her husband was *worried* about her. It was hard to believe. Joshua stroked one hand over her hair, and she felt the tangles as he passed them. For an instant, she thought he might kiss her. And then the moment passed.

"Come. Let us get you some rest."

She ran her fingers through the sweaty mess on her head, and heat rushed up into her face. "I know I look bad. I am so embarrassed. I promise I will take care to look better tomorrow."

"I want you to look *rested* tomorrow," Joshua corrected. "I have never complained about your looks." He gave her an odd scrutiny, his gaze traveling from her hair to her feet, but without scorn. "Hannah, it is time someone told you that you are a beautiful woman. I do not understand why you do not know that already."

She wanted to look away. There was no need for flattery. She knew better than anyone how lacking she was.

He seemed to be waiting for something, but she was too tired for games.

Joshua shook his head, and his shoulders drooped.

"I will do as you say," she said, hoping her obedience would take away the disappointment in his face.

"Go. There is nothing more for you to do tonight."

She hesitated at the door, and turned, but Joshua was already at the bed. He picked up the rag from the bowl on the floor, and, giving it a brisk squeeze, began wiping down the man.

"Hannah!" The low voice rang with urgency. "Hannah! Wake, please wake!"

Sleep was reluctant to let go. The voice came again, slipping through the darkness, nudging at her.

"Hannah. I need your help. Please wake up."

Memory burst through. Hannah sat upright, her heart pounding. The blankets slid downward. She grabbed for them blindly, remembered she had gone to bed still fully clothed, and let the coverings go.

Her eyes did not want to open. Joshua's hand rested on her shoulder. She had the strange urge to lean against him, solid support for her tired head, and let her body catch up to her mind. Light pushed at her lids, and she managed to get her eyelids apart.

Joshua was kneeling on one knee beside the bed. An oil lamp burned on the floor where he had placed it. "Hannah," he said in a low, insistent voice, "the woman is dying. I do not know what to do. Halel is with her now. We need you."

Death. The ultimate failure. Her husband's face was lined and grim. "Yes, I will come." Hannah swung her legs to the floor, and felt with her toes along the night-chilled stone for her sandals.

Joshua's cool touch came as a shock. He lifted her searching foot onto his bent knee, tilting Hannah off balance. She braced herself on elbows, staring in amazement as he tied the thin leather straps. He moved to the second foot, and did the same, then reached out a hand, this man who put her sandals on her feet so they would not get cold.

There was no time to think. She lifted her hand and set it lightly in Joshua's. His grip tightened and he pulled her up with him as he rose. He let go almost immediately. Hannah missed the warmth of that hand.

It came again, a gentle heat against the small of her back, urging her tired body forward. Joshua guided her from behind, his hand moving her past the linen curtain, out of the bedroom, moving quickly, pushed by the awfulness ahead.

And then she was outside. The stars blinked at her. The partial moon only gave the barest light to their steps. Despite the heat of the summer days, night wiped out what warmth the sun left behind, and Hannah shivered.

"I should have thought to bring you a mantle, but no matter. The hut is warm enough."

The thin, brittle grasses poked through her sandals as they hurried across the open space that separated the slaves' quarters from the main house. Most of the small dwellings were dark, but as they drew near, a dim glow showed behind the closed lattices on the house of sickness. A shadow moved across the window, and then the door opened.

The two men exchanged a glance, deep with anxiety, before Halel stepped backward.

Joshua had been right. The little house was indeed warm. The small metal brazier Hannah had donated when this struggle began sat filled with glowing coals. The bowls of rosemary and juniper berries, obviously recently replenished, still burned, adding their smoke to that from the brazier.

Through the gray haze, Hannah saw the couple on the bed. The man looked better, surely he did, but the woman . . .

Her rasping breaths were loud in the quiet house. They had no rhythm, coming one after another, then pausing to leave a desperate silence, before beginning again.

Hannah walked over to the bed, wanting to rush but unable, her steps heavy with despair. The small stool sat in its place beside the bed, and Hannah sank down on it.

"Hannah?" Joshua whispered her name, as though speaking aloud would be a profanity. "What do we do now?"

Hannah took the dry hand that lay unmoving on the sheet. It was cool, too cool, as if the body was dying already from the edges inward. The end could no longer be avoided. There were no more easy breaths. Every breath held a rattle, the long ominous stillness recurred before another gasp started the agony again.

A strange feeling of kinship, of understanding at the battle waged and lost, slipped through the heaviness around her heart. They all felt it, the three of them who had fought this war. They were in the presence of death.

"Please, no." She whispered her cry from the heart. "Please, please, no. What did I forget?"

Joshua's robe rustled as he knelt at her side. Twice this night he had gone down on his knees. "You hold no blame. I will not allow it. No one could have worked harder than you to keep them alive."

Tears slipped down her cheeks, and she swiped at them. Joshua's kind words were a balm she would consider later, on another day, when death was not so near. Now, just now, she could only mourn.

A big arm came around her shoulder. She felt Joshua breathe against her. "Her sickness was too much to fight. Look at the man!" She felt his gesture over her shoulder, saw him point to the far side of the bed. "He is better. If you had not fought so for them both, he would be like her. You – you are all that has kept him alive!"

But Hannah could only see the woman, only hear the rattles that grew both louder and slower. The baby, the woman's baby. Hannah had never even seen it, did not know how old it was or where it had been taken to keep it safe. And the husband, lying insensible beside his dying wife. He would never have the chance to bid her farewell.

Joshua moved the small oil lamp closer, and laid out on Hannah's clean table the pile of thin papyrus pages on which his brother had laboriously kept his records. Some of the edges had begun to fray, dried out by the heat of summer after summer, worn by many turnings. The overlapping horizontal sections of pressed stalks made neat lines for Levi's careful writing. He looked at his brother's familiar script.

Sales of grain, lists of vegetables sold, registers of planting times and estimated harvest. Levi's devotion to detail surprised him. For one so concerned with his accounts, Joshua could not understand why his brother let the farm fall into such a state.

Near the bottom of the shallow stack, on the oldest pages, he finally found the listing of the slaves. He set the rest of the pile aside, and began to read, hunting for the name Halel had given him. The woman, now dead, her body being wrapped for burial even as he sat here, looking at the pages that held her story. A name, Michal. A child born, a boy, unnamed in the record.

Practical considerations got in the way of proper grieving. Simple anxieties mounted up, one upon another. A death to record – the quill scratched across the paper – a burial place to be found, perhaps family to be notified.

The husband knew nothing, unaware with the feverish sickness. No one knew whether he would even live to hear.

Finally the child, still a baby, still well, somehow untouched by this grievous illness. Did he cry for his mother and wonder why she did not come? If the father died, someone would have to take it in until family could be traced.

Hannah would offer, he knew. She would take any child that came her way for however long she could have it. His own feelings on the idea, taking a child not his own . . . that still eluded him.

Joshua sighed, and rubbed his tired eyes, burning in the smoke from the little lamp. Faint sunrise blended into the lamplight. The smudged writing blurred as he tried to stay awake. Names, dates, children born.

And then he sat upright, and stared at the lines before him. Joshua went back a page and read again, more slowly. The dates took on an ominous sameness, slave record after slave record. He remembered the shed nearly barren of foodstuffs and seed.

"This cannot be," he said aloud. He checked the years again, and tried to count the months through the exhaustion that pulled at him. They were all

Hebrew, they were all governed by the Law. No Hebrew slave could be held longer than seven years.

If Levi's records were accurate, and they simply had to be, none of the slaves could be held for more than another three months. Joshua frowned at the numbers before him. Three months. He had only three months of help left.

There was one option. The Law provided for slaves who loved their masters to choose voluntary servitude for life. Those slaves bore the mark, a hole through the lobe of the ear.

Halel had such a hole. He had seen it.

Hannah was alone in the hut when he arrived, except for the husband, still insensible. And the body of the woman, wrapped in a single layer of fabric, ready for burial. Hannah should not be here, not in the presence of death. Impotent anger made Joshua's voice sharp. "Where is Halel?"

She turned around. Her eyes were still red, her face slack with exhaustion and sadness. "Outside somewhere. He did not say."

Joshua stepped out and scanned the area. In the first suggestion of morning he could see the dim span of bare, summer-dry fields stripped of their yield, the faint line of the wooden fence that edged the fields, the orchard, ripening fruit darker shapes in the branches, the pale hint of dusty ground separating the main house from these poor huts, toward the still-dark line of trees that made their own border behind the house. Halfway between the main house and the trees leading to the village, sat a large stone broader across than a man and upon the stone, still as the rock beneath him, was a shadow he recognized as Halel.

The older man must have heard his approach, for he turned as Joshua drew near. Both men were prohibited from entering the village for the seven days of purification for touching the dead. Hannah was prohibited now, as well.

The rising sun caught the small hole Joshua was looking for. "For whom did you pierce your ear? Was it my brother?"

Halel looked away. "I am sorry. No, it was not."

CHAPTER 12

"But if the servant shall plainly say, 'I love my master, my wife, and my children. I will not go out free;' then his master shall bring him . . . to the door or to the doorpost, and his master shall bore his ear through with an awl, and he shall serve him forever."

Exodus 21:5,6

Joshua sank down on the huge stone beside the man. "I thought as much."

They were silent for a moment, watching the sun rise, yet not watching at all. Halel spoke finally. "It was many years ago, early in the days of the war with Ammon." He turned his head and looked at Joshua. "I lost everything. Including my mind."

Joshua jerked in surprise.

"I had a wife, and children," Halel said, still in that quiet voice that was such a part of him. "Three girls, and finally one son." His voice trembled on that last word, and Joshua waited. "He was five." Again a pause. "My daughters were ten, eleven and thirteen. My wife and I, we had given up hope for a son." He smiled. "And then, there he was, a boy. He was finally big enough to be company for me."

Joshua's stomach knotted. He had wanted to get the man to talk. It appeared he was going to. And it would be bad.

"They came one perfect morning. It was spring, nearly time for the barley harvest. The winter had been good, lots of rain, and my soil was rich." For the first time since Joshua had met the man, Halel's voice hardened with anger, and an old hatred. "They came. They cared for nothing, not even a woman, or little children. My woman, my children. They threw them all inside the house, me as well, and burned it. They did not know I was not dead. My crops, nearly ready, and they burned the fields as well. Nothing mattered to them. They did not care that they were destroying food, wasting their own sustenance. They merely wanted to cause as much harm as they could. I got out through the smoke. I do not know why I fought to live."

The silence was thick and heavy.

"When it was over," Halel finally said, "I cared about nothing. I lived on wine, and whatever I could beg. Finally, I came to my senses. I had nothing left, not seed, not a single animal, not a house – nothing. So I sold myself into slavery. I was blessed with my master. He treated me well." He looked at Joshua from the corner of his eyes. "After a time, I found I still had the will to live. I never wanted another family, there were others in my line to care for my land and keep the inheritance. I could never endure another loss, but I could live. And that has been enough."

Halel was quiet for a moment, and Joshua did not want to interrupt. The floodgates had finally opened and he would not, could not stop his slave. There were still too many pieces to find.

"Then my master died," Halel said with so little emotion that Joshua understood, finally, what Halel's life had cost him. "He died, and I was free. But I did not want freedom. I knew what I was doing when I agreed to serve him for my life. I made that decision carefully. I was afraid of freedom, afraid I would become what I had been, afraid of the memories, so I sold myself back into slavery. Levi bought me."

"Do you know your time is almost over?"

Halel nodded. "I know."

"Did you know all the others are nearly done with their time, also?"

"Yes, I know that, too."

"I have to send each of the slaves away with a gift, and there is nothing left to give." Joshua looked at his hands, dangling between his legs. "I cannot spare any goats or sheep if I am to keep the farm functioning. And with that pitiful amount left in the shed, I certainly cannot spare any seed for them."

"Not and leave you with enough to carry on," Halel agreed.

"Not even enough for that, I fear. You saw. You need not speak with tact. I do not know what to do," Joshua confessed. For the first time in years, Joshua felt very young, and uncertain of his next step. "Halel, what happened here? Levi must have known it was time to send his slaves away. Why are there are no preparations for the slaves' freedom, or next year's planting? Where is the coin? Where is the food?"

The man inside the slaves' house lay still, but his breathing finally came in sweet evenness.

Hannah had won this battle, Joshua could see. She sat asleep on the uncomfortable low seat, her head fallen forward onto the bed, pillowed on her arms. Her skin looked gray in the dim morning light, coated with a shiny layer of sweat and the brazier ashes that drifted lazily on the air.

Joshua took advantage of her sleep to study her. Hannah's lashes lay in shadowy contrast to her fair skin, smooth despite the ash and dirt that almost disguised her beauty. Gracefully arched brows, a fine, slender nose, tumbled wheaten hair.

And dark circles under her closed eyes.

She had been thin when they married, but he saw hollows in her cheeks that had not been there before.

His sandals scuffed against the dirt floor as he stepped further in, and Hannah sat upright with a start. Her attention moved immediately to the man.

"He is doing well. *You* have done well," Joshua said softly.

It was not going to be a happy recovery, and Hannah knew it also. Neither would relish the task of telling the slave the fate of his wife. Joshua shoved the thought away. "I need to speak with you." He held out his hand, and waited.

His spirits lifted much too high when she stepped forward with no hesitation and took it, following him out the door into the morning. "I have been through Levi's records." He looked down at her face. The brightening sun showed her exhaustion clearly. As tired as she was, she would tell him the truth. "I did not know my brother was so meticulous."

"Yes. He wrote everything down." There was no smile of remembrance, no sign of fond memories. Her face showed no emotion, and her voice held no warmth.

Of course, she was beyond tired, and this was unfair of him. But he needed answers and to get them he could not let tenderness interfere. Halel's rock was a good enough place. He picked Hannah up, ignoring her gasp of surprise, and set her down on it. Behind her, small spots in the distance, he could see the slaves moving in the orchard at the far end of the field of dry stubble, picking the summer fruit and the grapes growing on their low vines. It was early in the day to be at work.

Joshua dragged his attention back to his wife. She waited patiently for him to speak – or just waited. The perfect wife, lovely in her soft-haired beauty, and submissive. She looked so innocent as her green eyes met his shyly.

"Levi's records show that all the slaves are due to be freed soon. All of them." He looked past her, at the slaves. Summer fruit, all he would have to show.

"Oh," she said, and he pulled his attention back to her. "I did not know it had been that long. Levi never spoke of it. I should have realized. They were already – I had – " She sighed, a heavy sigh rich with guilt, and looked down at the ground beneath her. He was coming to know that sound. "No," she said, her voice a mere whisper, "there is no excuse."

"Hannah – " Joshua tried to think of the right way to ask. "If – when – we free the slaves, I am sure you know they are to receive a gift. Levi must have stored money to take care of that. He would have known he had to purchase more slaves, and more animals. As far as grain for next year's planting – "

She interrupted before he had a chance to finish. "Where is it, Levi's money? Is that what you want to ask?"

"The very question, yes. Unless I can find his coin, I may not be able to buy you the flowers you wanted, not this year, maybe not for several years."

She shrugged. At least she was listening. "That is not a problem. The flowers are not important. The slaves are." There was no surprise in her voice, and no disappointment.

Joshua frowned. It was almost as if she never expected to get them at all. "Levi must have shown you where he kept his coins. It would be different if you could remember where they are. He sold his crops every year, did he not?"

"Of course. Every year."

"Levi must have given you monies to buy things at the market. Did you never see him take coins out, or put them back?" Hannah merely regarded him with her green eyes shuttered, holding secrets. "I saw you there among the market stalls from time to time. Clearly you had money to spend. He must have shown you where he put the profits."

She looked away. "No."

Joshua stared at the side of her face. "You never asked him?" That simply was not possible. Women always found a way to get gifts from their husbands. He knew. He had made jewelry for many of the village wives, he had heard them talk. Joshua could not keep the irritation from his voice. "No woman is that ignorant, Hannah! I do not believe you." The words choked him, but they were out.

She leapt off the rock with such suddenness that he jerked backward. Her eyes flashed fire at him, this shy wife of his. "I do not care what you believe, Joshua! You were not here! You were never here! You know nothing of me, or my marriage."

"Then tell me!" At last, he was about to get answers from her. "Are you waiting to see me fail? What is the meaning of this? Where is the money to keep my farm alive?"

Her eyes were still flashing. "I used the last of it for food!"

Food? "What food? Where?"

"I ate it all."

"All?" He looked at her thin body. "How can that be?"

"I had gone to the market for supplies the day he was found dead. The food was for him, but he was not here, so – I ate it instead."

Joshua slammed a fist on the rock. This time it was Hannah who jumped back. "A month ago? I am not talking about that kind of money! I need enough money to set up entire families on new land, not buy vegetables or spices. The sheds are empty. There are not even any dried fig cakes. There is nothing around here for any of us to eat beyond the next few weeks! And do not tell me you know nothing. Where did the coins come from, that you were able to shop in the village?" What would it take to get the truth from her? She backed away, so quickly she tripped over something and began to fall.

Joshua grabbed her. Her eyes were wide and alarmed, her face gone pasty. He forced himself to let go, even though he did not know if she was steadied, and stepped away. "I am not going to hurt you," he growled, and folded his arms so she could see they were no threat. "Just tell me why this farm is in such a bad state. Is that too much to ask? I just want the truth."

"I have given you the truth!" She eased a subtle step back, her face gone paler. "It was not my place to question him."

"You lived here. It is not a matter of position, but of observation. Did you not care to ask him *anything*? Explain this to me." There was iron in his voice. "The slaves' huts are falling to pieces. What has happened on this place? Why did you not go to the village elders? Why did you let these slaves suffer? Were you too concerned with your own comfort? Is that it? As long as there was food for your table, you did not care what happened to your people?"

He had let go, but his grip had been tight on her arm before he did. She wondered if it would leave bruises. But even that did not hurt as much as his accusations. Hurt her people? Ignore her people?

"What power do you think I had on this place? I did what I could to help them, but it was so little." Her voice surprised her by breaking. She swallowed hard, and cleared her throat. "I knew, believe me, I knew what they were enduring!"

He reached out, but there was no place to get further away, the rock was at her back. "You knew? I could forgive that if they did not live so close, if their shelters were on the other side of our land, but they are no more than fifty paces from this house." His voice was a growl, and the hair stood up on her arms.

She knew what came next. The hand was already on her arm, looking so solicitous from a distance but soon it would be squeezing so tight she could barely breathe, then the walk to the house that seemed easy but in fact she would barely feel the ground under her feet, his hand all that held her up – and then the rest...

She would not let it happen again! Hannah jerked her arm away, surprised that he let go so easily. "Look around you!" She waved her hand. "Would money for food fix the roofs? Straighten the fences? Stone the floors?" She took another step away, and he did not notice. "Have you looked inside my own shelves? Where is *my* food?" Her hand fell down by her side, suddenly too heavy to continue the gesture. "If you want answers, look around you!"

With the last of her courage, she turned her back on him and walked to the house, her legs shaking every step of the way.

CHAPTER 13

"Get the large pot, and boil stew."
2 Kings 4:38

Hannah crouched over the small fire burning just outside the door, and stirred the meal again, ignoring the ache in her back. The small pieces of meat she had cut up in such a hurry bubbled, finally cooking enough to send rich smells into the air. The lowering sun glared into her eyes.

She could not keep her mind on her work. She had nearly cut herself more than once, first while slicing the meat, and then peeling the turnips. Joshua's brooding silence worried her ever since their strange conversation by the rock. He had not followed her. When she was safely alone back at the house she had turned, to see him walking toward the fence behind which the slaves worked on the vines and fruit trees.

He had stayed outside for a long time, as the sun rose and the heat built, watching the slaves, talking to them for a long time. Hannah stopped her work several times to watch him. He even brought them water, a silent journey back to the house where he had not even seemed to notice her, and let them eat of the fruit they picked. She could not imagine Levi ever allowing such a liberty. But she had never checked.

Now she was outside, while he hid within the house, his presence like a dark cloud. He said nothing.

The screech of over-dried pivots from the door startled her upright, bumping the hot pot with her too-quick movement as she spun around to see Joshua in the doorway. The pot hanging on the three-legged stand swayed dangerously, spilling drops of boiling broth into the fire to sizzle and pop in its heat.

Joshua grabbed the thick cloth she used for protection, and in the same move had the stand braced and the pot still. He handed the cloth back to her. "You were not burned?"

Hannah shook her head. "No."

He nodded, and waved at the pot. "Please, do not let me disturb you."

He was not going to talk. Again. She nodded, and crouched back by the fire. Her wrist throbbed suddenly. She looked down, to find an angry red spot she had not felt until that moment. She cradled her arm close, hoping he would not notice. Old words echoed in Levi's voice. *You clumsy goat! Look before you do something! Will you never think first? You cause me such trouble! Why not just fall into the fire and be done with it?*

Joshua began an odd pacing in front of the house, passing back and forth. She could feel his gaze on her. She forced herself to look only at the stew, stirring carefully.

Joshua stopped beside her. "What is the matter with your arm?"

"It is nothing," she answered quickly. She dared one fleeting look. He caught her head before she could turn away, holding it still. It did not hurt. He knew how to hold without causing pain, she thought in surprise.

"Let me see it." He let go of her head and tugged her arm away from her side. The gentleness of his touch surprised her anew. "You are burned!"

"It is nothing serious. I doubt it will even blister." She tried to pull her arm free.

"It is already blistered," he scolded. "Let me get some water on it. Perhaps once it cools, it will feel better." As though that were the final word, he slipped back inside the house.

She stared at the door, bemused. He had not called her a name, had not implied or said a single word of accusation.

His large shape filled the doorway, and seemed to grow to monstrous proportions. She blinked, and the doorway became normal again, and he was merely a tall man, holding a bowl of water and a very large clean cloth.

"Sit."

She sat, surprised how good it felt to get down. He knelt at her side, set the clay bowl on the ground, ripped a strip off the cloth, and dumped it into the water. Joshua plucked the wet strip out and draped it, still dripping, onto the burn. Water ran along her arm and dripped onto the dry ground. It left a cold trail, so very cold. She shivered.

"Hannah? What is it? Are you well?"

Joshua was looking at her. Joshua. Not Levi. Levi was gone forever. It was Joshua now.

She nodded, and ignored the sudden whirling in her head. "Yes. I am perfectly well."

"I think the burn is better," he said, rose to his feet, taking the cloth and the water bowl with him, then disappeared into the house. She stared at the opened door, and listened as he moved about the room, set the basin on the table, a hollow thump. He was still angry, she guessed from the force of it. She held her breath as she tried to catch more sounds. Finally his sandal scraped. He was coming back.

He held up a skin of water, wetness shining on the outside. "We need something to drink."

The skin bulged and swelled as she looked at it, getting larger and larger, and she blinked in horror. As it had a moment ago, her sight became normal again, and the skin was its regular size. How strange, this had never happened before when she was tired. And twice?

He sat down on the ground. Hannah kept a wary eye on the waterskin, but it remained just that, a waterskin. She must get sleep soon. Somehow.

The smell of over-cooked stew interrupted her distracted thoughts. She looked down. A thin crust had formed over the top, orange at the edges with juices from carrots and lamb, but if she scooped carefully he would not notice.

She did not scoop carefully. She was tired of waiting for the real Joshua to come out, tired of waiting for the first blow, tired of wondering what would trigger his anger. Black bits from the bottom showed clearly. She held it out to him.

He looked at the bowl, then back at her, and held out his hand for the blackened stew. He tilted the bowl to his mouth, and took a draught. His gaze held her as he chewed without a flicker of emotion. Hannah held her breath as he took another gulp and another, eating without bread and without complaint. His golden eyes were cool, thoughtful, as he stared at her over the bowl's edge.

He handed it back. "More, please."

Hannah scooped more stew into his bowl with the long iron ladle he no doubt had made himself, then shoved the bowl at her husband. The world narrowed to a small point, just Joshua's face as he swallowed stew and watched her over the rim.

He handed her back the bowl, empty. "Eat," he said, something implacable in his voice. She dipped the iron ladle back into the hot stew, and stirred down to the bottom. Blackened chunks fell into her bowl. He had eaten without complaining, so could she. She raised the bowl to her mouth, and sucked in the broth. A few chunks of something hard and burned slipped in as well. She managed to chew them and swallow.

Joshua nodded. "You need food," he said softly. "You are getting much too thin. You were too thin before. Now you are like a shadow."

Hannah took another mouthful, wondering if he wanted her to mention the hard burned bits, wondering if she should apologize.

"Water?"

She nodded, and he poured the water into cups she had not seen him bring. But then, she had been fixated on the vision in the doorway. "Hannah?"

She met his gaze, her cup poised at her mouth.

"Do I beg forgiveness for my harsh words earlier at the rock? I watched you with the slave man and woman, I saw you fight for their lives. Those were not the actions of a selfish woman. I am still confused about what I find on my brother's farm, but forgive me for accusing you of not caring."

An apology? Hannah choked on a swallow of water. She had never heard a man apologize to a woman. No doubt they did, on occasion, when they had passed the point of easy forgiveness, but she did not know any man who had done such a thing, not even her brother when he had blithely sold her away while she was still grieving their parents.

The sun sank lower against the horizon, bathing them in the intimacy of twilight, gilding everything in a yellow glow, softening her husband's face. Joshua smiled at her, a gentle smile that urged her to talk, to lower her guard and confide in him. He only knew a small piece of the ugliness that had been here on this farm.

But this man was still a mystery and she had said far too much already.

The house had become almost too cool as the sun sank into darkness and the last of the day's heat fled. Joshua looked across the field toward the small hut at which they had spent so much time these last days. It was dark, no lamp sent its faint rays through the lattices. The husband must have been deemed well enough to sleep unattended.

The thought of sleep reminded him of the bed of rushes in the room behind him, the bed where Hannah finally slept free of the fear of interruptions. She needed this rest. How many days had it been since she had had a full night of sleep?

Somehow he could not move toward the bed. This still felt like his brother's house. He wished he dared move them back to the village.

It had been five days since they got here, if his count was accurate. Five days for Hannah to brood on Miriam and her outrageous, selfish flirting and work into exhaustion fighting for his slaves. Five days when she had not had a moment to herself, and how had he rewarded her? Joshua winced every time he heard his cruel words. *No woman is that ignorant! Do not tell me you know nothing! Are you waiting to see me fail? I do not believe you. Where is the money to keep my farm alive? Were you too concerned with your own comfort? As long as there was food for your table, you did not care what happened in the next hut?*

She was not selfish, far from it. He knew his brother, knew how much and how deeply Levi could love. And yet, how could he explain what had gone on in this farm? The big house in which he stood, and the empty food sheds and the pitiful huts for the slaves, his Hebrew brothers?

Hannah moaned, the sound sudden in the quiet house. What did she dream? He could not bear it if his harsh words followed her into sleep, tormenting her in the night as well as the day. What would it take to wipe them from her mind? Joshua moved toward the door of the room in which she slept. There was barely enough moonlight to make her out.

Hannah moaned again, the sound thick with pain.

Something was very wrong. The knowledge seeped slowly through his tired brain. He listened closer to her breathing. The breaths he heard were not calm and restful, but quick and uneven.

"Hannah?" He whispered her name.

She gave no response. Sleep held her fast. He touched her shoulder.

It burned his palm. Fever, searing her. He fought back panic. "Hannah? Can you hear me?"

She murmured something indistinct.

Joshua dashed for the curtain, fought his way through it, catching his hands in the folds as he tried to get out. Past the main room with the chairs, through the eating room, out to the fire burning low, his feet sliding with his hurry. He found the small sticks by the fire, grabbed what he could, stuck them in the fire and held his breath for them to catch. "Hurry, hurry," he begged them, and they lit. He ran back, remembered to hold the curtain, found the lamp. The flame wavered wildly, but it was his hands shaking the oil in the bottom.

His wife's face was still, her skin mottled red and death-white, the colors shifting in the flickering light. He put the lamp down before he could drop it, and bent over her. "Hannah, wake up. Please, wake up." His voice had no strength, the words a whisper on the air. It could not be, this could not be happening. Fear grabbed at his heart, and it skipped a beat.

She whimpered, "No, no, no."

He jerked back and looked down at her, but her eyes were closed. He hesitantly picked up her delicate hand, holding it with all the gentleness he could muster. He needed to feel her, to hold onto her, as if that would keep her with him. "Hannah? What do you mean, no?"

She muttered again, "No, please no." He echoed her words silently. Please, God, not now. I have only received her. Please do not let this be happening. He heard tears in her voice, pleadings from some memory locked inside. Her body tensed under his hand, and her legs moved, as if running. The whimperings became more urgent, and he sensed her sleep was filled with terror.

He should never have let her enter the slaves' hut. Hannah had been breathing in the very herbs and poultices that helped the man survive. Would they give her some protection from this fever? She had watched the slaves' lips, moistening them when they threatened to crack, spreading oil on them when the fever split them open. He touched her lips.

Her lips were dry and wrinkled, the last stage before they, too, split.

CHAPTER 14

"Love is strong as death."
Song of Solomon 8:6

Only moonlight lit his way as he dashed across the openness between the main house and the slaves' quarters. Gasping breaths kept him company, he who always had plenty of strength to spare, who now could not find enough air to fill his lungs.

He thought he knew which hut belonged to Halel. Things looked so different in the dark. It did not matter. Whoever lived behind the door at which he slipped and stumbled to a halt would be pulled into service.

After an eternal moment, the door opened, and the faint moonlight lit Halel as he peered out with bleary eyes. "My lord," he said with a raspy, sleeping voice, "what brings you here?" He blinked, shook his head as if to awaken himself, and a great yawn stretched his jaw.

Joshua saw the instant Halel truly woke. "What is it? What has happened?"

"Hannah is ill." Joshua's breathing had slowed enough to let him speak, but his heart was still terrified. "Please, will you come? I do not know where to start."

Without a word, Halel pulled the door wider and beckoned Joshua inside. It was totally dark within. Halel scuffed somewhere nearby, metal clinked, and Joshua could see the faint glow of coals in a metal fire holder as the old man lifted the lid.

Halel stuck a twig he had found somewhere in the blackness into the coals and it warmed, and burned. He lighted a lamp and the room was suddenly brighter. Joshua paid little attention to the furnishings other than to register a bed, a table, a chair. Clad only in a loincloth, Halel moved toward pegs in the wall on which robes hung.

"I must dress," he said with quiet modesty. "We will need help, I think."

"Tell me who would be best, and I will get them."

Halel pulled a robe over his head. His voice came out muffled. "Taleh." His head came out, and his arms fought for the sleeves. "If Javan will not let Taleh come, there is always Leah the midwife, but she is in the village, too far to go in a hurry, and she, too, has children." Halel slipped on a sandal, and reached for another, then rose. "Your place is here, and I know the way to their land, even in the dark."

"Yes." Joshua suddenly started to shake, trembling inside even though his legs still stood. He glanced down, expecting to see them shiver like the string on a lyre.

Halel stopped at the door, holding it open. "I will be back as quickly as I can. Wash down your wife." To Joshua's surprise, Halel touched his arm. "It is something, a start." Then he turned and hurried off, the lamp bobbing to light his way in the dark.

Water. Yes, wash her down. Joshua raced for the well. The bucket sat on the well cover. Joshua lifted the lid, and the smell of moisture wafted up on a rush of cool air. The water, when he pulled it up, was cool. Hannah had been so hot, the fire raging inside her. Joshua grabbed the bucket and ran for the house.

. . .

He heard her whimper when he first stepped inside the outer door. The oil lamp he had lit sent faint light around the edge of the doorway curtain. She whimpered again, a soft sound, full of pain, tearing another piece from his heart.

He hurried across the stone floor and shoved the curtain out of his way. Hannah moaned, and his bare feet slipped on a small puddle of water he had not even realized he spilled as he hurried to get to her. More chilly wetness spilled over the side of the bucket, sliding down his leg, bringing the skin alert with cold bumps.

"Please do not, please no." Hannah's voice stopped him as he set the bucket down by the bed. He looked over in surprise.

Her eyes were closed. He touched her face. "Hannah, I am here."

Her skin burned against his palm. He watched as a tear trickled from her eye. "No, no," she moaned. "I will be good."

Joshua forced himself to ignore her words. It was delirium. It need not have any more meaning than that.

No one would have done what he feared she was saying.

Hannah cried again, "No more, oh please, please." Joshua tried not to listen as he rummaged for a piece of cloth. He found a headdress and tore it violently. One piece, that was all he needed.

He plunged it into the water. It was straight from the well, but was it cold enough? Or was it too cold for her? Joshua pulled the covers back as Hannah moaned and cried. Her words were once more indistinct, mumbles that made no sense. Hannah's legs made a weak effort to draw up, and her arms curled toward her body. The very air must feel like ice on her burning body. Joshua looked down at the bucket of water, and shuddered.

He had to cool her, he knew it was the right thing to do, he could feel the heat pouring off her. Her skin exposed to the cold night air, he could hardly bring the cloth up to her fevered body. He had done it for the slaves and it seemed right, but now? On fragile Hannah it seemed too cruel.

At the first brush of the rag, Hannah cried out, and Joshua jerked away. How could he do this to her?

How could he not?

The rag was already warm. From one touch, one wipe of her body. He took a deep, bracing breath, and plunged the rag into the water again. Another breath for courage, and he put the wet cloth on her.

"No!"

He stopped instantly and stared down at Hannah.

Glazed eyes looked through him. "Why?"

There was no help from her. And now he feared there might be no help *for* her. "Hannah, you are burning up with fever. I must cool you. This is what you did for the slaves, do you remember?"

"Why?" She said it again, and started to cry. "Stop, please, I hurt." Her voice faded. Joshua felt a terrible relief. The mumbles were frightening, but not as much as what she said. Her tears kept coming. He washed them away in the awful stillness.

Pain pressed on her, pain everywhere. Hannah twisted to get away from it, but it sank talons into her bones.

Levi was beating her. Again, and again, each pound of the fist sending fire down into her bowels. "Please stop!"

A strange voice answered. "Hannah, I am here," and gentle butterfly wings touched her face.

Levi threw ice on her! She screamed, loudly, but could not hear herself. "What did I do?" She heard her voice, and sighed with relief that her ears heard again.

Golden eyes stared down at her.

"Why?" she asked the eyes, not knowing what the rest of the question was.

The eyes spoke, strange words about fever and cold slaves. It made no sense.

"Why?" she asked again, but the question faded once more. She tried to explain to the eyes, "It hurts," but they were not there, and Levi still poured ice onto her, drowning her in a winter river.

.   .   .

Joshua tried to shut out her sobs, so faint they hardly merited being called that. But they were caused by the cold water that was supposed to keep the fever at bay, and he had to ignore them, and ignore as well his doubts that he was doing the right thing. What else was there to do? She was already so hot, if she could not get cool, he feared she would be cooked alive from within.

"What did I do?" Her words came clear again, startling him. Just one sentence. *What did I do?*

Joshua stopped and looked down at Hannah. Beneath the fever's flush, her face was contorted by fear. She tried to lift a hand, too weak to finish the move, but he recognized it. Hannah was trying to block a blow. He stared at her, the rag forgotten in his hand. Her hand fell down by her side, and a tear slid down her face.

This was not a fever dream. Someone had hurt her. Her father? Brother? He knew of such things, but ... Hannah? Soft, delicate Hannah?

She mumbled something, her voice so low he had to bend down to hear it. "Please ..."

A bitter anger started, but he shoved it down. Instead, he used every bit of gentleness he possessed to stroke the cloth down his wife's burning body. And he stopped his ears to her whimpers, thinking only of the rag that warmed much too quickly, and the water in the bucket that was not as cool as when he started.

And of Halel, who should have been here by now. There were wild animals in the forest that separated his farm from Javan's, animals that woke and wandered in the night. He should have given Halel a sword.

He had sent his most valued slave alone, unarmed.

Hannah whimpered again. Joshua wet the rag another endless time, wiped his wife's body, and tried to keep the fears at bay.

Sandals scuffed at the doorway. In one quick move, Joshua flipped the linen covering over her. He hated to do that, hated knowing the heat from her body was trapped under even a thin blanket, feared undoing all his hard work, then turned, almost surprised to see Halel alive and unscathed.

"You made it back," he said stupidly.

"I have brought Taleh."

"Send her in." Joshua looked beyond Halel to the doorway.

Javan stepped into the room, bringing in strength, support and a scolding. "Did you think I would let my wife come into this desperate sickness alone? After a woman has already died, and the husband barely lives?" He shook his dark head, the silver strands catching the dim light from the oil lamp. He rubbed his hands briskly as though preparing for hard work. "She has raised six children. She knows all that is worth knowing about sickness, but she will watch from the doorway and we men will take the risks."

"Foolish man," a soft, feminine voice spoke up from behind Javan's vast shape. "As if I would risk you! I can hardly help if I cannot see what we are dealing with. You must at least let me have a look."

Taleh eased past Javan. His strong arms caught her before she got in far, and held. "I must get closer," Taleh insisted, caught tight within just one of Javan's arms. The muscle bulged against her struggles.

"No."

"It is enough that you are here," Joshua said, afraid that Javan would take Taleh away and leave him on his own. "I need your knowledge more than your presence at her side." He looked down at his wife, her breaths so faint he could hardly hear them. Was it his own dread, or had she grown worse in the moments since he had covered her? When he turned back to the door, his friends did not have time to hide their own fear.

Taleh peered intensely through the dim light. He met Taleh's gaze. Her black eyes, wide now with alarm, struck new fear in his heart. "I will need fresh water from the well," she said, brisk and decisive. "That water must be warm now, too warm to help."

Halel's voice came from the other room. "That is what I am here for. Let me go."

"Garlic and onions," Taleh said abruptly in an echo of Hannah's cures, as Halel's sandals scuffed away. Joshua's heart gave an extra, painful thump at the memory of his wife in the slave's hut, and he knew Taleh felt at that moment what Hannah had. Taleh's instructions continued, "If you do not have enough, we can send some with our own slaves. I will also have them bring marjoram leaves and honey. If you rub the mixture on the skin, it will produce a sweat."

Now that he had support, his fears poured out of his mouth. "She is burning up. The sun will rise when morning comes, and with it the heat. How will she live? She has no fluids in her to sweat away."

Taleh smiled at him, a tired smile. "Joshua, when the fever breaks, she will sweat, I promise. The body will find it somewhere. I have borne six children, and have seen all manner of sickness. They all manage to sweat when it is over. But since her body is not doing it now, we must try to do it for her." She straightened her shoulders with effort. "Have you listened to her lungs? Are they clear? No rattles?"

Joshua set aside the cloth, already too warm, obediently leaned over and laid his head on her chest, frighteningly hot and smelling like the well water. Her breaths were so faint, so light, they barely moved the body beneath him. "It sounds clear," he said, lifting his head off his wife. He wanted to leave it there, rest it on her and hope she could feel him there and sense his love.

Taleh was yawning when he looked over. She tried to catch it.

"You should be home." He could not believe those words came out of his mouth, and it did not stop. More foolish words that would send her away came out, as if his mouth worked on its own with no connection to him. "You have already given us much help." Not enough, not nearly enough, but now that the words were already in the air, courtesy and Javan would hardly allow him to cling to her robe and plead with her to stay.

"When I must sleep, I might try to sleep in the main room. You will need me near, and I can hardly leave."

You will need me near. She was as afraid of the outcome as he was. His heart turned to lead. He found Hannah's hand, and wrapped his own around it. She was alive now, and he would fight for her with his every breath.

Thank God for Taleh. And Javan, for allowing her to come and stay, but it was Taleh who knew what Hannah would have known, Taleh who wracked her memory for anything that would help. *I can hardly leave.* Joshua slipped back through the window into the room, holding the bucket carefully not to spill the precious cool water inside. He hoped Javan and Taleh still slept in the big room so they would be alert when he needed them. He tried to move as quietly as possible, reassuring himself that if Hannah had awakened during the few minutes he was out, Taleh or one of the two men would surely have heard her.

It was still quiet in the larger room where his three helpers had made rough beds. He set the bucket down next to Hannah, and poured himself some of the parsley tea Taleh had made for Hannah to drink. They had gotten such a small amount down her throat, and the tea had grown cold.

He felt himself smile at the incongruity, the water warming while the tea cooled. The smile flattened and drooped. Neither had done much good, the water or the tea.

A moan came from the bed. He nearly dropped the cup in surprise. "Hannah?" He whispered her name, and managed not to yell for the others.

"No."

The word came clearly, and he smiled for real. A little contrariness was surely a good thing. His legs buckled in relief, and he sat down with a plop on the bed. He grasped the nearest hot, slender hand tightly, brought it to his lips and kissed it, putting his heart into the gesture. "But yes, Hannah, it is you. And me, Joshua. Your husband." He felt he had to add those words, for fear she had forgotten him. "Can you talk to me?" The hand he held fluttered, a tiny movement. "Say something, Hannah," he begged. "Please, talk to me."

Hannah screamed. "No! Levi, no!"

Something thrashed in the other room.

Red flushed up his neck. Javan and Taleh stopped at the doorway, holding the curtain. Halel peering from behind them. Joshua spared them barely a glance.

"Stop, Levi!" Her voice was softer, but thick with terror. She must have used up her strength with the first scream. Joshua had to lean over to hear her. "Please. No more." She gave a dry sob. "I hurt."

CHAPTER 15

One witness shall not rise up against a man for any iniquity, or for any
sin that he sins. At the mouth of two witnesses, or at the mouth of three
witnesses, shall a matter be established.
Deuteronomy 19:15

"She cannot mean – " Joshua turned back to the bed where his wife lay, and ugly anger built. He did not know toward whom it was directed, only that it threatened to split him apart. *No, Levi, no, I hurt.* Words hard to misunderstand, harder still to understand.

"Cannot mean what, Joshua?" Javan asked. "She cannot be pleading for mercy from your brother?"

Joshua wanted to hit the man. He stood, glaring at this respected village elder, and his fists clenched. "She was his *wife*," he insisted, wanting to make them believe it. "He was my *brother*. I knew him."

"You have not been here much," Javan said quietly. "It is possible things happened that you never knew about."

His eyes were mild, and Joshua's rage grew against the pity there, the urge to lash out building inside him. "Hannah was his *wife*! This, *this* I cannot believe." His skin prickled, a flush of heat ran across his face. He could not look at Hannah right now, just kept his eyes on Javan, fighting the need to smash the pity in the man's face. "Levi? Hurt his wife?" A bitter laugh tore at his throat. "It is not possible." If only he could turn the world back and erase that one moment and those few words Hannah had cried out that changed his world, make them never happen! But they had.

Her feet moving feebly under the cover, the arm trying to block an imagined blow. What if Javan was right?

"No? What would convince you?" Taleh's voice interrupted his thoughts. Anger sparked through her words, anger that matched his own. "What would she have to do to prove it to you? Would you need to see the bruises? Feel the broken bones? Did you even pay *attention* to her when she walked through the village? She came often enough wrapped in too many clothes in the heat. Why would a woman do that in the summer? She was trying to hide what Levi had done! How could you not *notice*? Did you never even *look* at her? Your own brother's wife, and you never *saw* her?"

"Taleh!" Javan's voice cracked into the thick air.

Joshua could not answer her. He knew why he had not looked at Hannah when she came to the village.

"He had to learn eventually," she said to her husband, clearly unrepentant. "She never had to *tell* me anything, I knew. I saw her, I watched."

"Taleh." This time Javan's warning was clear, and she closed her mouth, pressing her lips into a stubborn line, as if keeping more angry words inside by effort.

"Please," a voice whispered from the bed, and Joshua whirled around. "Hannah?"

"Please stop," Hannah whimpered, and Joshua knew she was lost in her fever-dream once more. Her speech slid back into mumbles, locking Joshua out. He knelt on one knee, putting his ear close to her, hoping for words that made sense.

Hannah's breath was shallow and quick, and he thought he heard the first rattle. In a voice he did not recognize as his own, he whispered, "Taleh? Halel?" Halel was at his side, the argument was forgotten. "I hear rattles." He turned around to look at Taleh next to Javan in the doorway, but his vision blurred, the only clear thing he could still see was Taleh's worried face.

Taleh sank into herself. "Oh, no," she said softly. "I feared this. You must use poultices, any kind now, mustard, onion, whatever will bring heat to her chest."

"I saw her do that for the slaves." And one died, he thought, but he refused to say the words aloud, hated that they had even come to his mind.

"Stay with her. Try to get more tea down her, if she will swallow. I will make the poultices. I should have been doing that, instead of standing here talking," she said and was gone.

Joshua picked up the tea, cold as the night now, and lifted Hannah's head, trying to pour it down. He could not see that the temperature of the liquid mattered now, when Hannah was so hot.

She swallowed, and his throat felt thick with relief. Now that he needed their help so desperately, Joshua hated the anger he had felt when Javan and Taleh had tried to convince him to believe Hannah's rambles, these friends who had come in the dangerous dark. She was his wife, the woman he had waited for so many years, and she was near death.

But he did not want to believe her words. Or theirs. He would unravel that later. Now she had to live.

"What did I do?" Hannah was crying now, shallow sobs without tears, her words muddled and hard to understand because her body was so dry. He would have to get more tea into her.

"Monster," she said on another faint breath of air, but Joshua did not think she was seeing wild animals. "Kill me."

Pain pressed in. The monster sat on her chest, with Levi's face and Levi's cruel hands. Her throat hurt. "Go ahead," she told him. "Kill me and be done with it."

"Drink," someone said, and it was not Levi. How could he be gone when the weight was still on her chest?

"Drink," the new voice said again, and liquid filled her mouth. She swallowed before she could drown.

. . .

Kill me. The horrid words said in a whisper sounded like thunder in Joshua's ears.

Kill me. He did not know whether to rage or weep. Joshua held the cup to Hannah's lips and tried not to spill. It was difficult, with his hand shaking so badly. He had not imagined those words. *Kill me.*

It was all true. The whole night's ramblings made sense, the first pleading words, the agonized *why, I hurt, please no*, all congealed into one appalling, unavoidable answer.

Hannah, delicate, fragile Hannah, abused by his own brother. Just how bad had it been? Joshua thought for a moment he would be sick.

Someone cleared a throat in the doorway, and he whipped around.

It was Halel, holding the curtain open with his body. His brown eyes looked old, and when he met Joshua's gaze, there was compassion in them. "She has been talking," Halel said unnecessarily.

"Yes." Bile pooled in the back of Joshua's throat. He was shattered inside, his brother-love crushed beneath a truth he could not imagine how to accept.

"Now you know." Such simple words. Halel had known. All along. His eyes said so. He had heard what Joshua feared to find out.

Joshua could not meet his gaze. He turned his head away, and nodded.

Taleh appeared in the doorway behind Halel, a large bowl in her hands. It must have been hot, for she had wrapped it in a cloth. Halel took both bowl and cloth from her. Before she turned to leave, Joshua asked quickly, "Can you send your husband to me?"

She nodded, and melted into the darkness of the other room, letting the curtain close behind her with a quiet rustle.

Joshua took the bowl of mashed onions from Halel. His eyes began watering as the onion bit the air. It was just as well. It was something on which he could blame the tears pooling in his eyes.

Halel left, and Joshua reached a hand down into the poultice. Moving quickly, he spread the poultice mixture thick on Hannah's chest.

If she lived, what more would he learn?

. . .

Fire filled her. "No, not this! Please!" Heat poured into her around the weight
on her chest, and a strange pungency filled her mouth with every breath,
every cry. The air was tainted and thick. A mist swirled around her, wrapping her in gray and black.

"No, no," she moaned again at the monster and the mist, but more
weight came.

And yet, the weight seemed to lift her chest. How could that be, that the
weight made it easier to breathe? It was too confusing, and as the mist thick-
ened, Hannah could not fight it and slid into the darkness.

Javan slipped into the room. Despite his guilt and torment, Joshua noticed
his friend's eyes were dark hollows, made darker by the sleeplessness that left
bags beneath them, and by the onion. His own must look the same. "Yes,
Joshua? My wife tells me you wish to speak with me."

"Hannah has been talking again."

Javan nodded wisely. "This does not surprise me. I assume her words
have been – " he paused, looking for a word that would not insult,
"enlightening?"

"Too enlightening." Joshua shuddered. He hoped Javan did not see.

"I know this is hard for you." Javan walked boldly the rest of the way into
the room, and stopped behind Joshua.

"He was my *brother*, Javan," Joshua said. "I loved him. I admired him. I
wanted to *be* him, for the longest time, content with the inheritance, a happy
farmer, but I could not fight the need to work with metal, it was like a fire in
me from youth, and the farm weighted me down until I thought I would
break. Levi took the entire farm, my share and his own. He freed me, Javan.
Levi set me free." He sighed, but it hardly released the anguish inside. "I
thought he was happy, I thought he loved the farm. I would have sworn to it.
He made it possible for me to be what I am, to work with the metals, and
gold. I owe him everything." Joshua's chest ached, deep inside.

Words poured out of him, disbelief and grief spilling over into the chill air in the room. "What made my brother become this man? Did you know the sheds are nearly empty, there is nothing to plant, and winter is coming? My brother knew farming. He would not make such a mistake – unless there was a reason."

"I know one possibility. Not about the sheds, but the . . . other. Levi wanted an heir," Taleh said, appearing without warning in the doorway, but stopping there as if blocked by Javan's earlier words. "Hannah said that much, once. Just before Levi's death, she told me if she could give him a child, all would be well."

"A child?" Joshua clenched his hands and forced himself to keep them at his side. He tried to get the fists to release, but they would not. "Why not simply take another wife? It is so easy to find another woman and try with her. Abraham did, with Ishmael. It makes no sense. Why punish the land? And if he wanted an heir for it, why destroy something he would give to his child?"

Taleh sighed. "I do not pretend to understand such men."

He did not understand this either.

"Imagine the humiliation of discovering that the next wife did not conceive." Javan spoke slowly, as if he was testing the thought first. "It has been known. Several wives and no children? We cannot prove it, but to marry and find one barren woman after another is hardly reasonable. A man does not reason clearly when he fears his manliness is threatened. After all, the farm was at stake." Javan spoke with confidence now, seemingly finding his arguments sound.

"I have never heard of a barren man." Joshua could hardly believe his ears had heard right. Javan saying a man could be barren? The very thought was laughable – if he had been of a mood to laugh.

"I am not saying a man can be barren," Javan returned, "just that with several wives, surely *one* would conceive. Perhaps he, too, knew of such cases, and feared the fault was not all Hannah's. That even with a second wife, he would still lose the farm. All would know then that the defect had not been in Hannah. He may have lost all hope. Six years without a child certainly would do that."

"It was equally possible he could have had an heir with another woman."

"And equally possible he may not," Taleh said with a bitter voice. "A man like Levi could not take such a chance."

A man like Levi. He was Levi's brother. What had that done to Hannah, marrying the brother of the man who had tortured her so? It was supposed to be so simple. A little time to mourn her husband, a little kindness from him, and she would love him as he had loved her – the dream shattered into bits. "I have lost already," he said.

"Lost? Lost what?" Javan frowned at Joshua.

His secret was too heavy to keep inside. "You have never asked why I did not marry before. I have coveted my brother's wife these past six years." He did not want to see the condemnation on his friend's face, so turned to Taleh.

She was smiling.

The smile stung. "Did you not hear what I said? I have broken faith with the Commandments."

"No, not really," she said, her Ammonite history showing. "You did not act on it. I understand now why you stayed away from the farm." Her smile widened, and she met Javan's eyes. "Is it not wonderful, husband?"

"Perhaps not wonderful, but in this case, it is a good thing." A smile wrinkled his beard, but Joshua could see him trying to hide it. Then Javan gave a bellow of laughter. "No wonder you agreed to wed her so easily. I had been afraid for her, you see. After my wife told me what went on here, I was afraid you might be like Levi. He had deceived us for far too long. Why not suspect you as well?"

Javan looked over at Hannah as if he suddenly remembered where he was, but his smile still creased his face. "Truly, my friend, I never guessed, I never suspected you felt that way." His smile abruptly faded. "These years must have been hard for you, hiding such a secret. Perhaps it is better you did not know until Levi was dead what he had done. Had you known, the temptation to set things right might have been too much for you?" He made it a question.

Joshua did not answer. He did not know what he would have done. The Law had guided his very life, so much that giving up his part of the inheritance had already stained his conscience. What recourse would he have had and still lived with himself?

"I think, wife," Javan went on, turning to Taleh with tenderness in every line of his face, in his very posture, a closeness despite the width of the room that separated them, "that you may be right again. It is a very good thing."

Joshua could not believe his ears. "Have you not heard anything that has happened here? She will not want me! Can you remember the day we came for her? She was like a frightened deer. I thought it shyness, fool that I was. Only now can I look back and see the truth of that day. She never wanted to be married to me! I am Levi's brother!"

Javan shook his head. "But you are not Levi, and that is what will matter." He rested a great hand on Joshua's shoulder in the gesture that was becoming familiar. "I had not thought you the kind to give up so easily."

"I thought getting Hannah was a sign of God's forgiveness," Joshua said, and shifted away from Javan's comfort. He was not worthy, even if they could not see it. "Now I think this will be my punishment, to love a woman, to have a woman – if she lives – who will never love me in return. Fit punishment for coveting, will you agree?"

Joshua leaned on the wood fence and hoped it would hold. The night had been long and wearying, endless hot poultices to spread on his wife's body and endless cups of tea to tease down his wife's throat, and more trips to the well for cold water to sponge her off. His fingers did not know whether they were hot or cold.

He should be back in the room tending her, but he needed some time alone to think. He could not weigh the night's revelations with Taleh and Javan watching, and even worse, with Halel, the slave, uncomplaining when he surely had his own grievances to add to the burden of Levi's guilt.

Yes, Levi was guilty of whatever had hidden in Hannah's nightmares, a guilt for which he might never find an explanation. The storage shed should be brimming, and the flocks were not large enough to divide among the slaves when they were freed.

And Hannah, always Hannah, with her sad face and her fear.

Something had happened inside his brother, a poison that had corroded Levi like rust on iron, eating away at the strength, leaving it weak and rotten. Was that poison Hannah's barrenness? He had missed it somehow during these last six years, seeing only the surface, Levi bringing in the harvests, year after year, huge grain sacks piled on wagons and strapped to donkeys. He remembered standing in the doorway of his shop, filled with pride as his brother bargained with the traders and shopkeepers. He had seen the leather bags of coins trade hands, enough for grain seed and wood for roofs and fabric for robes.

Yet the slave's houses were crumbling, they had few clothes and little food. The puzzle turned over and over in his head.

Whatever else he was, the farmer Levi had been would have planned for this, keeping the money secure and the livestock plentiful for the day of the slaves' release. He had spent the gold on nothing. So where was it?

Levi was not here to ask.

Scuffing sounds drew near. He knew who it was without bothering to turn around. Javan stopped beside him, and leaned against the fence that Joshua had just worried might not hold one man's weight.

"Now that you finally see, Joshua," Javan said somberly, "what are you going to do about it?"

"I do not know." How like Javan to isolate the very thought that was eating away at him. "I do not know," he repeated.

Javan shifted his weight on the fence and waited for more. Or perhaps he just waited.

Joshua settled more firmly against the wooden pole. It had not fallen down yet, it would stand his weight for a little while longer. "As I said, I never wanted the farm. I liked some things about it, climbing the trees for the fruit harvests as a child, playing games with Levi, throwing fruit at him like spears until our parents caught us. Each time." His smile surprised him. He shook his head ruefully. "Perhaps my memory played false with me. There were good times here, but as I became an adult, I could not stay. I had another life in me." He sighed. "I did come, sometimes. I did help Levi. Sometimes."

Joshua looked at Javan, surprised he could even meet the man's eyes, his own shame was so great. "How did I miss what was happening to Hannah? I was on the land on occasion, not often, but I was here. And I was in the village. Taleh said Hannah walked there. How did others see what I did not? I looked at her with love, and I was too stupid to see what was before my own eyes!"

"Perhaps God shielded you." Javan crossed his legs at the ankle and put even more weight on the fence. Joshua thought he heard it creak. "You were wracked with guilt enough, how could you have survived if you knew what she was enduring?"

Joshua looked toward the house where his wife fought for her life. She had help right now, and he was no good for her, not until he had sorted this out in his mind – and his heart. "You asked that before. I would have killed him, Javan." He turned to the somber wise face. "I would have killed my own brother if I had known what he was doing to Hannah." His hands knotted into fists. "I almost wish I could still do it, yet he is beyond my reach."

Javan was silent for a moment, and then said, "My wife was kidnapped when she was about to give birth."

Joshua nodded. "I heard the story."

Javan scuffed the soil with the toe of his sandal. "The man was stoned," Javan said quietly. "I at least had that satisfaction, so I can understand."

Joshua did not want to talk about Hannah any more. It was too raw, and he had exposed himself enough. There were other worries easier to discuss in the early morning. Like . . . "Where did my brother hide his money?" The words burst out. "If I thought he had killed himself on purpose, I would think he left this mess to spite me, but his death was an accident, and I know he loved me. He would not have done this to me. And that means he knew he had to release his slaves." Joshua suddenly realized he was pounding one fist into the other hand, and stopped. "He knew the Law, he knew what was expected. I saw the wagons of grain he brought to market, I saw the gold he was paid. He had enough to send them off. He had enough! Where is it?"

Javan said nothing.

"He would not have done this!" He should not be defending his brother, but he could not stop. "I cannot explain everything, but he would have had a solution!"

Javan shrugged. "So what do you think it is?"

Joshua pushed himself away from the fence and started toward the house. He had been away from Hannah too long. The latest poultice and the tea Taleh had made for her must have had a chance to work. "I do not know yet, but I will find it."

CHAPTER 16

Jacob loved Rachel. He said, "I will serve you seven years for Rachel, your
younger daughter."
Laban said, "It is better that I give her to you, than that I should give her
to another man." . . .
Jacob served seven years for Rachel. They seemed to him but a few days,
for the love he had for her.
Genesis 29:18-20

Halel stopped chopping celery for a moment and listened closely. The soft sound came again, dried rushes crackling to movement. He dropped the knife and rushed into the sleeping room.

Hannah lay on her back, still as death, only the slight rise and fall of her chest telling that she lived. He watched closely, waiting for some change, some explanation for the rustle he had heard, shook his head at his foolishness and turned to go.

The sound came again.

He whirled around and stared at the still figure on the bed, willing her to do whatever she had done that made the sound. His eyes burned from not blinking, and then she moved one leg. Slightly, the barest movement, as if trying for comfort.

"Mistress Taleh!" It was hard to shout without raising the voice, but he managed to get the sound to carry.

He could feel her footsteps hurrying on the stone floor, leather sandals scraping, and then she stood at his side, in defiance of her husband's orders. "What was it, Halel?"

"I think she is waking!"

Taleh's impatience was palpable, shivering in the air. They both stared at the bed. "I see nothing," she said with discouragement.

"Wait," he told her. "Watch her legs."

Hannah did not move.

Taleh sighed with disappointment. "She was so weak when she became ill, and I fear she believed she had nothing to live for. She has no reason to fight." Her voice wobbled at the end.

He feared the same thing. Still, "I saw what I saw," he told Taleh stubbornly. "She will wake soon." Whether she wanted to or not, he hoped.

"I will stay near," Taleh said.

Something was on her chest, heavy and pressing down, and it hurt to breathe. She heard her name from far away.

"Hannah? Hannah, can you hear me?"

Halel? He sounded worried, almost frantic. Her mind replied, but no sound came from her dry mouth.

"Hannah, I am going to give you some water. Can you try to swallow?"

He needed an answer. She managed to whisper, "Yes." The effort it took frightened her.

Cool wetness slipped past her cracked lips and slid toward her parched throat. She wanted that water, craved it, but to her horror she could not swallow. Coughs tore at her chest, and added to the fire in her throat, and the precious moisture strangled her. The room spun while she gasped for air. Her lungs screamed to breathe. Strong arms lifted her upright.

Breath, sweet air. She savored it. Familiar scents carried a warning; garlic, onion, oregano, rosemary, juniper. The smells of a sickroom.

Missing memory returned in a rush, pounding in her skull, raising the hairs on her too-sensitive skin. The sick slaves, and the woman who died. She remembered feeding Joshua his evening meal, burning her hand on the kettle. Remembered him waiting and watching with that strange look in his eyes.

And then nothing.

The room moved once more. Someone was setting her back down, the bed touched her back and she was flat again. Her eyes opened at last. Her arms lay limp as dead things across her belly, her legs were stiff and weighty.

Halel smiled at her, a weary smile. "You had us very frightened. I did not think I had the skill to save you. But Taleh came." His smile faded. "We must give you water, and clearly you are not ready for a cup yet. If I put a rag soaked in water in your mouth, can you swallow?"

Yes, she thought, that might work.

Halel smiled as though he had heard her words. "I will try that." He headed for the doorway.

Her eyes closed again. She was too tired to keep them open. Her tongue stuck to the roof of her mouth.

Footsteps scuffed against the stone floor gritty with sand. Grit, scraping, the curtain swishing. Had no one cleaned the house, or wiped their sandals? How many had been through the room to bring that much of outside in and leave it on her floor? She smelled fresh cool air. Light flickered against her eyelids.

She caught the scent of water, and managed to open her mouth, like a baby bird. A cloth touched her lips, so cool it burned, but it was wet. She sighed with pleasure. The moisture slid across her tongue, slowly, and her throat opened to let it down. The fire in her throat eased a little.

More footsteps, pounding through the house, sliding to a stop beside her, a heavy thump and the bed shifted as someone sat down. A yawn where sleep still clung, someone just awakened to the news. It was Joshua, somehow she knew that despite the shortness of their time together. He picked up her hand and held it between both of his calloused palms. She felt his warmth above the fire in her skin, but could not turn to see him. She could only feel his touch.

Joshua did not let go of her hand. He did not speak, either, but his breath began to shudder, rough patches between the breaths, a trembling in and out, a near soundless sensation.

Was he weeping?

Lips touched the hand Joshua held, and stayed there. "I have been so afraid," he said softly, his voice ragged and thick. She felt the sound shiver through her, every word sending tingles across her skin. "I thought I had lost you. I do not know what – " his words stopped abruptly.

"You must get well for me." Joshua's voice came again, still rough and choked. "You must get well so you can sit beside me, and eat enough, and smile for me." There was a shivering pause, and then his voice came softer, almost hesitant. "I need you. You will survive." She thought his hand tightened ever so slightly on hers, emphasis to his words. "You are awake. That is a big thing with this sickness, I have learned. People in the village are ill, also. Javan and Taleh spread word, and found out. Several have died, not just our own slavewoman. So you see? You are one of the strong ones."

Strong? She did not think so, and if others wanted to believe it, then God and Joshua were going to have to be patient with her.

She was too tired to think any longer. Sleep tugged at her, and she slid gratefully into it.

CHAPTER 17

If your brother, a Hebrew man, or a Hebrew woman, is sold to you and serves you six years, then in the seventh year you shall let him go free from you. When you let him go free from you, you shall not let him go empty.

Deuteronomy 15:12, 13

Joshua strode across the field with purpose, to look at the olive trees, and the heavy sacks bursting with fruit. This harvest was well along, much of the fruit ripe and fragrant. The women were elsewhere, slicing the bounty of fruit to spread in the sun to dry for the long wet winter. There would be apples and raisins, olives boiled in vinegar and apricots cooked in flour and lemon. The walnut harvest promised to be rich, as well, and would add variety to the winter meals. They could be cooked in stews or stuffed into cuts in the meats and baked over the fire, mixed into bread – assuming he could buy enough wheat – or pressed into the dried fruit cakes.

To be taken with the slaves on their trips to their own soil when their time was over. The rest would have to be kept here, safely stored in the sheds. Even with the fruits, it seemed all too likely if he depended solely on the farm's yield, he might feed the slaves and send them on their way only to starve himself, he and his wife.

And if Hannah were ever to conceive, she would have to gain weight to carry any child in her womb.

Joshua knew if he could get seed, the soil would still be fertile. It had been good land, and he could not imagine Levi could destroy it unless he sowed it with salt. The burden of the work that waited pressed on him. The biggest job was the planting when the rains started.

It was all so pitiful, the poison anger left in his brother. He had punished everyone for something no one could prevent. Hannah's barrenness was simply a part of life.

He was going to need slaves again. Even if Hannah did conceive, it would be years and years before any child would be old enough to make a difference. The farm was big and needed help.

Now that Hannah was awake and his mind was not fixated on her, it kept swirling back to the need for coins. Coins and slaves, and the bags of money his brother kept bringing back from the market.

What had Levi done with them?

Sunlight warmed the very corners of the room, creeping through the closed lattices like a thief. From where she lay in the bed, her head and shoulders propped on goats' hair pillows to help her breathe, Hannah shifted her legs, appalled at how weak they were. At least they still worked. When she was able to stand and walk, they would get stronger. She should be grateful she survived.

She *was* grateful, of course she was.

The fever still simmered inside her, making her skin dry and tight, burning behind her eyes, but it had been worse. The awful fever-dreams were gone, leaving only the shadow of fear. She caught a sigh, afraid to breathe too deep for fear she would cough and Halel or Joshua or whoever else Joshua had assigned to watch over her, always ready to burst in at the slightest sound, might come to ensure she did not lose the ground she had gained.

She could not help thinking about Levi and what he might have done under similar circumstances.

She thought she remembered soft words from her new husband, words of encouragement, words of tenderness, words that had drifted through her mind and her dreams while the fever baked her. Words she had never heard from Levi. *I thought I had lost you. I need you.* And strangest of all, the sound of weeping.

Joshua would never know how much courage it had taken for her to insist on the help she needed with the slave woman, to tell him to hang the spices, and most frightening of all, to refuse his order to leave. Somewhere in that terrible time, a long-lost part of herself had been found, a woman with knowledge and even – wonder of wonders – a will of her own.

A woman she could like.

She remembered words Joshua said as they fought for the slaves' lives. *I need your help. What do we do now? Take care of yourself. The fault is not yours.* Now, *that* was a phrase she had never heard from Levi. For years it seemed as if everything had been her fault.

There was no comparison. Joshua was not Levi. She felt a smile form in her mind. She did not know exactly what Joshua was yet, but he was not Levi and that was a good thing.

At the sound of soft rustling, she looked up. She must have made noise, despite her care. Halel, not Joshua, stood in the opening, holding a clay cup. Water, no doubt. Again. Ever since she had awakened, people had been bringing her water.

"You must be thirsty," he said, as if it had to be so. "I have brought you water. It is cool, it has come straight from the well."

That had been easy to guess.

Halel smiled his calm smile as he set the cup down on the floor by the bedside, then leaned down to help her sit. "I can hold the cup for you, if you need it." He put the cup in her hand.

It felt heavy, but as it sat in her lap, her fingers curled around it, Hannah decided a woman who could stand up to Joshua could hold her own mug. Her arm shook as she held it, but she managed to lift it to her mouth. Accomplishment tingled through her as the cool moisture slid over her tongue. She could only hold it another heartbeat. Hannah gulped quickly, three swallows before her arm dropped back down. "No more, please. That was plenty."

Halel caught both hand and cup. "I disagree, but I will let that be enough for now." He rose to his feet, gave her a gentle smile, and slipped back behind the curtain, leaving her alone once more.

The room seemed barren after he had left. Not even the sound of Halel's footsteps and the clink of clay plates or bowls or cups against each other from the other room as he worked was company.

Weary darkness crept over her. She wanted Joshua to come in. He had not been here for more than a day, and there was no explanation for his sudden absence. How very odd it was that she, the cringing, cowering wife of Levi, should now want the company of a man. Perhaps not *want*, but she thought she missed his presence.

Or was it just the soft words that stuck in her mind she missed?

She knew he had seen her at her worst, but she was feeling a little better now, and she wanted a bath, she wanted to wash her hair, she wanted it combed smooth.

And she wanted him to come in and see her that way.

The curtain swished open. As if her mind had called him, Joshua stood in the doorway, holding the heavy folds of the fabric aside. A sheen of sweat covered his skin. His chest strained against the linen robe, and for the first time Hannah did not feel threatened by the size of a man – this man – by broad shoulders and bulging arms and legs. He looked . . . good, solid and strong and durable.

And Halel was still nearby.

She remembered somehow his touch on her skin, bringing coolness.

She stared up at him. There was yearning in his eyes, and a sadness. He caught her look and smiled. "You are better, I think." His gold eyes did not match the curve of his mouth.

She dropped her gaze. "Yes."

"Did I hear you tell Halel you cannot drink?" She looked up to see a tiny frown furrow between his eyes. It was gone quickly.

"No, I drank."

"Good. I am glad I misunderstood." He spoke in a soft, soothing voice. "You must not let the fever build again. We have worked so hard to get you to this point, I do not want to lose you now."

A giggle came from outside the window. Hannah jerked at the unlikely sound. A woman, young, not much more than a girl. Hannah did not recognize the voice. It could be one of Taleh's daughters, but she did not think so.

Especially not after looking back up at Joshua's face. The red color deepened and spread up from beneath his beard. He whirled toward the window, but the lattice was pulled shut, and only a slender shadow showed. He sighed, his broad chest lifting once.

"I have not seen Joshua at his shop for *days*," she said to someone outside the house, and Hannah turned back to the window, for some strange reason needing to hear every word. "I had heard of the sickness here, and simply *must* be sure he is well."

There was too much emotion in her voice, Hannah decided. And somehow it did not ring true.

Halel spoke. His voice was quiet, but the room was quieter and they could hear. "Joshua is well. We lost a slavewoman, mother of a young child."

"Oh, how sad," the girl said, but there was no sympathy.

"Joshua was never ill." Halel sounded sharp, a tone Hannah had never heard from him before. "It is Hannah we feared for."

"Indeed?" Now there was real interest. "And how is Hannah? Will she die?"

This woman would not shed a tear if I did die, Hannah thought, not unless the weeping would gain her something. A face popped into her mind, a faint memory of a girl and the kiln and Joshua saying kind words about her, but no name followed it. Hannah made herself raise her eyes and look at her husband. He stood with his back to her, listening as carefully as herself, his hands clenched.

"What is she scheming?" Hannah heard Joshua mutter. His jaw was tight, the muscles of his shoulders stiff and angry, to match his hands.

His shoulders and his hands did not lie. He did not look happy at all. He turned to face her and met her gaze fairly. "I must find out what she is doing here." He shook his head in disgust. "I may have to get some of the slaves to throw her off my land." Joshua stalked to the doorway, and flung the curtain aside with too much energy. Hannah heard a stitch snap. "She should have known better. I cannot believe she would think this would gain her anything . . ." his voice faded as he got too far away.

Hannah listened to his footsteps go out the building. The room was quiet again. She knew what pretense sounded like. Levi had pretended care, pretended concern, pretended happiness.

Joshua's angry reaction to their uninvited guest was real.

"Joshua!" The woman's voice was delighted. A laugh trilled. "Look at you! How well you look."

Hannah listened. Nothing could have prevented her, and she could hardly have avoided it. The pressure in her lungs grew as she struggled to get air quietly, so she could hear. She did not want to miss a word. A tickle threatened in her chest.

"My wife is ill. We are busy here. We do not have time for guests, and I cannot have her disturbed. I will not risk her recovery." Joshua sounded angry. "You know how dangerous it is to come here, where people have died! Does your father know where you are?"

"How could I stay away, Joshua? I have been so afraid! As for my father, he does not question my every move. I am free to go where I will."

"He *should* question you. He should show more interest in the mischief you plan so carefully. In fact, I am going to tell him this latest foolishness of yours. You have been looking for trouble, and I am ready to see that you find it! I have told you before I have the wife I want."

Scuffles came, and the giggle again, only to break off suddenly. "Joshua! You cannot do this to me!" There was genuine anger in her voice. "Put me down! My father will never forgive you! You will pay!"

Hannah heard a sharp slap, and a shrill, angry cry. "How dare you?"

And then a quiet male chuckle near the window, but not Joshua's. Halel.

The angry protests faded into the distance, the girl's getting more shrill the further away she went.

The cough Hannah had been fighting burst forth, tangling with a breath. She was paying for holding it in while she listened and her lungs, her throat, her head burned while she fought to get air. Footsteps came quickly through the house, closer and Halel hurried through the curtain.

"Hannah? Can you breathe?"

She choked and coughed, hoping for air to fill her chest. Halel came over and lifted her. His arms were not the broad ones of her husband, but once she was upright, the coughing eased.

He pulled something behind her, a pillow, then another, eased her back onto it, backed away, and watched her with worried eyes. Hannah wondered what she looked like after such a spasm. "Can you breathe now?"

Her breath smoothed. She tried to ignore the burning down her chest, and managed a single nod, frustrated anew at her weakness. "I have seen her once. What is her name again? Tell me what I missed."

He grinned, a rare thing. "That was Miriam. She thinks to wed Joshua, but he has had nothing to do with her." He looked sharply at her. "Her father thinks she can do no wrong, and has given her everything she ever asked for, but she did not get this – him. I do not know what it will take to open her father's eyes to what she is. The man is blind." He shook his head, much as Joshua had done.

She could remember what Miriam wore, the thin robe that let the sun show through, and wondered if she wore the same thing today. Joshua had backed up to avoid her touch then, but today he would have to touch her to carry her away. Jealousy burned inside. He was to touch only *her* now, and even if he was dragging Miriam off his land, Hannah did not want his hands on another woman. She felt a great stillness inside as she realized what she was thinking.

She remembered her feelings that awful first day all too well, the emptiness, the annoyance that Joshua had felt obligated to put on a show of happiness. She had heard some of his words from her hiding place behind the window, his protestations of joy.

They were only a burden then, with this marriage thrust upon both of them. But now Hannah wanted desperately to believe the words he had said to defend her. She wanted to be there when he presented Miriam to her father, and ached to hear what he would say.

She did not know if her husband even wanted her to be jealous over him. But she was.

It was a long trip through the woods. Well out of sight of the house, Joshua swung Miriam off his shoulder and onto her feet in one move, spun her around, and keeping a firm grip on her arm, pushed her ahead of him. Miriam cursed and cried, and called him names. Birds darted from trees ahead and to their sides, disturbed by her noise. Miriam's ranting served one purpose. It would be a brave animal who would venture close, and his sword was propped against the wall inside his brother's house.

The path seemed more open than it had when he walked to pick up his bride, as though there had been more movement through these woods. He thought back over the past week or more. There was the first trip to get Hannah, the return trip to the village, Javan and Taleh's journey home, another trip back to the farm to see the sick slaves, himself, Hannah and Halel, then Halel going for help – the path had indeed been busy.

It had been little used before. He thought of Hannah, isolated and alone, and his brother, keeping people away.

He did not slow. Miriam made a quick twist, turned her head toward him, and spat. The wet wad missed easily. "You are a monster," she shrieked. "How can you do this to an innocent woman?"

He doubted that very much. She may still be pure in body, although he believed that unlikely, but she was no innocent. She was as dishonorable as it was possible to be.

What a pity her father was so wealthy. Hophni held much land on the east of the village, and grew grapes for wine, olive trees for the oils and fruits, cows and sheep for meat and wool. Joshua had much the same on his land. Given time, perhaps he could hold the same wealth as Miriam's father.

Miriam needed something to occupy her. A husband with little money and several children would do nicely.

A husband with little money, and children. An idea began to form. He had a slave with a child who needed a mother, a fellow Israelite soon to be freed . . .

When they neared the edge of the forest, just before the cleared hills that surrounded the valley where the village sat, Joshua stopped. Crowding close to her back, he spoke into her ear. "I will not make you go through the village like a prisoner, but if you attempt to break free, I warn you, I will throw you over my shoulder yet again, and I will not care then who sees us. Do you understand?"

She nodded stiffly. Her body was rigid with anger – or plotting, he could not tell. No doubt she was waiting for her chance to run. He was more than a match for her. "Walk nicely," he warned, and started down the hill.

Sheep grazed on the hillside, as they had done as long as he could remember. A few sheep moved lazily away as they neared. The rest ignored them, and lay dozing in the heat, or chewing their cud and watching with bored eyes.

He could hear the village sounds, growing more distinct as they reached the valley plain and drew near the city gates. The hum of voices drifting from the marketplace, the hammer of carpenters, shrieks of laughter from children. Dogs barked, a lone rooster crowed, and donkeys coughed. The high stone walls cast welcome shade as they passed the gate and into the village. Long benches sat against the walls. A few older men, deciders of the village disputes, gray-bearded, some with balding heads open to the air, some with turbans to protect them from the sun as it moved across the sky, sat on the benches and leaned against the cool stone. There must have been no cases to hear today, for the men were alone.

He wondered if he would be before them soon, should Miriam and Hophni prove unreasonable, although what they would accuse him of, he did not know. Still, it would not do to underestimate the pair.

Miriam's father, despite his wealth, was not reckoned among the elders and based on his daughter's behavior, there was no question why. An elder needed to have his family reflect well on him. Joshua tightened his grip on her arm, and walked past the men, nodding at one who saw him.

"Where is your father at this time of the day?" He bent to look at Miriam's eyes, watching for deceptions.

"I do not know," she snapped at him. "There is no need to talk to him. I know now you have no feelings for me. And I no longer have any for you." She turned her head away.

Joshua caught her chin with his free hand, and pulled her face back to him. She closed her eyes.

She was lying, he knew, probably about everything. She knew exactly where her father was, and he doubted very much that he had seen the last of her. What was it going to take with her? "I can ask anyone where he is, but that might cause comment." She lifted her eyes, then quickly turned away but not before he saw a glint in them. Not only was she lying, she was indeed plotting. Joshua felt his jaw clench. "You may as well tell me. If you do not, someone else will."

"Then let them!" She jerked her chin free, and he let go.

He looked at Amos the carpenter. Amos looked from Joshua to Miriam, and pointed the way. Joshua thought he saw understanding on the other man's face. Had Miriam tried her wiles on someone else first? Not Amos, surely, for he had two wives, and eight sons.

Some of whom were marriageable age, and one or two already had wives.

"This will be good for Hophni," he heard Amos mutter as they turned to go. "It is past time."

Hophni was at the opposite edge of the village, watching over the cleaning of the two-level limestone trough for pressing grapes. Joshua could see the purple stain from the grape harvest in the trough, and coloring the water that soaked into the thirsty ground. No doubt Hophni's sheds were full of the new wine, neat rows of sheds whitewashed and gleaming in the sun.

He could have done the same. He had harvested the grapes, but his were becoming raisins for the winter. There was no surplus for wine this year. Next year would be different, Joshua vowed, and pulled Miriam with him.

Hophni did not seem to see them, although Joshua could not imagine how they could be missed, with Miriam's sullen face and his obvious grip on her arm, and his own anger that must radiate out like the roiling air before a storm. He had to call the man's name before he would turn. "Hophni? Have you a moment?"

He turned with a look of mild surprise, and nodded. "Joshua." His daughter got a fond smile. "Miriam." He looked back at Joshua. "I had not thought to see you two together so quickly after your wedding. I am pleased. Everyone will understand that a man needs someone to give him a son."

The words hit Joshua like a fist to the face. Since everyone knew Hannah was barren, no one would blink that he insulted her by taking another wife *mere weeks after wedding her?* His jaw hurt from clenching it. He forced it to release so he could answer. "I fear you do not understand, Hophni." Joshua let go of Miriam's arm. "You may go, Miriam."

She looked up at him, all feminine appeal now that Hophni was nearby to see and add his words' weight. Joshua glared at her with the rage that should have gone to her father. It was harder than he thought to keep his expression unwavering when she looked so like a child.

Maybe that was why he had let it get this far.

Miriam looked between her father and Joshua. Of course she wanted to stay, she knew this was going to be about her. If Hophni decided to let her remain, there was nothing he could do about it.

Miriam finally seemed to give in. She turned and walked toward the line of sheds.

With Miriam out of sight, Hophni asked, "What do I not understand, Joshua?"

She was probably waiting around the corner of the whitewashed wall of the nearest shed. Well, it would not hurt her to hear the first part of what he had to say. As for his sudden and still surprising idea, it would not be welcome, and no doubt Hophni would view it as the worst insult, but at least it would make his stand clear.

And he intended to make his stand on Miriam very clear.

"Miriam wants me to take her as a second wife," he started. Hophni nodded, his neatly trimmed graying beard bobbing, and rubbed his hands together, whether to dry them from the washing of the troughs or in hopeful glee, Joshua did not know. "I have a wife," Joshua went on.

"A barren wife," Hophni said with a callous lack of tact. "I have no objections to my daughter being a second wife. I know you would make her a good and decent husband, and that is all I ask for my daughter."

Joshua felt his hands fist, and forced himself to relax them. He could not lash out at Hophni. Callous thoughtlessness was not a crime. Beating was. Through gritted teeth, he growled, "I have no intentions of marrying another wife. I have the wife I want."

"But she is barren!" Hophni's face was a study in bafflement.

"I care not for that. I did not marry her for children, I did not marry her because I was obliged, I married her because I *wanted* to. Hannah is a fine woman, and a good wife. I am content with her. I do not know how to make it clear to your daughter, and now I must make it clear to you as well. I will *not* be taking another wife, not even for an heir."

"But even Abraham took Hagar, and Jacob took four wives!" Hophni stared at him as though doubting Joshua's sense. "See how they were blessed? If Hannah could not give Levi a child in six years of marriage, what makes you think you will fare any better?" He reached out to grasp Joshua's shoulder. "You now have the responsibility for the farm! You must have an heir!"

Joshua stepped back and tried to interrupt, but Hophni did not even pause. "I know you turned your back on the farm years ago, but you must see this is a sign from God! He wants you to have the farm, and therefore he wants you to have an heir, a son. Miriam is young, and has many years to bear children. One at least must be a boy!" He puffed out his chest, as if he already saw this coming grandson in his mind.

"I care not which of our ancestors took more than one wife. Do not shove them in my face. If Hannah has no child, we will turn the farm over to one of our slaves. Abraham was going to do that, also, if you remember."

Hophni gaped at Joshua, shocked, and stepped back as if Joshua were contaminated. "You do not want children?"

"Not if the wanting and not having makes my wife unhappy."

"Rachel claimed the children of her slave woman," Hophni said slowly. Joshua saw the shock slip away, and craftiness took its place. No wonder he had made himself wealthy. "I have seen Hannah's face when she looks at the children in the village. I have seen the yearning in her eyes. I think she would welcome a child in the house, no matter who gave it birth."

Hophni's words hit on the very thing Joshua himself knew, the one flaw in his argument. Had the slave man not survived, he knew Hannah would have joyfully claimed their child and raised it as her own. But an orphaned child was not its mother, and to have another woman in the house giving birth when she could not would be a burden he would never put on his wife. Even the thought of having another woman in the house when he finally had Hannah after all these years, the woman he had loved in secrecy all this time – it was impossible.

"Do you remember how Rachel suffered as Leah was giving birth to children? Would you ask me to subject my wife to the same thing? Do you remember the competition those two women had, taking slave girls and thrusting them upon Jacob, the feud that went on endlessly until Rachel died? Will my house become like his was, with endless servant girls being foisted upon me? Do you think I want that?" Joshua forced himself to take a deep breath. Just the thought of living in such circumstances was enough to make his head pound. "I will not argue history with you, Hophni. My decisions are good for my wife and I, and my mind is set. I do not want two wives! I do not know how much more clearly I can state it."

But there was one thing he could do that would convince Hophni, he remembered. He had a slave man, soon be freed and sent away with gifts, who would need a wife and mother for a small child.

Children would keep Miriam busy.

"I can perhaps help you find a husband for your daughter," he said slowly. He stepped back, casually. "Young, healthy – " soon, he soothed his conscience. The widowed slave was recovering. "Of good family." One would assume he was from good family. Who knew what put a man into slavery? Possibly the man had been a farmer, it was the work into which he had been sold. It would take hard labor on both parts to rebuild abandoned land. He bit back a smile at the thought.

Hophni drew himself up in affronted dignity. "I can find a husband for my daughter without your help."

"As you wish." Joshua finally could not help the smile that tugged at his lips, and was grateful for the beard that he hoped hid most of it. "Just know that her husband will not be me!"

He turned away, and walked back across the drying ground, toward the sheds with their carefully locked bars.

He reached the corner of the first shed safely when he heard sobs. He did not turn toward the sound, but kept walking. He had nothing to say to Miriam.

CHAPTER 18

"After he is sold he may be redeemed. One of his brothers may redeem him; . . . or any who is a close relative to him of his family may redeem him."

Leviticus 25:47-49

He had turned past the last of Hophni's sheds when he saw someone standing by the first potter's shop, watching and measuring him with a direct gaze and nothing of Miriam's flirtatiousness. A young woman he had never seen before.

He looked behind him to make certain there was no one else she might find so interesting. No, at the moment he was alone, the merchants in the back of their shops, out of sight,

She did not belong in the village. He had lived here for more than six years, and knew the people of the village quite well. She was not the daughter of anyone he knew, and she had a look about her as if she had lost her way, confused and a bit forlorn but not easily cowed.

"Hello," Joshua said when he drew near. "Who are you, and what are you doing here?"

"I was looking for someone to direct me to you." She still fixed him with her direct, expectant gaze

"Me?" Joshua forced down the urge to glare, but his muscles tensed nevertheless. Not another Miriam! "Why?"

"I am looking for someone, and I was told you might know where he is."

Joshua felt his shoulders relax. If she was looking for a different man, then she could have no interest in himself. "Who?" Joshua examined her more closely. Now that he had the time to stare, there was something almost familiar about her.

"My brother." She met him look for look. "Perhaps you have heard of him. His name is Reuben."

"Ah. Reuben." He nodded. He thought he recognized the name from Levi's lists. "I can promise nothing, but I do have a Reuben among my – ." he caught himself before the ugly word 'slaves' slipped out, instead turning to retrace his steps of the morning. "Come with me. We can see."

The girl followed close behind, through the streets, past the elders on their benches with the sun creeping closer as it rose higher and ate away the shade, and at last through the gates. Joshua slowed enough for her to keep pace easily as they followed the worn track up the hillside. The sheep that normally filled their way were grazing on the far side now, and they made easy time.

"What is your name?" Joshua asked abruptly, as they climbed up the hillside toward the woods.

"Hepsibah." She smiled up at Joshua, a sweet and impish smile. "I know who you are. You are Joshua. Miriam told me she was going to see a Joshua and she returned with you, so I can only guess that you are he."

He could only imagine what Miriam had told this young woman about him. He hoped Hepsibah had heard the conversation with Hophni. When the trees surrounded them, Joshua asked, "How long have you believed your brother belonged to me?" He looked down at the top of her head. She did not look up at him this time.

"Not until I heard about your marriage, and the name of your brother.

He was not the only possible slave-owner named Levi, but it was the right village, and the right name."

They walked in silence for a while through the trees. Birds twittered. "What sent your brother into slavery?" It was something he had been thinking about a lot in the last few days. Where had his slaves come from, and what had driven them to Levi?

"You may have had ample rains here," she answered easily, and without hesitation, "but on our side, the west side of the Jordan, we had drought for many years. Our parents wanted – needed – to keep the land, so Reuben and my other brothers offered to go into slavery." She swiped at a bush that leaned toward them. It bobbed as they passed. "I went into slavery as well, although my parents did not want me to. I was fortunate that a kindly family bought me. But now the rains have come, and we are all home. Reuben is the last to be found. My youngest brother was sent with me. None of the others could be spared right now." She grinned again. "He is not much help. He is too easily distracted by the shopkeepers and their daughters." Reuben's sister kept walking, swinging her hand with too much energy at leaves that waved within arm's reach in the breeze.

The possibility that had been tugging at his brain slipped out. "Would your brother like a wife, do you think?"

She stopped, leaving him walking on ahead. When he realized she was not beside him, Joshua turned, and laughed at the horror on her face. "No?"

"Not if you mean to wed him to Miriam!" She walked to join him. "You are thinking that, right? You are not serious, are you? This is a jest?"

"Not entirely," he said, and his laughter was gone. "Your family has enough money now, I am certain, even before my own gift is paid into the family chest, to make your brother a good pick for Hophni."

They began to move ahead again, only Hepsibah's steps were now stiff and angry. "I do not like her," she said, her words short. "If you try to convince him to accept her, I will tell him all I know of her – and I know a lot."

Joshua decided it was time to stop. "Very well. It was only a thought."

The rest of the walk was silent. Finally, the house came into view from behind the trees. Halel saw them coming as he dipped the bucket into the well for more water. He met them halfway, leaving the bucket by the well-cover, face stoic but questions in his eyes.

Joshua could guess what they might be, none of them flattering. "This is Reuben's sister, Hepsibah, here to redeem him," he told his slave. "She has been in the village, trying to find him."

Halel gave Joshua a sharp, relieved nod, and turned to Hepsibah. "I know your brother. He is a fine worker." He gestured toward the orchard.

Hepsibah's gaze swung to the trees. She went still, staring at the slaves, measuring each man with her eyes. Six full years was a long time. The brother she remembered would not be the man she sought. He might have been beardless and just beyond a boy when he was sold, only to be bearded and full-muscled now.

If Reuben had been younger, then Hepsibah would have changed out of all recognition.

She walked slowly forward as if in a dream, staring at the group of slaves around the trees so hard it seemed her eyes would fall out. She had thought she was ready for this, Joshua knew, remembering her brisk steps through the forest, but now that the time was here . . .

His heart hurt with sympathy. He followed behind her.

She stopped at the drooping wooden slats of the fence that marked the edge of the orchard, still too far away, he feared, to see clearly enough. Yet she made no move to climb over.

The slaves must have felt the force of her gaze, for they began turning to look as one nudged another and another and pointed her direction. Heads turned as men picked up the rumors and questions.

Hepsibah gasped, her hands going to cover her mouth, and then she shrieked, "Reuben!" She was over the fence before Joshua could give her a lift. He followed, not sure what else to do. He did not know what had triggered a memory, but whatever it had been was clear and sharp. And apparently accurate, he realized, as one of the slaves turned around, looking at the girl racing toward him with only mild curiosity. "Reuben!" Hepsibah called again, only her voice was strained with emotion and running.

She stopped a few cubits away, so quickly Joshua feared she would lose her balance. She was gasping, he could hear the air scouring her lungs as he drew up behind her. The slave who could only be Reuben looked past his sister to Joshua, one eyebrow raised.

Joshua could not say anything.

"Reuben?" The surety was gone from Hepsibah's voice. "Do you not know me?"

Reuben looked her over quickly, from head to foot, before coming back to her anxious, sad face. Red rimmed her eyes and the tip of her nose, and Joshua heard her sniff back tears. "Reuben, it is I." But she did not give her name, and a single fat tear rolled down her cheek.

Reuben's gaze sharpened, and fastened on her face. Joshua saw the very second the man guessed. "Hepsibah?" He only whispered it.

She nodded. Joshua felt Reuben's disbelief, and wished again he had walked away, leaving them to their reunion. "Hepsibah?" The name came out louder this time.

The air was still. Even the birds were quiet for a lone moment.

"It is you!" One quick glance to the heavens, and Joshua saw his mouth move in the soft words that looked like, "Thank you, dear God." Reuben reached for his sister, and tears filled his eyes.

Joshua turned away. This meeting was too private, and he had intruded enough already. He heard sobs strangling throats, and deep weeping, heart-deep, wrenching and tearing in the air.

A laugh rang out, wet and happy. He turned back around, to see Reuben swing his sister off her feet, to whirl her round and round, both of them laughing and crying and hugging. Finally he set her down. The first time for tears was over. There would be more tears, Joshua knew, for years to come, of years past that could not be regained, but now they could laugh. Reuben threw his head back on a shout of joy, and his gaze met Joshua's.

Reuben held out his hand as an equal, and Joshua stepped forward and took it for a brief clasp. The former slave – for Joshua knew the other man's slavery was done as of this moment – was smiling. "You have met my sister, I see," he said, and looked down at her again, in the circle of his arm.

"We have things to resolve, the two of us," Joshua said. "Please, you and your sister, come to the house."

There was a single heartbeat of tension, and then Joshua saw Reuben understand. "You are going to give a settlement on me? I am certain my sister brings payment for my last months of servitude. I wish to purchase my freedom."

"It is too close your time to accept any payment from you," Joshua insisted. "I will not permit it. But let us not argue in front of the others. Please, come to the house."

A palpable wave of sadness washed over him, and them, as slaves climbed from trees and walked away from their baskets filling with fruits to cluster at the fence and call farewells. "God bless, Reuben!" "Safe journeys, Reuben!" "We will miss you, Reuben!" There were embraces and handclasps and slaps on the back until Reuben and Hepsibah pulled away. Hands waved as they turned to go, and Joshua noticed that even the men were not ashamed to wipe tears from their faces.

Halel was waiting by the doorway to greet Reuben and his sister. He looked beyond them to Joshua, waiting for the nod before holding out a hand to invite them in. "Welcome to the house, my lord," he said, and Joshua stopped in his steps in surprise.

My lord? That was the greeting Halel used for Joshua and Javan. But then, Reuben was no longer a slave. Soon, all the slaves would have the same courtesy extended to them. Soon they, too, would be free to leave.

Reuben did not seem to find the greeting out of place. "Thank you, Halel. Today has been nothing but pleasure." No one looked at Joshua, for which he was grateful. He was happy for his former slave, of course he was.

But that left him with the same problems – who would take care of this farm after they were gone? And where would he find the money to hire more help?

Wherever he turned, there were only more burdens.

Halel brought wine and bread and fresh fig cakes. Joshua remembered the slave women making them. If the cakes were to last through the winter, the harvest would have to be a great one. Halel would certainly see this a joyful time and might well throw a like feast for every slave who left, and Joshua could hardly blame him. But how many cakes and fruit could they afford to eat in celebration?

Joshua looked at the table, at the happy faces around it, the meager abundance set before the little group. His first slave was leaving, hardly a thing to rejoice. Suddenly, he had to get away. He must have made some movement, for all the eyes in the room seemed to be fixed on him. "I must check on my wife," he said abruptly, and left.

He stopped outside the curtain, and drew his composure together. He wondered how Hannah would react when he appeared in her room. Hepsibah's arrival had delayed his visit, but he doubted even Halel had had time to acquaint her with what was happening. She had to hear the celebration, with Hepsibah's voice clear in the mix. Could she tell the difference between Reuben's sister and Miriam?

Hannah opened her eyes when he walked in. Her brows pulled down into a frown. "Where have you been?"

She sounded exactly like a jealous wife. How very wonderful. And unexpected. Joshua dared not smile for fear he was wrong. "I brought Miriam back to her father – and offended him badly, I fear. I offered him one of our slaves as husband for her."

Hannah blinked, and a smile slowly curved her lips. "Did you really?"

Joshua's heart leapt. This was the first sign of Hannah's humor. He smiled himself. It became a laugh, more of relief, but she did not need to know that. "Yes, I really did." He remembered his guests, and the rest of his news. "The very slave I had in mind is being claimed by his family today. His sister was waiting in the village, and I brought her back with me. They wait in the other room. Halel is feeding them."

He remembered the payment owed Reuben. "His seven years ends in one month. I cannot let his family give me money for his freedom, not this close to his time, and even more so for what he suffered under Levi. I hope you agree."

Hannah gave him a surprised look. He suddenly realized Halel, Javan and Taleh knew his eyes had been opened to his brother's true nature, but he did not remember ever telling his own wife. He did not feel like discussing it now. There would be plenty of time later, when the house was not full of guests. "I came because I thought I should tell you what was happening. I knew you could hear the voices, and did not want you to think you had been forgotten."

. . .

Reuben was quiet as he walked with Joshua away from the house. This situation was different from the release of the other slaves. Ruben was in a position to purchase his freedom, none of the others could. Joshua still did not know what the other man would do when they reached the sheepfold. He could count, he knew what this would cost the floundering farm. But the offer must be made.

The pen loomed before them, the wooden poles drooping between their posts. One or two appeared ready to fall out of the holes in the uprights. The fences would have to be replaced before they did collapse and let the sheep out. If only he could find one thing that had been cared for!

The sheep bleated as they approached, and crowded the fence. He should have brought something to feed them, Joshua thought, even an apple or a handful of grain.

"Take two, one male and one female," he said abruptly, and winced at the harsh sounds of the words.

Reuben looked between the animals and Joshua. He braced his arms on the wooden pole and examined the flock eating contentedly before them. "I am a free man now, of my own accord." Reuben met his gaze straight on. Joshua could not read what he saw there. "You expect me to refuse?"

"I hope you will not." Joshua hoped he sounded convincing. He had known from the moment he found the slave list the test it would be of his faith, follow the commands of the Law and hope his God would provide. He wished his heart was in this particular command. What did it say of him, that now the time was here it was so hard to obey? The flock would be thinned to nothing with all the slaves to follow.

"I need nothing from you," Reuben said quietly. "I am free now, and my family can pay you full price, if they even need sheep. I do not believe they do. My father is a born farmer. Only another drought could hurt him now, and even then, not for long, if my sister's report can be believed."

A slow smile started in Reuben's eyes, and moved to his mouth. "I think you need this giving more than I the receiving. Sheep will only slow our journey. But I will take your two animals," Reuben surprised him by agreeing. "I will accept your gift. It is just compensation for hard years and you have been fair."

Joshua surprised himself by smiling. "I am glad." *He had been fair.* High praise from an unwilling slave. His heart lightened just enough to let him not count the flock.

Reuben put a hand on Joshua's shoulder, a gesture of friendship that surprised Joshua as much as Reuben's agreement. "You are not Levi. I knew that days ago. In fact, it is hard to believe you share the same parents. Seldom have two brothers been more different. The other slaves would agree with me."

Joshua shook his head. "I have done a few things for them, but that is a long way from winning their respect. They tolerate me, that is all. Perhaps they even fear me. They look at me and know that if they displease me, I might well turn on them as my brother did."

"No," Reuben said, sharp and angry. "You are wrong there. They know you are not Levi. They do not fear you." A smile lifted one corner of Reuben's mouth.

It felt good to hear Reuben's words of respect. Joshua took a chance. If anyone would give him the answers he sought, it was this man. "Reuben, I saw Levi come through the village these past years with donkeys piled with sacks of grain and bales of wool, baskets of fruit. I find no signs of where the money from the sales went. If he bought grain for the coming planting, which there would hardly be need to do if he was careful to set some aside from his harvests, where is it? And where are the dried fruits?"

Once he started, Joshua decided to tell it all. "The monies did not go into the houses, I can see that. It did not go into the fences or the sheds. Yet I saw him sell his harvests. You were here, I was not. Take a guess. Where would my brother hide the coins? And why?"

CHAPTER 19

You shall furnish him liberally out of your flock, out of your threshing
floor, and out of your wine press.
Deuteronomy 15:14

Reuben sighed. "I think it went into drink. That was the only explanation I could find, in my more charitable moments, for his actions."

"I disagree," Joshua said, knowing how stubborn he sounded but holding his opinion nonetheless. "Drunkenness is not so easy to hide. I may not have been here much, but he did come to see me from time to time, and I never smelled it on him. I even served him wine when he came to visit me in the village, and never did he overindulge. Yes, he was drunk when he drowned because of the empty wineskin, I know that, but it was not a common thing with him. He did something with the money, but not that."

"I never saw your brother with coins. Not going to the market, and not coming back." Reuben backed up to the pole and leaned against it, staring off into space.

Once again, as he watched Reuben foolishly brace himself on the warping wooden fence, Joshua hoped the pole would hold. It would not surprise him if it simply fell over from the pressure of Reuben's body and bring the rest of the fence with him. It had held for Javan, but one of these days, if not repaired, someone would land face first in the sheepfold.

Reuben continued, staring off toward the far woods, "You saw Levi sell his harvests. I never saw him come back with coins. So where between the village and his house would he hide them?"

Reuben shifted away from the pole and faced Joshua with his whole body. His voice was rough and impatient. "Ask yourself this, Joshua. Levi was losing all his slaves in only months. There is no seed for this winter's planting, yet he had made good harvests and put the money into nothing we can find. So think on this: no slaves, a farm left to rot, and plenty of coin. Where was he going?"

"Going?" Joshua shook his head, not wanting to follow Reuben's reasoning. "What do you mean?"

Reuben folded his arms, frustration in every line of his body. "Joshua. It is obvious. I know you think you owe him loyalty, after all he was your brother, and if anyone understands what one will do for family it is I, but as someone who suffered under him, listen to my words. I would not have guessed this but now I know monies are missing, I believe he was shutting down this farm, and hiding his money where none but he could find it. Why would he do that, unless he had planned to run away?"

Joshua thrust out his hand for something solid, closed it on the nearest fencepost and clung as he stared at Reuben. Obscene awareness grew. All the slaves freed, all the animals portioned, the remaining seed divided up with the animals, carried off by the slaves as they went to their homes.

His throat closed. His mouth went dry. Sickness pooled in his belly and black dots swam before his eyes. He was the heir. Live or dead, should Levi not want the farm, it would come to him. Levi knew that. Everyone in Israel knew that. Would Levi have done this to him, his only brother? His head could not turn to survey the land, to scan what was there, but he did not need to because the images of decay were burned into his brain.

Heat built in his chest, searing, pounding, blazing heat pushing and burning, screaming for a way out. The noise in his head was so loud he thought surely he must be howling into the air.

And then the sound in his head pounded against his ears and he realized the noise had not been just inside, it had torn from his throat while he bellowed his rage. As the sound died away, the spots in front of his eyes faded into colors of green, brown, and blue, warm eyes looked back into his own, dark hair over a face strong and tanned, and Joshua felt his mind clear.

"Forgive me." His ears still rang from the pressure within and without. "I have been more of a fool than I could have dreamed." His legs felt as if they would give way; he locked his knees and prayed they would hold him upright. What a fool he would look to collapse ignominiously in the dirt, although it was nothing more than he deserved.

"You know, of course, that there is almost no seed left." His throat burned as the words came out. "It now makes sense. There was very little to send, appropriate for someone who clearly thought as little of his slaves as I now see he did, and if you are right and Levi intended to leave, what did he need of seed?"

Reuben's hand clasped Joshua's shoulder, the weight oddly helping to hold him up. "I am sorry, my friend."

One last bit of ugliness finally shifted to the forefront of his mind where he could no longer be ignored. "What would Levi do with Hannah?" The question seemed wrong somehow but he did not know why the image of the two of them walking away together would not come together in his mind. He could only see Levi disappearing alone. He did not realize he was speaking aloud until Reuben answered.

"Oh, come, man." Anger creased Reuben's face and drew lines between his brows. "Look at what's in front of you! Your brother hated his wife! What makes you think he wanted to be burdened with her? You asked my opinion. I have never seen a man treat his wife as badly as Levi treated Hannah. He had no intention of bringing her with him."

He thought about what Reuben had said with dispassionate distance. There was nothing in him that even wanted to defend Levi. It made sense. It all made sense now.

The villagers hardly knew Levi. His brother could have been gone a long time before they would have missed him. There was always the chance Joshua would have realized it had been far too long since the last visit, but by then Levi would have hidden his tracks too well.

Unless he missed his guess, Hannah would have been hiding from her husband, possibly injured, which seemed to be her normal state, and Levi might well be gone for several days before she realized he was not coming back. How long would she wait before she gathered enough courage to report Levi's absence?

But Levi had died instead, of some drunken stupor, perhaps brought on by a guilty conscience. Or perhaps it was his last celebration, a final salute to the land he obviously had come to despise.

Regardless, Joshua had the farm, run-down, scarred, and empty. Levi, more than anyone else, knew how much of a punishment that would have been. Was it just watching Joshua's freedom from the endless drudgery of the farm? Or had Levi – Heaven forbid – guessed Joshua's aching secret over Hannah?

He would never know.

He felt scourged with the evidence of his brother's bitterness, even from the grave. His very insides hurt, as badly as they had when he realized Levi had beaten Hannah. Without raising a fist, his brother had beaten him as well. The broken fences, the empty fields, the missing grain, all were whips Levi had used against him. How many years had his brother been planning revenge? He had succeeded beyond his wildest dreams.

Reuben had been waiting, without speaking, as Joshua's mind whirled. The air had been silent, as if everything was waiting for Joshua to mourn. He turned back to the sheepfold with its sagging bars and leaning poles, and Reuben, watching with sympathetic eyes. He should have welcomed the sympathy, God knew he needed it, but it grated on his raw senses. "Have you chosen your sheep?" His voice sounded like wood scraped across rough gravel.

Reuben merely looked back at him. "I will look over the flock again," he said slowly, and turned to the fold behind him.

·   ·   ·

Reuben was gone, with his sister and the two sheep. Joshua watched them fade into the forest, the sheep fat gray shapes in the underbrush, the sack of today's fruit harvest making a warped lump on Reuben's back. Anyone would be happy to give them shelter for the night, and Hepsibah and the youngest brother, Joshua found out, had indeed arrived with enough to pay their way.

His hand dropped from its last wave, and he turned back to the house. The slaves, gathered behind him to bid their last farewells once more, turned wearily toward their bitter sheds.

Hannah was standing in the doorway of the house. He stopped, then hurried toward her. "What are you doing?" he snapped. "You have no business out of bed! Do you wish to get sick all over again? You look like you could collapse right at my feet!"

Her knuckles were white on the door frame, and dark circles ringed her eyes. Her face was the color of milk. He did not wait for her to speak, but swung her off her feet into his arms. "Had I known you wanted to bid them farewell, I would have brought them to you. You should have said something, rather than run such a risk!"

They were nearly at the curtain when he realized he was scolding her, undoing all the hard work he had put into winning her trust. He looked down at her, ready to apologize – and she smiled at him.

He stopped in midstep, fixed into place by the simple curve of her lips.

"I did not want to put you to more work, and I am tired of being visited in my bed."

"You need not reproach me further. I have not visited you enough. I have left your care to the others, and I am sorry." How tempting it was to invite himself to stay! But she was still not well enough for anyone to visit long, least of all him alone. What stress she must be under just being around him!

How could his brother even think of abandoning her?

"If you are feeling well enough to drag yourself out of bed, I will bring you things to do to keep you busy. You can hold a needle, or wind wool and linen, perhaps." He forced his gaze away, and shouldered the curtain aside.

.   .   .

She had been thinking while he was out with Reuben. Softer words came back from when she was sick – sicker than now, at least – words he would have had no reason to say because he did not think she could hear them. Words she had thought she recalled earlier that had been forgotten in the rush of the day. Words that had made her think he might welcome a greeting. *You must get well so you can sit beside me.*

How did one ask a husband to sit and talk? He was going to bring her *sewing*? What had she done, that he would rather bring her work than spend time with her? He had told Miriam that she was the wife he wanted. If that was the case, why was he away so much?

And how did she get him to stay?

She reached up and touched his cheek, hoping he did not feel her fingers tremble.

Joshua looked down, surprise clear on his face.

Hannah could not smile again. She was afraid to ask, but she held his look with a desperate ferocity, afraid that if she turned him away this time, she would never get another chance. "I heard what you told Miriam." Her heart beat so hard her head ached. "I thank you for your kind words."

A red flush rose up his cheeks, and Hannah could tell he knew it. He gave an odd grunt and an abrupt nod, set her down gently on the bed, and pulled the covers up over her. His face was very serious as he picked up one of the pillows and set it on the floor next to the bed. He lowered his big body down on it, and Hannah hid a smile as he dwarfed the soft cushion, his legs sticking up almost to his ears as he wrapped his arms around them and tried to keep his balance.

"I do need to ask you a question," he said quietly, looking deep into her eyes as if trying to read her mind.

She nodded, wondering why he had to be so serious.

"I have asked you before about the coins Levi should have brought home. Halel does not know where they are, Reuben never saw them, hardly a surprise for one who was a slave. Reuben gave me something to think about." He lowered his legs, and leaned back on one hand. "I accuse you of nothing, I would not do that again. However, you may have seen things you did not realize. Did Levi ever do anything different when he came back from selling his goods?"

She did not want to talk about Levi. But she had done so much wrong with this husband, and if he wanted to talk about Levi, they would talk about Levi. "I do not want to hurt you, he was your brother, but I have been told that my mouth spoke when I was sick and not aware of it. I wish I could have spared you that knowledge."

Joshua looked steadily back at her. "It seems both our tongues have been speaking without thinking."

Was that good, or bad? She went back to the subject. "The only thing I can tell you is that the last few times Levi went alone to sell his goods, and I did think it strange because often the load was very large, much larger than I thought one man could manage. He let the slaves load the grain on his donkeys, but he wanted to go alone."

Joshua suddenly raised his head. "They were his own donkeys? I have not seen one since I arrived."

Hannah blinked, struck by this question. She had not seen them either, but then she had not been looking. "You have not seen them?"

Joshua shook his head. "No. Do you think he might have sold them?"

"Why would he? In fact, if there was one thing on the land Levi seemed grateful for, it was those two animals. Plowing and pulling and carrying everything. He could not have functioned without them."

Joshua rose briskly, brushing off his hands against his robe. "I do not want you to worry. This farm is my responsibility, and I will take care of it. All I ask is that, if you remember anything else, you must tell me immediately."

Hannah nodded, her throat tight as she watched Joshua walk toward the curtain. Their time together was over.

CHAPTER 20

When she was brought out, she sent to her father-in-law, saying, "I am with child by the man who owns these."
Genesis 38:25

Joshua sat on the large stone and let the chill night air seep into his bones. He should be in the house keeping watch on his wife. But his mind needed the crisp air to think.

The coins were not going to suddenly appear. Whatever his brother had done with them, they were gone and it was foolish to keep pining after them.

He had a skill and it was time to use that skill to make the money he needed. Much as he wanted to keep the two parts of his life separate, keep the coins he made with his metals for buying more metal and use the earnings from his farm for the farm, the choice was gone. The slaves had to be paid when they left, and he would simply have to hire workers to do the planting for the spring crops.

Joshua pushed himself off the rock and brushed off his robe, then crossed the expanse toward the house, the brittle grasses that grew sparsely across the area poking into his sandals. The sky overhead was dark, clouds blotting out all but the rarest glimpses of moon and stars, He did not need their pale light to see his way back, he knew this path. How many times had he traveled it these last few days? That rock had become his thinking rock, a place where he could be alone with his worries.

When he was not questioning other people at it. He grimaced.

The house was quiet when he slipped back inside, Hannah's steady breathing in the sleeping room only a ripple in the still air. Levi's chair had been shoved against the outer wall, with hers next to it to make room for his helpers. His own pile of blankets, the only thing in the room he truly felt was his even though they had belonged to this house first, lay in the corner where he had staked his territory for the past days. The blankets Javan and Taleh had used were put away in a fat woven basket that made a squat shape directly opposite where he slept.

Alone.

Halel had returned to sleeping in his own hut now that Hannah did not need someone watching over her every instant. That brought its own quandary, because it had been easy to sleep in a separate room when she was so desperately ill and there were guests seemingly in every corner of the house, witness to every interchange between husband and wife. Now that she was well enough to be left alone, it was expected that he be at his wife's side.

There were so many reasons why he would not, not yet. She had barely recovered. He would like her to at least be able to walk to the door without turning the color of milk before he resumed his place.

His place. Once. One night.

But of a sudden she seemed to want him near her. It was a wondrous thing. He had not wooed her, just the opposite. He had abandoned her for most of the morning to take Miriam to the village, only to return with another woman, had a feast without her and lastly scolded her for leaving her bed. Hardly a way to express love. He would not have faulted her for slapping him. If she had been well, if he knew that shy touch had truly been meant, he would have returned it with interest, but he was strong enough to know that was not the time.

Perhaps he would have to remove her back to his house in the village before he could start his marriage clean and untainted again.

But right now, he needed sleep so he could be at the shop in the morning and begin making items to sell. There were a few villagers who had requested things done but set their requests aside when Levi died, a few copper pots and mugs, a new iron latch to replace one that had finally snapped from use, some harness clasps for oxen. He spread his roll of blankets out, lay down, and wrapped himself for warmth.

What a tangle this marriage was! Neither of them was happy here. If only God did not require the land to be kept. He would gladly sell it to anyone who asked and wipe it from his life. He stared at the ceiling above him, paler black against the night.

It took a long time to relax.

Hannah sighed and stretched, feeling the day pull her into wakefulness. The room had grown too light to continue sleeping, another sign that she was getting well. Joshua said she was one of the strong ones, and had not added anything about all the work she was missing.

It seemed God had truly given her a different kind of man.

Even before she opened her eyes, she heard someone else breathing. It was a sensation she had grown used to. Now all she had to do was get her eyes opened and find out which one of her caretakers it was.

"Hannah? Hannah, I must go back to the village."

Hannah's eyes popped open. Tightness choked her throat, as if someone had clamped a hand around it and squeezed. On the last whisper of air she had, she whispered, "You are leaving me?"

He crouched beside the bed and took her hand. She had never grown used to how gentle such calloused hands could be.

"Just for a while, just until I can purchase wheat and slaves. I will be back as time permits." He lifted her hand to his lips, his beard tickling her skin. His beard was neatly trimmed. She should have noticed that right away. "I will make sure there are people here to watch over you. I will not leave you unattended. And I will work hard, I will keep this time as short as I can. You must concentrate on getting well. I expect to see you back to yourself. Now I must leave, I must begin right away."

Footsteps scuffed behind the curtain. Hannah blinked, and rubbed sleep from her eyes. How surprising that she had slept after Joshua left. Surely such news should have kept her awake. She held her breath, trying to hear something familiar, but the steps had a different rhythm than she had heard since she had waked from the illness. She could not get accustomed to people wandering into her room. It was as if all her most private secrets had been exposed.

The curtain billowed and opened, and a woman peeked around. Only her head and her hands, holding a bowl that steamed something whose fragrance had not yet reached her, were visible.

Hannah did not know her.

Brown hair slid from under the headdress she wore, brown eyes that matched the hair in color met Hannah's curious gaze straight on. The woman's skin had seen too much sun, her nose was burned and a layer had begun to flake off. Hannah now could smell the broth in the bowl she held.

The woman's eyes glanced around, as if checking to see if there was anyone else sharing the room. The survey took little more than a blink. "My lady?" Since it was just the two of them, the woman spoke with more confidence, and smiled, an appealing smile when connected with the flaking skin, so like a child's who had not come in when called and paid the sun's price.

"Come in. Please." Despite being faced with someone totally unknown, it was not so hard to smile back. "What is your name?"

"Tirzah," the woman said, and stepped fully inside the curtain.

The bowl sent its fragrance more strongly into the air, and Hannah's mouth watered. She recognized garlic and onion, and smiled. There had been so much onion and garlic used about the farm lately for healing, and borrowed from others when their own supply ran out, that it was a wonder anyone anywhere around had any to spare for something so simple as eating. What a good sign, she thought, to be hungry. Maybe there would be something solid enough to chew. "I am Hannah." How hard, and yet how simple, to make friends, especially when they came bearing food.

"Yes," Tirzah said, her voice warm and gentle. "I know. I have watched you for years. I live here, you know."

"No, I did not know." Her attention abandoned the bowl, and went back to the woman's face. They had watched her, she had watched none of them. "I am sorry." Sorry. What a small word. "I do not know . . . any of you. I did not know the woman who died."

Tirzah's face lost its smile. "It was very sad. I am sorry you did not know her. She and her husband had such hopes for when they were freed. He was ambitious, and hard-working. They would have had success."

"I do not know how to apologize," Hannah said, and wished Levi were in front of her. This time she would not stand passively and listen and obey. She wanted to scream her rage at him, to pound him with her fists, to throw things at him. Their slaves had suffered and died because of him and his bitter anger. He had been poison, and the whole farm had paid a high price. "I did not know how difficult your lives were. I was too selfish."

Something of Hannah's thoughts must have shown, for the other woman smiled a grim smile. "Selfish? Never think that! We all wondered how long you would be able to survive him. I am glad you were not the one who died. We worried that we might bear the burden of bloodguilt if he killed you. We all knew it was possible, but none of us had the power to step in. We were slaves. Who would believe us? For so long, I have wanted you to know you had supporters. All we could do was hope and pray for you, but there were many times we wished we dared interfere."

Hannah was so surprised at Tirzah's words that for a moment she could not respond, just stare at her as the words buzzed in her ears. *They* had worried about *her*? They had wanted to protect her? Her face heated, she felt the red burn under her skin. She did not want to even think about that time, but being here in this house where it all happened kept the memories near the surface, tormenting her even though the husband was not the same.

Tirzah walked up to the little table, and set the bowl down. She turned slowly. Hannah suspected she was weighing her words.

"There were so many other clues. You had no guests. No one came to visit, and it was clear you visited no one. You would look out at the fields and we could feel you yearn for release just as we did, as clearly as if you shouted your need to the heaven. The two of you, you and Levi, were so seldom together, and when you were, there was a – " she hesitated " – a stiffness. And the times you could barely move." Tirzah stopped on a quick, indrawn breath. "It did not take much to guess what was happening."

Hannah nodded, and let it go. Tirzah wanted to save her some pride, Hannah knew, and she was grateful. "I must eat, my husband tells me," she said, changing the subject, and Tirzah nodded. She lifted Hannah upright in the bed with easy strength that bespoke hard work, and placed the bowl in her hands, waiting to step back until she was certain Hannah had the energy to hold it.

The broth was lightly spiced, with a hint of lamb flavoring among the healing herbs. "Have you children?" Hannah asked between swallows of the delicate soup. Oh, it was so good.

Tirzah smiled a mother's proud smile. "Two so far. Both boys. They are four and six, but we hope to have more." Then she seemed to realize what she had said, and blushed.

Everyone reacted with so much discomfort around her when children were mentioned, Hannah thought wearily. They all knew how painful the subject was, and avoided talking about their own children unless absolutely necessary. If only they knew how she craved to hear of children, even secondhand. She had never been able to decide which was worse, to see others with their babies and endure the ache of emptiness, or to have everyone else pretend children did not exist, simply for her sake.

"Joshua hopes for children," she said, and made herself swallow another mouthful, but it was suddenly tasteless.

Tirzah brightened. "He is right to hope. Who is to say whether it was

Levi who was barren and not you at all. It would be a fitting reversal, would you agree?"

"Levi?" Hannah stared at her. "Levi barren? But it is women who are barren, not men."

Tirzah laughed, a light, merry sound. "Oh, my lady! Why do you think our God would give a woman a second chance, unless he knew another could succeed? To give a barren woman false hope would be cruel, and I do not believe God would do such a thing. I know of cases like yours where the wife was fruitful with the brother. Where I lived before I went into slavery there was a case just like yours. The second husband gave her six children, one after another, and she had been empty for many years. Why would she suddenly conceive? It could not have been her fault that she had no child with her first husband. Not when she had such success with the second. The same could easily happen with you. You must never give up hope. Never!" Her face was fierce with conviction.

To her surprise, Hannah felt her spirits lift. "I will get well," she said aloud, "and perhaps my womb will heal also."

"Perhaps your womb was never ill," Tirzah said sharply, and took the nearly empty bowl from Hannah's hands. "Would you like me to wash your hair?"

Clean hair. Hannah plucked at the strands. Taleh had washed it shortly after she came back to herself, but no one had done it since and it felt thick and heavy with oil. She had been so ill for so long, Joshua probably had forgotten how she looked the day they were wed, when she was clean and dressed in her finest. He had not lain with her since she became ill. In fact, they had not lain together since arriving here, which meant they had but one night together. If she looked healthy and smelled fresh, that might lure him into their bed.

And maybe, oh maybe, there could be a child.

But she must not hope that far ahead. Just to start their marriage would be enough for now.

"Yes, please. I want to feel clean." Hannah felt the bedding under her. She had been on the coverlets so long, if they smelled she had probably grown used to it. "Can I bathe all over? And can we change the bedclothes?"

Tirzah grinned at her. "*You* cannot, but *I* can, and I certainly will." She put Hannah's thoughts into words. "You want to tempt your husband to give you that child. Certainly, I will wash you."

The water Tirzah brought in was warm and smelled clean even before Hannah felt it on her skin. Having a woman who was comfortable bathing children, like Taleh had been, kept the blushes away while she was so exposed.

With every stroke of the soapy cloth, Hannah's spirit's lifted. How nice it was to no longer smell herself, to have water scented with rose petals replace the odor of sickness. Tirzah scrubbed her hair until it squeaked, then combed it through with a trace of oil, and even massaged her aching muscles with more of the same. When she was done, except for the last lingering fever and the weakness that left her drained and shaking, no trace of the deadly illness could be seen on her body.

Hannah braced herself on Tirzah's shoulder as she was moved to a pillow on the floor for the bed changing. She leaned against the rough stone wall, her wet hair wrapped in a dry cloth, a blanket tucked around her to avoid any chill on her still moist skin, and watched and wished while Tirzah replaced each layer of covers.

If only she could get well in a day and get rid of this awful weakness, someone else to bathe her, to clean for her, to remove sweat-soaked blankets and rid the room of the musty scent of sickness. Hannah could smell the difference in the room, clean hair, skin, coverlets. "Thank you, Tirzah," she said for the dozenth time as Tirzah eased her back into the bed.

Tirzah smiled back, her brown eyes gentle, her skin shiny from her exertions. "That is why I am here." The smile faded. "You do not appreciate how very close you came to death. You need sleep. I will be nearby. Call if you need anything, and I will come." Then she swished out of the curtain and left Hannah to her cleanness and her thoughts.

A child. Tirzah thought it so simple a prospect. For the first time in years, Hannah imagined a little body squirming in her arms, tiny fingers to grasp her own. A tiny head cradled in her hands, tiny feet to kick against her belly, a little one to prattle at her during the day as she worked.

It was a dangerous dream. She might begin to believe it was possible.

No, far better not to dream. The day she felt movement inside her was the day she would let herself believe. Until that day, there would be no hope, no wishful thinking when she was alone.

As now. Hannah tensed in the silence of the house, so quiet it was like a living thing. No Tirzah, who had promised to stay nearby, no Halel, who had been her support ever since Levi died, and most of all, no Joshua, who said he had chosen her of his own free will.

She looked at the lattice and gauged the level of the sun coming through it. She was supposed to be sleeping. Tirzah might peer in and expect to find her doing that very thing. Sleep was the farthest thing from her mind.

Joshua was. He drifted into her thoughts at the slightest encouragement.

He was back in the village, back at his kiln, his true work. How easy it would be for him to stay there. When she had married him, she had put the farm behind her. She did not want to come back here at all, would not have without great need. He might not wish to return, either, despite his promises.

But now she could see him here. Do not paint a picture of him in the village, she scolded herself. Think of him wandering the land, clearing the field of stones that would chip the plow blade. Think of him chopping trees for wood for heat for the cool days and nights ahead.

And in the vision in her mind, a small shape was always beside him.

Hope, once planted, was not so easy to erase, she discovered.

Joshua worked the bellows and the kiln glowed orange. It felt good to be back here, doing what he loved, behind his own house that he had worked to build, at his own oven, by his own anvil. Here, he could leave his brother behind – except for now, he thought grimly, when Levi's problems once again crept in. But for Levi, he would be with Hannah – in Levi's house.

His life was what it was now, and he would learn to take the good with the bad. A reason to come back to the work he loved, even if only for a little while, knowing this time it was not to forget her. That she was waiting for him. That she still lived when others had died of the very same illness. Those were the good.

He wiped the sweat from his forehead with an equally sweaty forearm. The sun was directly overhead, turning his small working area into a kiln almost as hot as what stood before him.

He picked up the tongs, and carefully pulled the glowing lump of iron from the coals. Placing it carefully against the anvil, he picked up his hammer and began to work. The sound echoed back from the buildings nearby, familiar and loud.

Beating metals into submission was a good way to think. How many times had he been here, taking his frustrations out on his work, alone with his thoughts? The noise became a rhythm, iron submitting to his will, unlike the farm.

His stomach protested being ignored. He looked down at the ax, and nodded his satisfaction. He could certainly afford a few moments to eat now. He set the hammer down on the ground, and flexed the cramps out of his hand. He had been away from his work too long. Normally a morning's work would not cause him this discomfort. He would have to remember that in the future. If he was going to keep both his lives, he would have to make a point of devoting equal time to each.

"I heard the tale, but did not believe it."

Joshua's head whipped around. Hophni stood there, arms folded in satisfaction over his ample belly. "Hophni." This was a complication he had not anticipated. The sound of his hammer ringing against the anvil was surely enough to alert the whole village to his presence here. He just did not think it the village's business that he was back.

Apparently, it was.

"So you have become tired of your new wife already, have you? Is this the same man who told my daughter he was happy with his marriage? After causing her such a wound, you dared to come back here so soon and announce to the whole village that you have abandoned Hannah?" Tension radiated from Hophni like a bad smell.

Joshua felt his hands curl tight, a normal state, he was discovering, around this man. "I have not abandoned my wife."

If Hophni had been glaring before, it was nothing to the hot gaze that pinned Joshua now. "Oh no? Then what are you doing in the village, when we all know that your wife is still back at the farm? The sound of your anvil has alerted the whole village to your presence here."

The back of Joshua's neck prickled, and he turned around to see what caused the sensation. It gave him a chance to look away from Miriam's father. Sure enough, Hophni had spoken the truth – this time. A collection of faces stared at him around the ubiquitous olive trees and whitewashed house corners, concern written on every one.

CHAPTER 21

When Rachel saw that she bore Jacob no children, Rachel envied her
sister. She said to Jacob, "Give me children, or else I will die."
Genesis 30:1

Hannah woke early, the sun through the closed lattice just a thin line along the top of the wall. She had listened for Joshua last night when the house was quiet enough to hear the slightest movement. Owls hooted from the nearby woods, now and then a sheep would bleat, a soft conversation that quickly passed back into stillness. As the sun had slipped away and the room went dark, the curtain just a whisper of lightness in the faint illumination of the moon, she stared into the dark. *Joshua, come back.*

He was in the village. Two days was not enough time to expect him back, she knew that, at least her mind knew that, but her heart did not seem to. It was not so very far away, part of an hour's journey at most. In the blackest moments, the cruel and lonely part of the night, he might as well have been on the moon.

She had been beaten into weak spinelessness by Levi, but Joshua had given her reason to hope. He had listened to her as they nursed the sick slaves, had done her bidding – imagine that! He had done *her* bidding! He had insisted she care for herself when she had grown too tired to think, and if Halel, Javan and Taleh – and the whispers of words that slipped through her mind – were to be believed, he had watched over her while she lay sick and insensible.

Hannah edged onto an elbow, and pushed herself upright. The room did not spin around her as it had the day of Reuben's leaving, and that was a good thing.

Should he be here, she was not at all convinced she dared make the first move toward him, but she could at least stand in the door and wait. Perhaps the weakness in her body was a good thing for now. It would let her courage catch up to her strength.

Please let him have come home.

Hannah looked down at her arms. It was obvious even at a single glance how much weight she had lost. Tirzah was right, how very close she had come to death. She grasped the short post at the head of the bed and stood slowly. Her legs were wobbly but they worked, and much better than her previous effort.

Her lips curved, and that simple movement triggered a lightness around her heart. She was smiling. No one would drag her back to that place that Levi had left her. Her body was mending, and she was determined her spirit would mend, too.

Perhaps she had Tirzah to thank for that. Someone else who saw through Levi, and mourned him almost as little as she did herself.

She let go of the short post and pulled herself to her full height, listening carefully over her breaths and the thudding of her heart. It hammered as hard as if she had been running, and she supposed for her worn-down body, this might well be that much exertion. There was no sound in either of the other two rooms.

"Hello?" She waited for someone to respond. "Tirzah?" No answer. "Halel, are you here?"

Only silence greeted her words.

She smelled the faintest drift of smoke from the firepit outside, just what she would expect from a banked fire. Likely no one had come to stir it up. The air had a distinct chill, warning of winter's rains and the time of planting.

She tugged the top blanket off the bed, a soft gray woolen weave, pulled it around her and walked slowly toward the door. The only way to get strong was to get up and make the trembling muscles work.

One hand braced on the wall, Hannah crept into the main room. Halel had his own hut, as did Tirzah, and Javan and Taleh had gone back to their home and their children three days ago or more. If she fell because of this ill-advised effort, how long would she lay before anyone came and found her? Her arm was heavy from bracing it against the wall, and her palm felt the rough stone edges. She had to sit down soon or she really *would* fall.

Her blood pounded against her skin as she made her way slowly into the eating room, sank down on the bench by the table and closed her eyes. She must look like a bent twig, all curved over her arms where they rested on the table's top. Hannah wished she had a back to lean against. It was all she could do not to let her head drop on her hands, but she had made it to the table, and even managed to sit upright, more than she could have done before Joshua left, and by herself, too.

Feet scuffed on the doorstep. Hannah's heart lurched and her eyes flew open. Tirzah walked in, holding a clay pitcher of water so fresh and cold there was a skim of moisture on its outside. Two little boys followed her, one about eight, the other closer to four or five. They looked freshly washed, their hair was still damp, their little robes crisp from a recent laundering and as clean as it was possible, the stains obviously having been there so long nothing would remove them. Their feet were bare, their toes pink from the crisp air. She did not know if that meant they had no sandals or if they preferred to go without.

"Good day, Hannah," Tirzah said, looking only slightly surprised. "So you are up."

"I could not stay in bed any longer," Hannah replied, and smiled. "I cannot stand to be there another day. I must get strong again, and I cannot do that in my bed."

"I had thought I should get you up this day, anyway. You are too quick for me, but that is good."

The two boys seemed fascinated by the stone floor beneath their feet. They wiggled their toes on the floor, and slid them back and forth as if testing its smoothness. No doubt they were only familiar with packed dirt floors like the one inside the shed where the slave woman had died. There were going to be small gritty footprints all over the floor for their mother to clean.

Maybe Tirzah would not get to the sweeping until tomorrow. This house needed the footprints of children, even if they were only borrowed for a time.

Still holding the wet pitcher, Tirzah walked over to the shelf of plates, picking out a cup. Without turning around from her efforts, she said sternly, "David, touch nothing, do you hear me?" The older boy nodded glumly. Water splashed into the cup.

Tirzah brought the filled cup over and set it in front of Hannah, then propped her hands on her hips. Very much the mother, she scolded gently, "You are as pale as whitewash. Drink."

Hannah managed another smile. Two and the day was still new. Tirzah had endured slavery, and managed to keep her spirits joyful. If anyone was going to take her mind off Joshua, it would be her. "Yes, mother."

Tirzah grinned. "If I can handle my two boys, I am certainly up to you." She pointed to the water cup Hannah held loosely. "Drink. And you need to eat for the day, especially since you feel well enough to get up and move around. I will cook you something that will build your strength."

Titters came from the little boys, no doubt enjoying their mother scolding someone of Hannah's stature. Hannah glanced over and smiled at them, surprised and pleased that it came easily. Her smile prompted another spate of stifled laughter.

Sweet children. Longing came over her, fierce and sharp as a stab in the heart.

Tirzah looked her over with a measuring gaze. "As long as you do not feel like you are going to collapse, you may stay up." She looked over at her two boys, and back to Hannah. "I may have a chore easy enough for you. May I leave them with you while I am out at the fire? The three of you can keep each other company and I – " she looked over at the oldest boy, " – can finish cooking without worrying about someone tipping the pot over."

David scowled and his mouth compressed as if he knew whatever he meant to say would only get him in more trouble.

Hannah nodded, and smothered her nerves. What did she know about entertaining two little boys? But Tirzah apparently trusted her, and she owed so much in repayment. "If they are willing?"

The boys looked slightly alarmed, the younger one's eyes round as the moon.

"They would be happy to," their mother said firmly, pinning them in her unyielding gaze. "Very well. That is settled." She ignored the tension in her sons' young bodies. "Be good. I will ask if you were."

Then she left them alone.

Hannah looked at the boys, and they looked back. She wondered which of them was the most nervous. Begin at the beginning, she thought. "You – " she pointed at David, "are David." He nodded warily. "But who are you?" As she leaned her head down a little, just enough to catch the eye of the youngest but not enough to lose her balance and fall flat on her nose, Hannah felt the room give a warning tilt.

Tirzah was right. She needed food more than she had realized when she forced herself out of bed. Her strength had better last long enough to let Tirzah finish the meal! And what would the boys do if she began to lose her balance?

There was a long pause. She hoped they did not notice her fingers clenched, one on the table edge and the other on the bench, propping her up. David gave his brother a sharp nudge. "Stop it," the littlest snapped in a sharp whisper, and nudged back.

"Tell her your name," David whispered loudly.

"Israel," the younger one said. If Hannah had not been paying close attention she would not have heard him.

The two boys glanced at each other, and a whole conversation seemed to pass in that one quick look. The oldest, David, cleared his throat and wound his hands together. "We were not supposed to ask, but can we see your house?"

Hannah smiled even as her heart went out to these two little slaves who had missed so much in their brief lives. "Of course you may," she said.

But the boys were already across the room, their bare feet slapping the stone floor. The house was only three rooms but must seem like a palace to them, she thought as the sounds from the other rooms came louder. The words mostly consisted of, "Look at this!"

Hannah followed the sound of their path through the main room and into the sleeping quarters, trying to imagine what it looked like in their eyes. It was a good thing now that Levi had not allowed her anything decorative, because she strongly suspected it would be picked up and handled. She would hate to have these lively boys scolded.

Was this what it would be like to have children in the house? She held the voices in her heart, their higher timbre, only to suddenly sit upright at a scuffling that sounded like pushes, followed by a hissing that sounded like scolding and no doubt presaged one or the other running to mother to tell a tale.

The other door in the main room suddenly scraped open, and a strangled double gasp sounded. Hannah's heart lurched to a stop, and then began pounding in her ears.

"Well, who do we have here?" A familiar voice, but old, not young. Halel, come to see her for the first time since Tirzah had been assigned.

She had to give Joshua time. He had the right to come home without feeling guilt when he was working so hard for all of them. She had not known when he first left how very much she would miss him. That had come as a bit of a surprise. Was still a surprise.

"Greetings, Halel! What are you doing here?" That from David.

A younger, higher voice piped up. "We were told we could look. We have not touched a thing."

Hannah wondered at the truthfulness of that statement.

"No? Very good. Your parents will be pleased." Halel's voice had always been calming and gentle, but the soft, warm tones, deep and male, only reminded her of the one she longed to hear.

Hannah took advantage of the sudden spate of chatter to clear the thickness away from her throat before anyone came in and she was forced to speak. Tirzah would think her children had been misbehaving. Halel would think her fever had gone back up. Tirzah would take her children away. Halel would put her back to bed.

She had spent far too much of her life being alone. Today she had guests, and she would enjoy them.

People abruptly seem to converge from everywhere. Tirzah walked in from the outer door holding a heavy pot, the handle protected by the folds of her outer garments. Steam rose from its top. Halel and the two boys came in from the other door. The noise in the room seemed to multiply of itself.

"David, Israel, come help. Please set out the bowls." The pot landed on the table with a heavy thump. The fragrance drifted across Hannah and the lightheadedness of a moment ago came back. She smelled mutton and leeks. Bits of leaves showed in the rich broth, and carrots. Her mouth began to water. Tirzah must have been up before the sun to cook such a meal for them to break their fast.

Tirzah had been so cautious with what she was allowed to eat. It had only been broth, broth, and more broth. She had not actually chewed food since before she became ill. Ah, to have a bite.

Halel sat down at the table on the opposite bench, and Hannah suddenly realized what was happening. There were people in her kitchen, not slaves but friends, and no one would ask them to leave. In fact, Joshua had been the one to invite them in. He could not possibly realize what a gift that had been. She would never again need to eat alone.

Tirzah set a bowl down in front of her, and Hannah nodded her thanks. She dared not open her mouth at the moment. Emotion was too close to the surface.

There was food in front of her, but her throat was too tight right now to eat.

The neighbors were watching again. Joshua pretended he did not see the eyes peeking from between the lattices of the house on the right side of his own as he tightened the last strap of leather around the sickle handle. How unfortunate it was that the windows looked out over his kiln. The white stone house that bespoke years of attention held an elderly couple, husband and wife, neither of whom had enough to do. He knew, because every time he lifted his head up from his anvil they were watching. If they had done so before his marriage, he had never noticed. They had the ubiquitous olive trees that every home cherished, but they did not seem to want to watch openly while picking the ripe olives, and when they were out checking the status of the remaining harvest, they managed to almost completely ignore him.

On his left in the mud-brick house that had seen much use, where the whitewash was peeling and the lattices had been bent and snapped by the brood of children, the mother was frequently in the back with her children, as she was right now. If she was not picking left-over apricots from the two trees they boasted or chipping away at the hard ground where last year's garden had been, the ground still much too hard from the summer sun to yield much to her efforts, she was tossing a ball to the little ones or teaching the older children some new game. None of that fooled him, however. She had become quite good at doing two things at once, whatever the chore of the moment was and simultaneously watching him. She openly disapproved of him being here alone, but had not come over yet to express her opinion, and that blatant censure pruned her face with scowling wrinkles at this very moment.

Funny, Joshua had paid very little attention to them prior to this. Now, however, even his skin seemed sensitive to the looks he was getting.

Completing his current sale was hardly interesting enough to warrant this much attention. He wished the money had come in more quickly, so he would be able to return to the farm. He had been away far too long. Joshua dragged his attention back to the man in front of him, and the sharp implement he had just finished.

"I hope it works well for you." Joshua handed over the heavy sickle. He accepted the coins in return, trying not to show his satisfaction when the heavy gold settled in his palm. This would buy another bag of seed. He was certain he had enough now, at last, to send with the freed slaves, but still not enough to plant his own land. He would need what he had earned over again for that.

"It was good of you to finish it for me, although I have no real use for it until next spring's harvest." Hazael's eyes asked a dozen questions, but he kept them to himself, a tact for which Joshua was most grateful.

Clearly some believed either Hannah had died and he was working his grief away or that he had found no satisfaction in his new wife and this was a most convenient way to keep peace. It was no one's concern but his own, and he refused to tell anyone that his brother had left the farm destitute and that his desire for his wife had driven him here for her own safety. He could not risk getting her pregnant until she was well enough to carry the child. On his few – far too few – visits back, she still looked much too thin. The color was not yet in her cheeks.

Javan, who knew the situation better than anyone else, had even given him some sideways glances, but made no other comment. That would change soon, Joshua knew. He had not expected it to take this long to accumulate the coins. Work had not been there for the asking. He had had to go out and remind people of the things they needed, walk through the village and look for hanging hinges or broken latches without *looking* like he was looking.

The clouds had begun to march across the sky, empty yet but promising rain soon, and he had nothing to plant.

Hazael lifted the sickle carefully over his shoulder, gave Joshua a brief nod, and left through the gap between the houses, weaving through all the olive trees to the street beyond.

CHAPTER 22

You shall be blessed in the fruit of your body, the fruit of your ground, the fruit of your animals, the increase of your livestock, and the young of your flock.
Deuteronomy 28:4

Hannah walked through the grove of olive trees with Halel, and wished the sun was stronger today. Of course, even if it had been the heat of summer, under the trees where they were it would have been cool. This time of year, as summer slipped into autumn, it was downright cold in the shade. The sun slipped behind a cloud, and the wind cut through her light cloak.

"The rains will come soon," she said, and basked in the knowledge of what those rains meant. Until these past weeks, Hannah had not appreciated the true extent of how dependent they were on its bounty. It was one thing to know, it was quite another to see the bare fields crack and the tree leaves curl.

A sudden wave of dizziness caught her off guard and she grabbed for the nearest trunk. The bark was gnarled and rough beneath her hand. Heavy clusters of olives bounced off her head, but she dared not let go long enough to brush them aside.

Her feet tingled in the warm, thickly strapped sandals Joshua had sent for her as the numbness spread. She seemed not to have recovered her strength from her illness, though a month and more had passed, and from time to time her body reminded her of just how close she had come to death.

Everyone had to work now.

"You are not going to faint, are you?" Halel leaned close and bent his head to peered at her.

"No, I will be fine." If Halel knew that she was having these weakness spells yet, he would not allow her to come out into the orchards, or the fields, and learn what she needed to learn, the backbreaking work that the poor slaves had gone through during the years of her ignorance.

Her head rang and buzzed with all the information she was trying to stuff into it. Harvesting dates, figs, olives, apricots (which fruit had mostly been done before he began her education), making raisins from grapes (although it was just the last bits of the crop, as well), feeding sheep, so many things she had taken for granted because there had always been someone else to do it.

Dates, for instance. Dates sat in the baskets piled high at the traders stalls, probably having fallen safely to the ground from their lofty heights. But no. She had watched the men lop off thick fronds to make a rudimentary staircase as they climbed into the towering palms to harvest the dates, balancing out on the stalky stems so high up they were like ants, all the while her heart was stuck firmly in her throat. "They are used to this. They do this every year," Halel reassured her repeatedly, but it had not helped.

The fig trees were much better. At less than one third the height of palms she did not have the fear of the slaves tumbling to their death, and the simplest way to harvest was to swing long wooden poles while standing firmly on the ground, letting the fruit fall into long stretches of cloth laid about the base. "This," she remembered telling Halel as she watched, "is the way to harvest." She even thought it might be fun helping them knock the ripe figs from the trees, but Halel said that was better left to those with experience.

He was right, of course he was right. They needed everything, every date, every apricot, even every small basket of nuts collected from the forests around their land.

There had been some good news. They found several bundles of wool in one of the locked sheds, right inside the door where one might walk right past it and forget it was there. They all knew the wool in the shed would not last forever, but the slaves would at least be able to leave in warm clothes. There was only one loom, but several of the women already had spindles, and Hannah would look over and see them sitting in the sun twirling the spindles and making long stretches of yarn. She even joined them when she could, squeezing her visits between her training sessions with Halel.

It also gave her a chance to hide the dizzy spells. No one seemed to care if she put a hand to balance herself. They often did the same thing, rubbing their backs or rolling their heads to release the strain in their necks.

One of the slavewomen did it more often than the others. And she had just confessed she was pregnant.

It was just a coincidence, Hannah told herself, that they both shared this one symptom. It had been a very bad illness, and she could not expect herself to be back to normal. She had not had her monthly course yet, but she knew it happened that way with women sometimes after having come so close to death. It did not necessarily mean she was pregnant, although the possibility teased her more and more. She held the hope in abeyance. It was much too early to believe.

The pleasant chats among the women were like a rest for her over-worked mind, stuffed with the finer points of running a farm and learning to make decisions on her own.

"Tomorrow you will start learning how to press out olive oil." Halel looked over a basket filled to the brim with olives under one of the trees, and nodded with satisfaction. "Levi sold most of the olives before. Nothing I said dissuaded him. It was a foolish thing to do. There is no need to buy olive oil when one can make one's own."

Hannah shuddered. She remembered all too clearly trying to carry home clay jars filled with olive oil. She always needed it after he had injured her. Only he never used the oil to bind her wounds. No, that she had had to do herself.

Enough of Levi! It was impossible to get away from him completely, their every effort was geared toward recovering from the damage he had done. Still, long stretches would go by when he never crossed her mind. Every time he did, she felt stained by his poison.

Like now. Joshua's very absence was Levi's fault. She wished she knew what Levi had planned had he not drunk himself into the river. Undoubtedly he would have invented some new torture for her. With the slaves gone, would he have strapped her behind a plow and made her push the heavy thing through the ground? Or would he have made her climb up for the dates?

Think of Joshua, she scolded herself. Even though his absence hurt, he had put his stamp on this farm. She but looked out the window and would see the places he had been as he struggled to learn the extent of the damage to the land – and to the slaves. Halel's rock was saturated with his absence, no longer a place to go to think but instead a place to miss him. His memory was in the orchards through which she walked. It was in the sheds where her new produce was being kept. It was around the slave houses that she now visited on a regular basis.

She could not even go into the village now because he was there. If he saw her there, he would scold her. She was to get well, she was not to over-exert herself. He said that with a straight face, while the sweat poured off him from his own exertions and the village echoed with the sound of his hammer on iron. She had noticed the sound when she reached the hill outside the village and broke free of the trees, but did not realize what it was until she walked up to his house. People had told her that sometimes they heard the sound way into the night.

Nothing she did convinced him she was well. She did not want him to worry any more than he already did. His work was dangerous. It was up to her to worry about him. She did not risk injury if she worried. Joshua did. So now all the tasks that involved going to the village were given to the slaves, and they were instructed to bring only good news.

Fortunately there was enough of that to distract him.

"Hannah, are you listening?"

Hannah jumped. "I am sorry, Halel. No, my mind was elsewhere."

Halel raised an eyebrow. "Are you sure you are well? Joshua will be most upset with me if you become sick again. I constantly receive questions from him about your welfare. I have begun to lie. If he knew I had you out in the orchards like this, I fear I would lose all his trust."

Hannah had to laugh. "He is on all our minds, is he not?" She shook her head and wrapped her cloak a little tighter. "Do you think we will have an early winter? Is it just me, or is the day really cold?"

A frown deepened the lines on Halel's already wrinkled forehead and then was gone. "Summer has grown old and tired, it is true. As for winter, it is too early to say." In a voice that was too casual, he asked, "Do you think the women need help with their weaving? I am sure it is warmer there. They are working in the sun."

Hannah propped her free hand on her hip. "Halel, I am not ill." If these strange lingering dizzy spells were all she had, she should be grateful. If the dizzy spells were in fact from the illness, and not something else . . . She pushed the desperate hope out of her mind. "But if it will make you feel better, I will send someone back to the house for a warmer cloak."

Halel shook his head. "You are still pale, Hannah. And Joshua worries about you."

"Yes, Halel, I know that." Hannah smiled as she looked at the new sandals on her feet. "But we all must work to save the farm. His job is in the village. Mine is here." Hannah tried to remember what they had been talking about before her mind drifted away. Olive oil. "Do we even have an olive press? I do not believe I ever saw one around here. My father had a very small one in the house when I was young, nothing that would handle the amount we have here, but even in the early days of my marriage to Levi, I do not believe I ever saw him use one."

Halel shook his head. "It still feels strange speak disparagingly of one's master, and especially to his wife."

"Widow," Hannah corrected.

Halel reached into the basket at their feet and scooped out a handful of olives. He picked out one of the fattest, and bit carefully into it. The bitter fruit puckered his mouth, but he nodded with satisfaction. "They are juicy," he said, the words sounding muffled. "We will get plenty of oil from this harvest, probably even enough to send small jars with the slaves when they go."

Yes, everyone had their release firmly in mind.

No matter how many times the question hovered on her lips, Hannah never asked Halel if he would leave with the rest. She could not bear to think how lonely she would be if he did go.

Halel went still, then slowly dropped the handful of olives back into the basket. His gaze went past Hannah and focused on something in the distance, and a smile slowly lit his face. Even his beard tilted upward around his mouth. Hannah turned to see what it was that had brought such happiness to his face.

In the distance, coming up the path away from the woods, was Joshua. He did not seem to be looking for them, because he was making his way directly to the house. He did not even glance toward the slave cabins, he would never see her and Halel here in the olive grove.

Hannah's heart lurched, and began pounding the drum beat in her chest. The dizziness came back, and she took the steps backward to lean against the trunk, hoping that Halel would not notice.

"Master! Master Joshua!" Halel's shout bellowed across the orchard and through the sheepfold, but Hannah did not know if Joshua had heard until she saw her husband's head turn. He raised his hand in acknowledgement, changed direction and began walking toward them.

She did not want her husband to learn of this latest weakness. She forced herself to take deep breaths, and gradually the dizziness faded. At least the shade from the tree would hide any pallor. She was not really concealing anything from him.

Not yet. If only she had begged the women for more information! It could not be, not after only one time, not after six years of barrenness, and she dared not get her hopes up for fear of the crushing despair she would suffer if it were not true but Joshua was here now, and the urge to confide was suddenly a wound in her heart.

If anyone was to know, Joshua deserved to be the first and she did not want details to start floating around that might not be true.

It seemed to take forever for Joshua to reach them. The distance was not that great, but there were two fences for him to climb. Had he noticed the work they had put in, cleaning out the brush around the poles? How surprised he would be to find out that so much of the effort they had done had been her idea. One of the empty sheds had even been torn apart, and the wood used to patch the holes in the roofs on the slaves' houses. It was so much safer than going out into the woods to fell trees.

His face was lined, Hannah noticed when he stopped in front of them, although it could be just the dappled shade from the olive branches. But she did not think so.

The dark curls just above his ears showed sprinkles of grey. Hannah fought the urge to reach out and touch them, smooth them back. Just the thought of such familiarity brought heat to her face. They had an audience, and such a gesture was too new to share. The first time she did something so intimate must be for just the two of them.

Would this new husband welcome such a touch some day? She prayed she would be brave enough to do it, for the urge to give in to such little familiarities became stronger every time she saw him.

"It is good to see you both. You look well, my wife. As do you, Halel."

The shade – and the blush that heated her face – had done their job.

"Please, sit down." Joshua suited his words to action, and beat them to the ground. Hannah sank down gratefully.

"I came to read the records again. I had forgotten how much time was left before I must release more slaves." Joshua plucked at the dirt at his side, and scooped some up in his hand, drawing idle lines through it with one finger.

Tiny scorch marks dotted the tops of his hands, and up his arms. Hannah looked at those tiny burns and felt them on her heart. There almost certainly had to be more elsewhere on his body. She remembered that first day, such short months ago and yet such a long time, when she had stood near his kiln and felt the heat as she worked the bellows.

How badly had those tiny marks hurt? She remembered the day she made the stew, when she had bumped against the hot pot and Joshua had brought cold water to put on her hand. If she had been there, she would have put cold water on his burns. For as many as there were, he must have shrugged the pain off and let the hot sparks sizzle while he worked.

"The farm looks good," Joshua said. His voice sounded rough.

"We have done much. We burned the shed where the slavewoman died, as you ordered."

"I am glad to see it gone. The illness was not leprosy, when we would have had to burn it, but if destroying it is good for leprosy, it is good for this." Joshua coughed twice. "It is the dust," he said when he saw Hannah.

"I will have one of the slaves bring you water." Halel rose, and gestured to someone, then sat back down. "It will be here soon."

Hannah felt a flash of fear at the cough. She had coughed when the sickness had been heavy on her. The cough had been slow to leave. He had stayed well during her illness, was it catching up to him now that he was tired and burned? What would she do if he died?

"We cannot change the fact of the missing grain, but the rest of the harvests have done quite well." Halel reached over and plucked some olives from the basket. "This is the first harvest of olives. See how plump they are?"

Joshua picked one up and weighed it in his hand. "They are good size. I would like to dry half in the sun, as that is my favorite treat, and press the others. We should have enough for a fair sized flask of oil for each family, and a sack of dried olives as well for the journey. I would like to keep half the harvest for myself, to eat and to sell."

"I will begin right away, and save some for you. We can send them with the slaves on their next trip to the village." Hannah looked at the grey hairs again. That visit would need to be soon. Olive oil was used to heal the outside, perhaps the fruit would do the same on the inside.

"Your wife is learning about running the farm." Halel sat up straighter, like a proud teacher. "I taught her about both the date and fig harvests. She is an apt pupil."

"You did *what!* Do not tell me you let her up in the trees?" Joshua glared at Halel, almost before he had finished speaking. "I thought you were taking care of her."

"He is," Hannah snapped, at the same time Halel said, "Of course not."

They were talking about her, she was best qualified to discuss her health. Leaving out one small detail. "You cannot expect me to stay in bed. I have been well for weeks now." Again, leaving out that same small detail.

"I would never let her do anything dangerous, my lord." Halel looked offended. "Skilled work is best left to those with such skills."

"I am glad to hear it. Your words frightened me. I did not mean to offend. I fear it will take some time before I no longer worry about her."

"That is good." Halel's beard curved in the shape of a small smile. "But as you can see, she is well and strong. And learning quickly. She will be a great help to you now. You have been away a long time, if you will excuse my boldness, and you will have new slaves. It will be good to have another person to work alongside you."

Joshua looked down at her even from his seated position, and Hannah looked up at him. He was so close, and she had missed him so much!

He finally broke the connection between them, and turned back to Halel. "What about the grape harvest?"

Hannah stopped paying attention. Words swirled around her, Halel's voice, Joshua's voice. Only the deep timbre, the cadence she had come to identify with him. She would have to soak up that sound for the weeks ahead when he would be gone again.

Please, God, let his work be done soon, and please let there be a child.

"Well, I have the records yet to check. After that I must be going." Joshua stood and brushed off his robe.

She and Halel rose with him. He had been here, he had seen the farm was still functioning, and now he must leave again. She could not be selfish and think only of her needs. Remember the women weaving the winter clothes, remember the slaves out working among the olives and figs and dates. Remember they would only have what the farm produced, unless her husband could earn enough to provide more. Working with heavy metals and fire as his hair added grey.

"Be careful," she managed, and clamped her mouth shut on any plead-ings. *We will manage somehow. Come back soon.* Joshua had enough burdens to carry right now. She would let him go back to the village without guilt to make him careless, to cause more tiny burns on his skin.

"Hannah. I am always careful. This is what I do." Joshua put his hands on her shoulders, and looked deep into her eyes. "You must promise to take good care of yourself." His finger traced under her eyes gently. "I see dark circles here. You are not getting enough sleep. You must promise me to sleep."

"Yes." She would not tell him how sleep fled, or how many times she woke in the night haunted by his absence, tormented by the need to confide in him, by the breathless hope that trembled across her with every unexpected wave of dizziness.

God, please let him go before the hold on my tongue is broken and I give him precious hope that may only be snatched away.

He kissed her forehead gently, held her away for one more look, then turned and walked slowly back through the trees toward the house and the news those papyrus sheets held.

Joshua waited while the trader measured the grain with agonizing slowness. The sun beat against his face, blinding him. He was so tired he saw spots before his eyes, and the glare of the sun bounced against them, and pounded in his head. It had been six weeks of constant work, of waking before the sun was fully up to begin melting the iron and copper and bronze, six weeks of swinging the hammer until his shoulders burned and his skin shuddered even after he was in bed, six weeks of pouring hot metal into molds, of making new molds for new designs of candleholders or lamps or buckles or harnesses, anything that would bring in coins for the grain and new flocks. Six weeks of staying at the kiln trying to work from the faint glow of the hot fire long after the sun had set and the sky had grown dark.

Six weeks of bartering for any spare metals anyone had, six weeks of tiny work with gold and silver when his eyes were so tired they struggled to see the holes to thread through, making small beads string on smaller wires for women who loved jewelry and paid well.

Precious coins, mounting up slowly but faithfully.

He had used his entire pile of metal, of iron and bronze, making pots and swords, and locks and hinge pins for doors, the items getting smaller and smaller as the pile diminished. He had no gold left for women's pretty things either, no silver, no copper. Not even anything for his own wife.

He only hoped the pile of coins in his pouch was enough to send the slaves away, if not satisfied, at least not disgruntled. The autumn rains were coming. The first storms had already passed, and this was the last caravan to come through. He needed every sale he made. He needed whatever was left of this grain to plant for the spring harvest. He had no coins to buy more metals to make more goods to sell for more grain and more flocks and more slaves – the circle went around and around and it all depended on whether he had earned enough coin for this load of grain.

His eyelids drooped and he had to force them to stay open to watch the trader measure and count. He leaned against a pole driven into the soil to hold the cover strung over the trader's stall, and watched the grain pile on the scale. The side with the weights slowly rose to balance the grain, and Joshua watched as carefully as a man past exhaustion could. He had to stay awake, no matter how sleep pulled at him. He could not risk being cheated.

But he wanted sleep now more than anything. Sleep and Hannah.

Hannah, who had haunted him these past weeks. He slept in his lonely bed night after night, awoke to the strangely familiar sounds of the village, and wished for her shape beside him.

He had managed only three visits to the farm, quick trips to see the harvests, check the records and count the days before it was time for the next group to of slaves to be freed. He had not stayed the night, it was not a comfortable place for him. Hannah had said little either time, only stared at him with unfathomable eyes, and he was afraid to reach beyond that look.

The merchant clapped his hands, and Joshua was startled upright. "Ah. It is equal," the man said, and tilted the large scale to pour the grain into the waiting sack. "This is the last one. It is good grain, no? You will have fields heavy with wheat and barley in the spring. I hope you have many slaves to bring in the harvest. If you get good rains, you will bless the good fortune that brought you to my stall." The last of the grains whispered into the bulging sack. The merchant rolled the edges down, and stuck the long metal pins into the fabric, weaving them in and out until the pins were tight. "There! I will come in the spring, and you can tell me how rich the harvests were, and I will buy your surplus."

Joshua nodded, and stepped forward to load the last sack onto the wagon he had borrowed from Javan's farm on his last trip. His feet slipped as he tried to heave it onto the wagon bed.

"Careful, there," the trader said, his voice alarmed, and lurched forward to grab the other end of sack. "Here, now, I do not wish to see my grain all over the ground."

Joshua was embarrassed at the help, he had managed the other sacks unaided, but this was one sack too many. With the other man's help the sack thumped into the bed easily. He hung onto the wagon side for a moment while the spots danced before his eyes, blurring the merchant's face again. "Thank you."

The borrowed oxen shifted restlessly, feeling the load pull on the harness, their hooves clumping on the ground. Joshua climbed into the bed of the wagon and wobbled back and forth as he wove his way through the bulging sacks to the front. Normally he would walk beside the wagon, but not this time. It would never do to collapse on the trail and have the wagon leave him behind, a very real possibility now. "They know their way home," Javan had assured him after a piercing look when he left the team and wagon at Joshua's house last night. Joshua sensed Javan's worry, but had been too hired to care. "If you fall asleep on the way home, they will just come to my land, and I will take it from there."

The merchant looked up at him with the same worry on his face. "It is good grain," Joshua allowed the man, then flicked the slender twig onto the backs of the oxen. "Hup," he called, and the wagon creaked forward.

His small village house was filled with everything he had managed to purchase with his trade, mounds of wheat and barley seed, and vegetables to grace the table, cucumbers, melons, artichokes, beans, and spices, bay, coriander, mint, mustard, and dill.

Today he was going home. Not his village house, except for long enough to load everything into the wagon. No, he was going to Hannah.

Hannah was his real home, he knew, had always known.

Today their lives together could really begin.

After he got some sleep, that is. He gave a snort of laughter. People at the stalls through which he traveled looked over. A sure sign of his exhaustion, he thought, that everything was funny.

He stopped in front of his house and climbed over the wagon's edge. His legs buckled when he landed. He grabbed at the wagon once more and just stood there until his legs could straighten.

He still had a dozen sacks of grain as big or bigger than the ones just purchased to load, plus the smaller packets of food seeds.

This was folly, carrying a dozen more sacks of grain out to the wagon in his state, but what else could he do? The clouds were coming, and if he went to sleep now, he might sleep for days. He could not risk having it rain while he slept, getting the grain wet and having it spoil. The sooner he got it to the farm and into the sheds, the better. Joshua tied the reins to his awning and hoped nothing spooked the oxen and their already-heavy load. If they took off, they could pull the whole house down.

"Twelve sacks," he muttered aloud to himself, hoping the words would give him strength. "Just twelve sacks of grain and then home to Hannah."

CHAPTER 23

There is nothing better for a man than that he should eat and drink, and make his soul enjoy good in his labor. This also I saw, that it is from the hand of God.

Ecclesiastes 2:24

The farm's house came into view behind the waving branches of the trees. The clouds hung low, full of rain, but it had not begun yet. It would, though, and soon. The lowering sun had vanished behind the heavy grayness when he was barely started on the long path. He had looked up between the waving trees as the wind picked up to see the clouds roll in, higher and higher, bright tops reflecting the sun they hid and their dark bellies heavy with moisture. Joshua hurried the team, hoping he would beat the rains and keep the seeds dry until they could be planted.

He saw his menslaves out in the fields, small human specks in the distance in their undyed ivory-colored robes, appearing between the flailing branches of the warning wind and then disappearing behind the next tree as he guided the wagon along the path. Even at this distance, he could see they were dutifully chopping at what stubble remained in the fields, getting it ready to plow under when the rains softened the ground. The wind caught at the broken stalks and whipped them into the air, but the slaves just brushed the bits out of the hair and off their faces and kept the iron staffs and hoes going.

The slave houses looked better, freshly whitewashed and with the new roofs he had noticed on his last visit. Each even had a parapet around the roof's edge to keep anyone from falling off, hardly necessary on such small buildings but a requirement of the Law nonetheless. He had no idea where the wood had come from, he had not asked before, but that did not stop the surge of pride in Halel, who had taken these responsibilities on himself, responsibilities that belonged with Joshua.

The fences, however, still sagged, he saw when the wagon passed the small scrub at the forest's end and he got a good look at what the bushes had hidden. The wood seemed to have split further in the weeks he had been gone. Something had to be done with them so the sheep would be safe during the cold, wet time ahead when they had to be kept to their folds. Something more substantial that would last winter after winter.

An idea slipped into his weary brain as the wagon came out from the forest's edge into the opening and creaked across the expanse toward them, an idea he should have had weeks ago. Not wood, no, these fences would be stone. And unless Levi had done something else with that field from more than two months ago, he thought he knew where to find just what he needed.

What a fool he was not to have thought of it earlier!

He heard a shout of welcome. Halel was in the field, his gray hair standing out amidst the group, his arm waving with enthusiasm. How like Halel, Joshua thought, to work alongside his fellow slaves rather than sitting somewhere and telling them what to do. Joshua lifted his own arm, heavy with weariness, in response, beckoning everyone in. Hoes and staffs went over shoulders as the group drew together and started toward the fence, their feet stirring up the chaff for the wind to catch again. They were all going to be busy, the seeds had to get into someplace dry and quickly.

As he drew nearer, the oxen plodding along the rough ground, rocks grinding underneath the wooden wheels, Joshua wondered again what had happened to Levi's donkeys. He had managed to forget that particular worry during the past weeks but now, driving Javan's wagon with Javan's oxen, seeing the fields stretching out toward the far woods, all of them needing to be plowed and planted, it came back. It would require several animals at least to get the fields finished, now that the rains were on the way.

Halel hurried across the fields over the fences. Joshua kept the oxen moving, past the house and beyond, toward the barren sheds. It took a moment to realize one was missing, the stone floor pulled up and stacked in neat piles. So that was where the wood for repairs had come from! They had torn down a shed to find what they needed, and at no cost, too. A smile quirked his mouth.

Halel caught up to him by the first shed, the infamous one where Joshua had originally discovered the extent of the disaster here, the old man's heaving breaths audible even as the shuffling oxen eased to a stop and the wagon's creaking gave a last moan. "You were able to buy seed! Look how much!" Then he switched his gaze to Joshua's face and sobered, his expression as worried as Javan's last night and the merchant's at the market. "How hard you had to work, to accomplish this." His voice was hushed. "I can see it beneath your eyes."

Joshua shrugged. "Can we get most of this planted before everyone has to be freed? I cannot do this alone."

Halel looked up at the heavy sky, and back at the laden wagon. "If we all work. Nothing will be done today, the rains are too close, but tomorrow – it is a new beginning. There is life on this farm now." He gave Joshua a warm smile. "Yes, this farm is full of life again. It will be a fine place to raise children."

"If God wills," Joshua added.

The first splats of rain hit. Joshua looked up and a heavy drop slapped his forehead. "I want the seeds in the storage shed." Slaves appeared at the corner of his eye, their steps brisk as they, too, felt the first plops of wetness. No one had to tell them what to do. Several clambered up onto the wagon beside Joshua. The sacks that had taken the last of his strength slid off the wagon bed one after another, and the wagon shifted as the load lightened.

The heavy sacks were vanishing quickly, the slaves hurrying inside to dump each successive one. The seeds would be dry here while they waited for the rain to soften the ground, on the stone floor Joshua's father had thought to build in better, happier days.

Out again, into the strengthening torrent, to get another sack, the men's robes darkening with the sheets of wet. Back into the shed, dumping the sacks just inside the doorway before they would rot. They all worked quickly. Thunder shook the ground beneath their feet, water streamed down the sides of the oxen, and they tossed their massive heads in irritation.

The last sack, and his legs were shaking, the muscles of his arms tight and sore.

"Open one of the other sheds," Joshua shouted at whoever was listening, and grabbed the reins, tugging on the beasts. He hoped he would stay upright. How humiliating to fall flat on his face in the mud. But thankfully the oxen moved readily, just as eager to get out of the rain as Joshua and the slaves were. The door of one of the sheds swung open, and a slaveman rushed out to grab the reins beside Joshua. The rain poured down their faces, into their eyes, down their legs, pooled in their sandals and soaked the leather leads as they fought to unhitch the wagon.

The rain chilled Joshua and the sudden cold woke him up from his sleep-starved state. "Take the beasts and the wagon into shelter," he called over the wet drumming on the roofs, the wagon bed, the ground, and even his head, the drops stinging as they hit. Mud squished over the soles of his sandals. The slaveman grabbed the reins and pulled the animals free. The big oxen nearly ran him over rushing for the open door and the shelter within regardless of the strangeness of this new shed.

Joshua helped push the wagon to the protected side of the improvised barn. The rain washed his hair down into his eyes and his robe slapped against his legs. Each step, the wet linen stuck and clung stickily to his arms and chest, impeding his movement.

At last the doors were sealed, everything was safe. "Go home," he shouted, and the men could run for their own houses.

He looked at his house, shrouded in the silver sheets of rain falling around him, and just stood there, his legs shuddering, his vision blurred from more than the rain. It was done, with God's help he had earned enough to start.

Halel slapped him on the back, a squishy sound, splashing more water onto his neck. "Go to her," he shouted, and turned toward his own house, hurrying on his old legs through the mud and wet.

Joshua pushed his hair out of his eyes and squinted at the door, shut tight against the weather.

He hunched his shoulders against the rain's force and, with the very last of his energy draining off him like the rain, slogged through the soggy ground toward the house, hoping he could stand long enough to greet her.

Hannah watched through the lattice slats as Joshua came across the span between the sheds and the house, the rain pounding on his shoulders and his dark hair, blackened by water, washing over his forehead. He made no attempt to run, not like the slaves whose racing feet splashed puddles up over their knees, the bottoms of their robes brown with the mud they churned up as they ran toward their small homes and waiting families. Children dashed out into the rain to meet their fathers with joyous shrieks, delighted of an excuse to play in the wet.

She had wondered once if she would ever be able to rush to him without being asked, just let her feet fly across the fields to his side. She wanted to do that very thing now, but her feet felt stuck to the floor as if soled with bitumen.

The dizziness that had been a nuisance just two weeks ago was now her every moment's companion, and nausea accompanied each quick gesture. They had been together once, just one time in the two short months of their marriage, and that one lone time had borne fruit.

She guarded the fragile life inside her with fiery jealousy. Nothing must be allowed to interfere. The times when she would have to sit down suddenly or grab for the nearest tree or post or wall had begun coming with increasing speed, and they scared her.

It was possible the hard work she did about the farm, all of the knowledge she worked to pack into her head until she had grown too tired to think, had been too much of a strain. It was also possible that the desperate illness had damaged her body as well, making it too difficult to carry this child, but she would fight with her last breath to see that nothing happened.

He was getting closer, still trudging through the mud as calmly as though it were dry ground. The rain had not let up. She pushed open the door and waited calmly as the wind blew cold, wet drops against her legs and arms and face, and said nothing as he drew closer. He did not look up until he had almost reached her. She marveled that he did not walk into the door.

And then she looked at his face. And gasped. He truly did look ill. His face was pale beneath the tanned skin, his normally golden eyes were sunken and red-rimmed, and lines creased his skin that had not been there before.

"What happened to you?" Her words were shrill.

"I am tired." He grabbed the door and braced himself against it as he pushed passed her as if she was not there. "I need to sleep."

Tired! How tired would he have to be to look like *that*? Hannah pulled the door shut behind him, and shoved the latch into the catch, then hurried behind him, her bare feet growing cold from stepping in his wet prints. He staggered as he went into the main room, and stopped, as if he could not remember which way to turn.

For only a heartbeat she hesitated, then reached out and caught his arm, slipping it over her shoulder. He was so heavy! He stumbled once, and she glanced up at his face. His eyes were nearly shut.

She would have to lead him. She staggered through the sitting room, past the bench and chairs, past the shelves where they kept the blankets and the drying cloths she would have to collect before he truly became ill from cold, caught the curtain for the sleeping room with her free arm and swung it around the pair of them, hoping it cleared his tall head. He ducked just in time – or else his head sagged further.

She stopped him near the bed, and took advantage of a brief moment to catch her breath when his arm slid down and away. "Take off your clothes before you lie down." Hannah slipped out to the shelves, grabbed the warmest blanket and two drying cloths. He was so wet, one cloth would never be enough.

She turned to go back and looked around the room where they had never spent any time together, the chairs they had never sat across from each other on as husband and wife. What a strange marriage this had been!

At least he would know their first child had been conceived in his own house in the village, before all the worries had descended upon them.

But first things first. She carried her bundle into the sleeping room, only to find him standing there exactly as she had left him. "Why did you not take your wet things off?" she snapped before she even walked around him, instantly angry at herself for the sound in her voice, but his appearance frightened her. She tossed the dry pile onto the bed and turned around.

Joshua still stood there, eyes closed, looking as if he had fallen asleep on his feet.

What was wrong with him? Her worry transformed instantly into alarm. "Joshua? Did you hear me?"

He opened his eyes, and rubbed a hand over his face. It trembled. Her strong husband was shaking?

"Sit down. Right now!" She pushed him to the edge of the bed, but he made no attempt to sit. "Joshua, you look ill. Are you sick?"

"No." Hannah could hardly hear the word, but at least he answered.

Thankfully his skin was cool when she pulled his robe off. If he had caught the fever, not even the rain would have cooled him. She threw the wet robe into the corner. It landed with an audible splat. His inner garment around his loins was equally as wet. "Wrap this around you." She handed him one of the drying cloths. He finally moved on his own, untying his inner garment and letting it drop, then tying the dry cloth around his middle.

Hannah stared at his chest. His ribs were showing. "Joshua, have you not eaten?" Cold bumps covered his skin. She wrapped one cloth around his shoulders and rubbed vigorously. Moisture began to spot the cloth, but the bumps were fading and his skin warmed under her hands.

His hair dripped more water onto the cloth. His chest was dry enough, she judged, and warm enough. She flipped the cloth up over his head, catching the dark strands and stopping their constant drip that would have undone all her efforts.

"Of course I have eaten." Finally he sat down, his head drooping between his shoulders, the cloth covering his face and muting his words. It appeared the only thing that held him upright were his arms as they rested on his legs. "I have been working night and day to buy the seed. There was no time to cook." His voice was so quiet she had to listen hard to hear him, as if words were too much effort.

She grabbed the second cloth and knelt, wiping his legs, colder even than his chest had been. With a deep breath, he began talking again. "I have been eating whatever I found in the market that was quick – and of little cost. Every coin had to be saved for the seed."

Working night and day? "Did you sleep at all?"

"Yes. Some." It seemed he had used all his energy for the last spurt of words.

"Oh, Joshua, why did you not send word?" She rested her hands on his knees and peered up at his face. "I would have told any of the slaves and they would have carried you whatever you asked." She turned back to his hair and the cloth that was doing nothing as it hung loose over his face, and squeezed the strands into the cloth. It immediately was wet through, so she took it off and replaced it with the second one, scrubbing it across his scalp. When his hair felt dry enough, she set both cloths aside and smoothed the dark strands away from his face. They were only slightly damp, it would be good enough.

His eyes opened wide, as if for the first time since he got there he saw what he was looking at. They were glazed with something, illness, exhaustion, but they *saw* her – at last. "There was no need. Everyone here had other worries."

"Joshua, you look ill!"

"I am well. The fever is gone from the village." He flopped backward onto the bed, lying sideways with his feet still on the floor. "I am so tired. I love you but I have to sleep."

With that, he was out like a blown candle. Hannah watched it happen as she stood there, stunned, watched his muscles go limp, watched the tension seep away from his face, from around his mouth, watched his hands uncurl into the mattress beneath him.

I love you. Did he really say those words? Wonderful, amazing, unbelievable words?

I love you. Who said that to a wife who had waited for weeks – for her whole life – to hear those words, and then fell asleep? *Did you mean it*, she wanted to ask. *How long have you loved me?* But she would not – could not – disturb his sleep, when he so clearly needed it. *Say them again, please tell me you meant them.*

I love you. Her heart softened, just as his muscles had, the pain seeping away as the words sank gently into it.

She dragged his feet onto the bed, opened the blanket she had brought in and draped it over him while that tender, unexpected, unsolicited phrase spun and echoed in her brain.

"I love you, too, Joshua," she whispered. "And I have such news for you when you wake."

CHAPTER 24

May . . . a full reward be given to you.
Ruth 2:12

The bed rustled and creaked faintly from the other room. The second time it happened, Hannah straightened from the table she had been washing assiduously and stood there, irresolute. Did she go back in and feel his forehead again? Her husband had not been overly warm the last time she had checked on him, but he had slept for nearly a full day. Surely that could not be normal. Yet without a fever, she had nothing to nurse.

The quail that bubbled in the pot outside over the fire, a small one Halel had surprised in the woods and brought to her for Joshua, sent its fragrance into the air. The rich, meaty scent must reach as far as Joshua's bed, although if it woke him, it had taken long enough for him to notice. Or was it the bread's warm smell, fading from this morning's baking but still tempting?

Joshua stumbled into the eating room, rubbing sleep from his face, still wearing the drying cloth around his middle. The mattress covering had pressed lines in the shape of straw and tree cones into his face. He stretched broadly just inside the door, his muscles, as hard and ropey as layers of grapevines grown around a cedar, pulling tight in a feast for the eyes. The yawn that accompanied his impressive stretch was loud and long. As Hannah watched him, she knew he was unaware she stood there watching.

His arms, the sleep released, dropped to his side, and his eyes finally opened most of the way. He blinked. "Hannah. I did not realize you were there."

They both stared at each other and waited. The silence grew awkward. His eyes were clear, the dark circles gone. His face was fresh, the color good again. *We are having a child.* She had practiced the words, the right way to break the wondrous news, and now that an opportunity was here, all her perfect phrases vanished like smoke on a windy day.

Joshua finally broke the stillness, much to Hannah's relief. "Where is Halel?"

"He has been out hunting this morning. He might be with the slaves in the field, or he might be back in the woods." She forced herself to look at Joshua, despite the sudden wave of shyness that made her want to hide her face.

Joshua nodded again. "I think my sack of clothes was stored with the grain in the sheds. After I collect it and dress, I will check the fields for him."

He finally moved, but his steps kept going, to the door and beyond. He stopped by the fire with the bubbling quail. The pot splashed broth out, that spit and sizzled in the flames. He took a deep breath and Hannah could see him savoring the aroma of nearly-done meat. He looked over at her. "The meat will be done when I get back?"

Go over to him, her thoughts urged, her heart urged, and she set the rag down on the table, and pulled her big stirring spoon off the nail in the wall. It was the perfect excuse to stand close to him. Maybe the perfect moment could come and the words would pop back into her head. She scooped down inside the pot and lifted out a piece of meat, pretending to analyze it carefully. It was most obviously done. "Yes, it will easily be done when you get back."

Joshua took the wooden bucket that she had used to get water to fill the stew pot, and walked the whole distance to the shed in his bare feet. Hannah winced, imagining the chill he must be getting from the cold, damp ground. He disappeared inside, and she heard the odd thump of heavy sacks being shifted before he reappeared with the bucket in one hand, a lumpy sack in the other. The journey continued to the well.

She pretended to stir the meat as she watched Joshua lower the bucket. He unhooked the dripping bucket and started back. His stride was loose and strong, eating up the distance. He smiled as he walked past, but he did not speak.

Another opportunity squandered.

Hannah collected two bowls and filled them, carrying them inside to set them on the table. She broke off some bread to set by his bowl with fig cakes and dates, then filled his cup with water from the jug. It had grown nicely cool overnight, it would be refreshing for him. She sat to wait.

When he came out from their sleeping quarters, fully dressed again, he saw the small spread she had laid for him, and smiled. "It smells good." He caught the opposite bench with his foot and pulled it out. When he sat down the air seemed to leave the room. He took up so much space! She had forgotten how large he was.

He bowed his head for the blessing. How strange it was to have someone else bless the food. They had never had a chance – really – to set this pattern, or at least, had never taken advantage of the opportunities that might have been. She had grown used to doing that herself.

He relished the soup, closing his eyes to savor every bite. He looked at her and smiled. "I have missed your cooking."

"There is plenty. Eat as much as you like."

"I will." He went back to his eating, glancing up every few bites to smile again.

Hannah took the moment to stare at him, and admire his strong-boned face now that healthy color was back. He had lost weight, but his dark hair was healthy with shine, and curled around the bottom.

This was not the time to spring her news on him, she thought. She would have to let him enjoy the food lest he choke with shock. Her pregnancy had come as a surprise to her, how much more so to him! He had said he had gone hungry while he was in the village. She knew she was being cowardly, but there was a time for everything and she told herself this was not it.

Three bowls later, he rubbed his stomach and sighed with contentment. "I have not eaten like that in weeks. I look forward to many more meals with you." He reached across the table and took her hand, holding it gently.

This is the time, she thought, and her stomach knotted tight. She took a deep breath and cleared her throat.

Someone knocked sharply at the door.

"I hope that is Halel. I have much planned for today." Joshua pushed himself away from the table, the bench scraping sharply on the floor. He looked at her, but she could see his mind had already moved on to other things. "No doubt you have much to do as well. I doubt I will be back for the midday meal, but I hope to join you this evening, and we can eat together again."

With that, he pulled open the door. Just as he had expected, Halel waited him. "Ah, yes, Halel, plan to work." He pulled the door shut behind him.

And Hannah sat there, alone, looking down at her own bowl of soup.

The scrub forest closed around them as Joshua moved Halel toward the field he and Levi had worked on such a short time ago. "My brother was removing rocks from an unused field. My parents had intended someday that one of us build a house there and we would share the whole land together. We forgot this parcel, or at least I had until Levi called for me just days before he died. I thought since all the fences must be replaced, what better thing to replace them with than all those stones? Since we have Javan's oxen, if several of the men could begin plowing, the rest of the men could help carry the rocks back to the fences." Joshua pushed a branch out of the way and held it for Halel. "I have so little time. Soon the others will all have to go, I should use them for this heavy work while I have them."

The bushes caught at their legs and snagged their robes, now that the leaves were gone and only the branches and stalks remained, but the forest was narrow and soon they stepped into the meadow.

"This was never used. It was just a path to the stream. There were far too many rocks to be good for anything." Joshua shook his head as memories washed over him, and grief clenched his heart and tightened his throat. He remembered that day, before he knew what his brother had been hiding, himself and his brother working hard to pull the rocks out of the ground. He scanned the meadow. Nothing had changed. The rocks were still piled in small white hills among the long grass, exactly as they had been when he left. One of the white mounds was larger than the others and he remembered the big rock with the small hole he had found on his way out of the meadow.

It was still there, of course, as it no doubt would be a hundred and a thousand years from now, so deeply was it sunk into the ground. He shoved the undeserved grief away and squinted closer at the pile of limestone chunks beside the big rock. Out of every rock pile in the meadow, only this one had changed. Joshua could see even from here that the small rock chips around its base had grown. A lot.

He did not want to think about Levi, he did not want to remember happier days, did not want to hear again in his mind the teasing as they worked their ways across this meadow. Now when he thought of his brother he could only think of Hannah, fragile Hannah, being beaten by Levi. The meadow seemed tainted, dark and evil despite the sun that shined down from the sky and glinted off the drops from yesterday's rain still remaining on the brittle grass at his feet.

But Levi had brought him here to work hard that day, knowing all the while it was the path to the river where short days later he sat to drink himself drunk. No one had yet come up with an explanation for the boat near his body, a boat just as few people recognized.

And the rocks. With all those slaves, Levi could have asked them for help, Joshua had even wondered it that day. *Why not use them instead?*

Knowing what he now knew, the answer came quickly.

Levi did not want the slaves to know what was going on here. No, he had asked his trusting brother to come help him, his brother who would never question anything he did.

So what *was* going on here?

The large rock drew him, his feet moved him toward the it, crossing the stubbly ground without thought, just instinct, like a bird heading across the sky. He had peered inside that day, when he noticed the rock bits lying around the ground. He had thought the hole was made merely to keep food cool on the warm days.

But so many rocks mounded right there would only be used to cover something. The large rock was so very big. Limestone was soft, easy to hollow out, and often used as a grave.

A grave. He wanted to push the thought aside, wanted to pretend it had never crept into his mind, but it had and once in he could not push it aside. No emotions, only reason. Emotion had blinded him for too long.

He knelt beside the dark opening and hoped no animal had made it its home.

Mounded rocks, and a hole in the largest boulder in the whole meadow. Levi drunk and drowned in the river, the skin of wine empty. No seed, no plans for the following year, slaves to be released, and Hannah.

Joshua took a deep breath, and said a quick prayer that he would not see inside what he feared. Then he lay on his belly, and peered inside. The sun could not reach to the back of the hole, but there was enough daylight so if he looked he could make out its size. A large hole, large enough for a person.

Bile pooled in the back of his throat, and he swallowed hard. He wanted to drop his head on the ground and weep, but it was not ground beneath his head, it was rock. Carved rock roughly chipped to hollow out a hole.

He was looking at a roughly hewn grave.

He knew if he asked any of the slaves, none would know anything about this. No, this was Levi's doing, Levi's plan.

Things were beginning to make an ugly, evil kind of sense. A beaten wife that no one even seemed to know, or would hardly miss, a boat by the river, slaves free and on their way, no animals to pull a plow and no seed left to spoil.

At least the farm would not have been overrun by rats! Although he hardly thought that had been Levi's intention.

His eyes blurred, his chest heaved and strange sounds burst past the control of his throat, wretched sounds, grieving sounds. He lay there, his heart tearing, his throat burning, and realized he was weeping.

He did not know how long he lay there, his control shattered, before his grief finally emptied itself. He rubbed his face on his sleeve and blinked and cleared his throat. It would not do to have Halel see him like this. Although perhaps Halel had heard him, and stayed on the other side of the meadow to allow him privacy.

His vision cleared and he squinted at the back of the hole. In the far back some darker shadows caught his eye, and he scooted himself further in, pulling with his elbows, and pushing with his toes.

Leather, filled with something hard. He tugged and that leather thing separated into two, two leather sacks filled with something that clinked as he pulled it. He found the strings, wrapped them around his fist and eased himself back, listening to the clinking inside as he moved.

He knew what he would find. He knew those sounds, he had earned enough coins over the years to recognize their rattle when he heard it. The sun was obscenely bright on his eyes when he knelt and looked at the bags still attached to his hands. They were larger in the sunlight than it seemed in the dimness.

He just stayed there and looked at those bulging sacks, the leather beginning to age into brown, not quite ready to open them up and find out just how much Levi had hidden. He still felt ready to fly apart, his skin felt too tight for his body, his heart pounded as though the threat were right in front of him.

He could feel the anger simmering inside, bitterness at the desperate weeks of work, of fear, wondering how he was going to make this farm function again. All totally unnecessary.

And all the while, Hannah, the love of his life, gentle, broken Hannah. When she saw this, she would know one more reason not to trust.

And he had thought he had lost her before?

"What is that?"

Joshua jumped, his heart making a wild lurch inside his chest. He whirled around so quickly fire lashed down his neck. His elbow caught the stone opening with an audible thunk, and he winced as this new pain joined the first. "Halel!" He shook the strings off his hand, and rubbed the annoying pain on his elbow.

Joshua shaded his eyes against the sun and looked up at Halel, but Halel was not looking back at him. No, those bulging sacks at Joshua's knees grabbed both of their attention today.

The bitterness in Joshua's chest began to bubble again, rising up like poison to loosen his tongue. "Coins. Levi's coins. His profits from – how many harvests? All here! I am sure the sale of the donkeys we cannot find is here as well." He slapped his hand down fiercely against the sacks, the sting not even registering now.

Halel said nothing. Joshua could no longer look at him, no matter that the other man was not looking back. He grabbed the top sack, and pulled it open. The string was sticky, and a strange smell wafted up, warming in the sun. He lifted his hand to his nose and sniffed.

"Wine." Dried and spoiled wine, spilled while shoving the sacks into the hole. No doubt the last thing Levi had done before going out to sit by the stream and wait for – what? The slaves to go to sleep? Hannah to go to sleep? Whatever Levi had been waiting for, it had been just enough time for him to drink himself drunk and fall in.

"A celebration." Halel spoke the word flatly.

"Yes. Of course, yes. If he did not want the farm, why did he take my part at all? Or did he want it at first and change his mind?" He looked up against the sun and at Halel once more. "He was leaving. He knew I would get it all, just as he had years ago." Inside his chest, every beat of his heart was painful. "This is a grave. All the rocks – he was going to hide her here, and seal the grave. No doubt late at night, when all the slaves were asleep."

Halel was looking back now. "She had become quite good at hiding."

"I believe you." His hand was resting on the sack again. He snatched it away when he realized what he had done, then slowly set his hand on it again. These coins were his now, to settle on the slaves soon freed, to buy more slaves, and donkeys, even oxen, to buy more gold for his kiln. Enough for flowers for Hannah's garden and more. "These are mine now."

He went back to work on the string and it gave way. The sack fell open and the sun caught the glint of gold upon gold, a mound of it, and this was only one of the sacks. He re-wrapped the gold and with sudden decision retied the string. He picked up both sacks, marveled at their weight, and got to his feet. Dirt stuck on his robe and legs, but he did not stop to brush it away.

Hannah looked up from the large washing pan to see her husband come through the woods, Halel beside him. Something was very wrong, though. They walked somberly as though to a funeral. She rose slowly and cautiously and leaned against the side of the house as she watched them draw closer. The sense of wrongness deepened. Their faces were as grim as their posture. Joshua had something hanging over his shoulder, something clearly heavy. Two somethings, she saw as the men passed the sheds and their forms grew more distinct.

The two exchanged a glance. Joshua gave Halel a nod, and they separated, Halel turned right while Joshua turned left, toward her. Even at this distance she could see him bracing himself.

Her stomach clenched, her heartbeat changed into an ominous thudding. Something must have shown on her face, because Joshua's expression softened instantly. "Do not be afraid." He did not raise a hand toward her, did not even move a step closer. He motioned toward her little stool by the washing pan. "I think it would be best if you sat down."

Grayness dimmed the sunshine. She groped for the side of the house and hoped her legs would make it to the stool. Joshua still did not know, and he already had some terrible concern on his mind.

Joshua hovered an arm's reach away, and she felt his worry, so like when she was ill. It was a sweet sensation for her, but she must be frightening him, it was all on his face. She would ease his mind as soon as she could, just not this moment. She wanted to watch his joy when she told him, not see a blur. She sat down, grateful she was able to do it with some semblance of grace. Joshua found a dry patch of ground and sat down, his legs crossed in front of him. She knew why he did that, it was a position from which he could not rise easily. One more way he was trying to make her feel relaxed. It was not necessary any longer. Color eased back into the day.

He cleared his throat. It was so easy to meet his gaze. There was a sadness there, a burden she did not understand. "We went to get stone for fences. I need to replace the wood before the fences crumble and the sheep get out. I remembered the meadow I was supposed to inherit. Levi and I had begun clearing the rocks, shortly before he died." His eyebrows went up. "Do you remember the day? You hid in the house? The last time I was here?"

"Yes." She did not remember him so much as the beating. Perhaps someday that memory would fade, but it was still clear.

"We found the rocks. They are still waiting there." He gave a shrug. "They will make good fences."

Joshua put the things he was carrying on his lap. They clinked, the strange noise pulling her attention away from his face. "We found something else." His fingers played with strings that tied the sacks shut.

There were two sacks, leather sacks all awkwardly shaped. Whatever was inside was bumpy and rough. And clinked. Her gaze flew up to meet Joshua's. "I understood you had spent all the money you made."

"This is not my gold. Or more precisely," he corrected himself, "this *was* not my gold. I have a story I must tell you, and it is not a pretty one." He suddenly rose, his movements stiff and jerky. The bags that had been on his lap tumbled to the ground, the contents clinking and rattling as they rolled. "I cannot sit still and tell you the story." He glanced down at her, and away again. "You know we had been looking for Levi's money. I regret more than I can say that I accused you of knowing where was. Levi had hidden it."

His hands opened and clenched and he began pacing in front of her right, into the muddy water, a sharp turn to the left, past her again, leaving wet tracks until he did another sharp turn and began retracing his steps once more. "There is a meadow to the right of the – our – property. It has been there for a long, long time, but I imagine Levi never showed you where it was. My parents meant it someday to be a place for me to build my own house, and Levi and I were to share the land. He would reside here in this house, and I would build my own house in the meadow."

He stopped abruptly, and took a deep breath, then blew it out almost fiercely. "Last summer, he called me to come help him remove rocks. The meadow is full of rocks. One, too large to be moved, had been hollowed – but just a little. It bothered me, but I put it from my mind and told myself it was just to protect food on hot summer days." He began pacing again.

"I was such a fool!" Joshua shouted the words, and Hannah jerked. She put a hand down to brace herself. "It was a grave!" He knelt down in front of her, the fringe of his robe straddling washing-water wet and dry ground. "Hannah, he was going to kill you. I found the coins inside that rock. The hollow is no longer small, for food, but large, a fully completed grave, with plenty of rock to seal the entrance. If you smell the sacks, you will smell wine on them. Whether he was celebrating, or needed it for courage, we will never know. He had no intentions of keeping this farm going. He did not care that the slaves had to be released. He did not care that there was no seed for me when I had to take over the farm, as he obviously knew I would. He was going to leave me an empty house, and a barren farm."

He jumped back up to his feet and his hands were clenched once more. He did not look at her. His teeth were gritted as he ground out, "And to think I loved him all these years. He bought my part of the farm so that I could go into metalwork, and all this time how he must have hated me!"

Hannah looked up at her husband and tried to make sense of what he was saying. "Levi had planned to run away?" And then part of what he had just said became clear. "A grave?" Her voice squeaked at the end.

He nodded, and slowly turned around. His eyes had gone red rimmed and bleak. "It is small, no bigger than for a woman. After what you said when you were sick, it has to be for you." Moisture built in those red-rimmed eyes. "Hannah, I am so sorry. I was not going to tell you, but I want there to be openness between us. I will not protect or defend him, or keep his secrets."

It was good that she was already sitting, because for a long moment the dizziness threatened and her stomach rebelled. *A grave.* And then clarity returned, and an odd strength. She had won. Through Levi's own folly, she had won more than she could ever have dreamed. "I am glad he is dead, then."

He made a strange noise, half laugh, half groan. "Odd as it sounds, so am I. Now. I trusted him, I believed in him, I gave him all the credit for my release from this very farm. And all the while, he was plotting the most vicious revenge. I would get it back, but in the worst possible condition."

Hannah thought about it for a moment, remembering the horrible early days of her marriage. She had never known what drove Levi to his rages. Maybe Joshua was right, but Levi had seemed happy with the farm. Just not with her. She sometimes wondered if there was a different woman he had wanted, a woman out of reach, possibly dead or married. It was only as the months passed without pregnancy that he had found a weapon, the most hurtful accusation of all, to hurl at her. She looked at her husband's stance, shoulders drooping, face gray and numb, and shook her head. "No, I do not think Levi had this in mind all the time. Just after I proved barren."

Only she was not barren any longer, she thought with the growing euphoria that settled on her every time she realized the miracle happening within her, but bit the words back. This terrible knowledge he was facing had to be resolved, accepted and shed like a worn cloak before they could turn to the coming child.

"Perhaps. But perhaps not. I think now that we will never know just how badly and how long his fury festered." Joshua took one step toward her, and then another, but stopped just out of reach. His eyes were so sad Hannah bled for him.

"He wastes our time," she said firmly, and believed it. She got to her feet carefully, wanting to be upright for this. God had permitted her a release. Now it was time for Joshua to receive the same. "I think of Levi's death as a gift. He is gone, and we are free."

The bleakness had not left his eyes. "Can you forgive that easily? I do not think I can, maybe not ever. The things I have learned about him are burned in my mind like a brand." He reached out for her but his hand stopped before she could catch it, and fell back to his side.

"I do not want him in my head ever again," Hannah said slowly, the thoughts just forming in her mind. "Is that forgiving? It would be easier if he came to us to ask our pardon, but he is gone, it is beyond him now."

"Even if he asked, I do not think I could give it. He would have to repent of his horrors. The Law requires just compensation for theft, four times as much. How could he return fourfold stolen spirits and broken bodies? You most of all, but the slaves and their houses, the squalor he condemned them to live. How does he beg forgiveness for that? Would he even want to? He has left a poison behind for us. How can you look at me and not see him?"

Joshua's eyes closed, as if he could not look at her while he spoke. "I am here and I am his brother." He opened them again, and they glistened with tears. "You might say today that you can put him from your mind, but the first time I accidentally swing my arm and you remember his blows, or catch your shoulders to pull you to me, or raise my voice – what then? I cannot promise never to get angry, husbands and wives do, I am told. What then, Hannah?"

"You are not Levi." A smile tugged at her heart and began to rise upward.

Joshua shook his head fiercely. "We are not fighting now." His eyes narrowed at her. "Did you hear me? *We are not going to fight now.* We are going to think. We must face this, Hannah. Levi has left his mark on both of us. And you must know that it was never my intention to remain on the farm. I am not a natural farmer. What happens the first time the crops fail? What happens if the rains do not come? If winter bites too strongly and the crops die and I get angry because I am trapped here? What then? Will you look at me and be afraid because I am Levi's brother?"

He did not want to be on the farm? Neither did she, but for two very different reasons. For her, it was the memories, he was right about that. Hannah looked at him, at those sad eyes, and thought. This was too important for a quick reply. They were married, but she had not allowed it to move forward, at least not when he was near. Her illness had been a protection for her, keeping him away. Now she was well. She had grown to love him from a distance. Could she love him up close? Perhaps she could have run to him in the rain last night, and her dizziness had been a convenient excuse.

No. The dizziness was all too real, and she had not been afraid of him last night. She was not afraid of him now. Hannah took a deep breath. "If the farm has troubles, we will live carefully and pray for rain, or for warm temperatures in the winter. And we will teach our children to do the same."

Joshua shook his head, his golden eyes still bleak. "But there might not be children. I give you my word now that I will never reproach you for your barrenness. I believe Levi did. I am not Levi and someday perhaps you will believe that."

Hannah began to laugh. "I most certainly know you are not Levi. I am with child." The words came out before she could ease him into the knowledge.

Joshua went white, then red. "With child? Are you certain? It is not possible!" He sucked in a breath, noisily. "So quickly? Once? Just one time?"

Hannah struggled to control the laughter that wanted to bubble outward and encompass him. "Is that not what this marriage was supposed to do? Succeed where the other one failed? Levi failed – in every way. You succeeded! Not just with the babe." Her hand slid down to cradle where the baby would soon make itself known to all. "With me." Her other hand went up to stroke his face, his beard, surprisingly soft, his lips that slid a kiss onto her roving hand, his straight nose, his eyebrows, and his rich dark hair with the tendency to curl unexpectedly. Oh, to be free to touch! "Joshua, you made me feel safe when I never thought I would feel safe again."

Joshua took her hands, and lifted them one after the other to his lips. "I must tell you a secret I have been keeping for nearly seven years. You said once I never came here, I did not know what happened on this farm. There is a reason for that. I fell in love with you the day you married my brother. I broke one of the Ten Commandments. I coveted my brother's wife. I had to stay away. I could not keep faith and do otherwise. Having met you, I could not take another woman to my house. Perhaps someday I would have been ready to say goodbye to my dream, but it had not happened yet, and I, I guess I too must be grateful that Levi drank himself into the river."

Hannah stared at him, all thought in her brain wiped away by his confession. He loved her. More than six years, he had loved her. All those terrible years with Levi, someone had loved her. So much, no other woman had been in his life.

"I wish – how I wish – that I could have spared you." He let out a big breath, maybe the one he had taken earlier, and smiled. It was small, but it was a start. "You are pale. Perhaps you should lie down."

She smiled back at him. "Perhaps I should. Perhaps you should, too. You have had a severe shock today, more than one. You must need time to recover, do you not think so, my love?" The first time she had said those words, and they came out so easily, as if her heart had been practicing them all this time.

One arm went around her shoulder. Joshua gave a shout of laughter, and caught her legs in one strong arm, lifting her with surprising grace. The sky whirled around her, but it was a good sensation. She kept her eyes on Joshua's face, his smiling lips and nice trimmed beard, the high cheekbones, the dark curl that flopped over his forehead in a so-familiar way, and his golden eyes that left her face only long enough to be sure of his path over the threshhold. They crossed the eating room, and passed through the main room with its lattices wide so anyone who wished could see, and finally there it was, the curtain, before which Joshua lowered her with exquisite care.

"What would you like first, my wife?"

She looked into Joshua's eyes, full of concern – and yes, love, it must have been there all the time – and said, "A kiss?"

He smiled at her, and the last traces of sadness finally left his eyes. "Any time you wish." He leaned forward, framed her face in his gentle hands, and gave her what she wanted.

EPILOGUE

Joshua sat beside Hannah's bed and held her hand, feeling more helpless than he ever had before. Her lips were white, and her face was red as she suffered.

"What is wrong?" he asked Leah, the village midwife, from where she sat at the other end of the bed.

She glared at him. "Nothing is wrong! This is what a birth looks like." She stood and propped her hands on her hips. "Joshua, if you cannot be helpful, go outside and keep Javan and Halel company! Your wife and I are busy just now." She sat back down and ignored him.

Joshua felt red rush up his face.

Taleh rubbed his shoulder in sympathy. "Javan was as frightened as you with our first."

Leah looked up. "But Javan had cause to worry, if you recall. You had, after all, just been kidnapped and ridden across the country."

"And back," Taleh laughed.

How could they joke about this? His wife was suffering! It was not funny!

Taleh tugged on his arm. "Go, visit with Javan and ask him for the story. It will distract you."

Joshua sat harder. "I cannot leave my wife."

"Then stop talking about disaster," Taleh snapped, and Joshua realized both women were serious.

"It is going right?" He begged for reassurance.

"It is going fast," Leah said, "and if you are going to be here, you will have to stay out of the way." Her hands reached under the blanket they had draped across Hannah's midsection, as if there was something he had not seen before under there, and rested it on the bulge that was his wife's belly, her whole attention trained on what came through her palms. She gave a nod. The time for modesty must have passed, for she shoved the blanket up away from the mound of Hannah's stomach.

Hannah lurched upright, and Leah snapped, "Get her up! It is time for the stool!"

Taleh left his side and moved around to the bottom of the bed, to pick up the birthing stool they had brought with them when Joshua had sent his newest, fastest slave to the village for the midwife this morning. Levi's gold had bought everything they needed, and there was gold to spare.

Joshua had been surprised to see Taleh arrive with her. It took both of them, he saw quickly, to carry a midwife's supplies.

Taleh set the stool next to him, and said, "I will take her other arm. You lift her – carefully. We must get her on here quickly."

"I had not expected this so fast for a first one," Leah muttered.

Was that good? Faster *must* be better. Joshua could hardly wait for this to be over. It was already midday, and Hannah had been suffering like this since she awoke with the first pain at sunrise.

Hannah stiffened when he tried to turn her toward the birthing stool, and grabbed at his robe, catching his chest hairs with her fingers. Joshua bit back a yelp, and felt some hairs pull out. Taleh reached across Hannah and pried those fingers off his robe. He looked up in gratitude, and saw her biting the inside of her cheek to hide the grin.

He would smile about it later – perhaps.

Taleh guided Hannah's hands to the stout poles that rose on either side of the sturdy chair. The wood was dark with the sweat of many birthing mother's hands. Hannah grabbed the poles with a grip so tight her hands went white and a deep groan started down near the bulge of her belly.

He could not move away. He did not know what to do, but he could not take his hands off his wife, and eased her head back onto his belly, holding it there, stroking her face and hoping he did the right thing.

Leah pushed past Taleh, and knelt before Hannah's knees, splayed apart by the shape of the birthing stool. Hannah arched against the strong back of the chair, and pushed her feet flat on the floor, but it had been designed for that very thing and stayed solidly in place.

Leah held her hands out, and Joshua saw a bloody round thing with dark hair begin to emerge. A head, all small and perfect. Their child was really coming. He could only stare in amazement as a body, all loose limbs and slippery, slid out at Hannah's startled shriek. Leah flipped it over and slid her finger into the mouth, scooping out a gray-white slime.

The baby gurgled, its arms poked out in thrashing effort, and a sharp cry came out of its mouth.

Leah and Taleh laughed with joy. Hannah sighed against his body, and to his amazement, she laughed too, tired but joy-filled. One hand left the grip and reached up, to grab at Joshua's robe again. He looked down at Hannah looking up at him. "I gave birth," she said, and there was wonder in her voice.

She had turned to him first, before even seeing her child. The miracle that was his marriage clenched at his heart. Joshua knelt at her side, and took her other hand. "Yes, you did."

They both turned as one to see their first child.

"A daughter," Leah pronounced, and reached for the knife to separate Hannah from her child. "You have a little girl."

Joshua laughed. A little Hannah. Nothing could have please him more.

"We will have to try again for a son," Hannah said, and Leah placed the baby in her arms. Its little arms thrashed the air, its little legs curled up tight to its belly. It kept its eyes squeezed tight, as if afraid to see the world. Leah quickly wiped a clean cloth across its face, it opened its eyes at last as if it had been waiting for that very thing, and of a sudden Joshua saw his wife's features in smaller form look up at him.

She smiled at him. "But maybe not for a while. Now – " the twinkle he loved was muted but still shone in her eyes – "you must hold your daughter."

He sat down next to her, so carefully, needing to be at her side. Hannah, his wife, his gift. He pressed a kiss to her mouth. "I love you."

Then, only then, he took the little bundle in his arms.

ABOUT THE AUTHOR

Mary Ellen Boyd is a romance author whose passions are in Regency and most important to herself, Biblical fiction, although if the muse strikes, she will happily branch into other genres. Her special passion is building a fictional story around a factual account. She is always on the lookout for another tidbit that begs to become a novel.

She lives in the beautiful state of Minnesota (and yes, it does get hot there in the summer). She and her husband have been happily married since 1982, in May, the prettiest month of the year. They have one son, who is now married himself to his high school sweetheart.

Her website is www.maryellenboyd.com.

Made in United States
Orlando, FL
18 August 2024

50468802R10130